Matthew 'Ollie' Ollerton is a former Special Forces soldier and was one of the founding Directing Staff on Channel 4's hit show *SAS: Who Dares Wins.*

Ollie's military career began at the age of 18 when he joined the Royal Marine Commandos and toured operationally in Northern Ireland and in Iraq for Operation Desert Storm. He subsequently spent six years in the Special Boat Service rising to team leader, before working in Iraq as a private security contractor and carrying out anti-child-trafficking charity work in Southeast Asia.

Ollie now spends his time as an entrepreneur running multiple companies including Break-Point, Battle Ready and has a busy public speaking business. He is passionate about helping veterans through the Break-Point Academy and lends his support to many veteran charities.

His books, *Break Point* and *Battle Ready*, have both been *Sunday Times* bestsellers. *Scar Tissue* is his first novel.

BY THE SAME AUTHOR

Break Point
Battle Ready

SCAR TISSUE

EVERY BATTLE LEAVES ITS MARK

OLLIE OLLERTON

BLINK
bringing you closer

First published in the UK by Blink Publishing
An imprint of Bonnier Books UK
80-81 Wimpole Street, London, WIG 9RE
Owned by Bonnier Books
Sveavägen 56, Stockholm, Sweden

facebook.com/blinkpublishing
twitter.com/blinkpublishing

Hardback – 9781-7-88703-80-2
Trade Paperback – 978-1-788703-81-9
Paperback – 978-1-788703-82-6
Ebook – 978-1-788703-83-3

A CIP catalogue of this book is available from the British Library.

Designed and set by envy.net
Printed and bound by Clays Ltd, Elcograf S.p.A

Copyright © Matthew Ollerton, 2020

First published by Blink Publishing in 2020.
This edition first published by Blink Publishing in 2021.

MIX
Paper from
responsible sources
FSC® C018072

Blink Publishing is an imprint of Bonnier Books UK
www.bonnierbooks.co.uk

This book is dedicated to the men, women and children of Iraq who welcomed me with open arms. Thank you for your love and hospitality through the times depicted in this book. I pray that you see the sun at dusk and dawn and forgive those that took more than they deserved.

PROLOGUE

Dad, we need to speak. It's urgent.

But the text message had arrived at night, which was the wrong time for Alex Abbott. Night time was when the other guy was in charge. The drunk guy. And the drunk guy was way too busy for text messages. Reading them. Replying to them. Remembering them, even.

And so, by the time of the next afternoon, when finally Abbott had surfaced and was contemplating a black hole where yesterday should have been, it was too late.

He had tried the number, and in a voice that quavered with emotion and guilt, left a message, saying, 'Nathan, it's Dad, getting back to you. What is it, mate? What's the problem?'

And, two days later, was still waiting for a reply.

CHAPTER 1

High above the municipality of Morelos in the state of Mexico, a Cessna drew a line across the clear blue sky. Inside, two skydivers clad in bright red jumpsuits made final adjustments to their rigs. Body cams were checked, goggles adjusted. Gloved hands went to helmets, checking the fit. Each turned so that the other could inspect their rig and examine the AAD, the automatic activation device designed to deploy a reserve chute should the main one fail.

All done.

A green light blinked on. The pilot gave them a thumbs-up over his shoulder. They were at the right altitude of sixteen thousand feet, bang over the drop zone. It was time.

'Ready?' asked Number One. His hand was on the activation button of the para door, but he waited for Number Two's reply before he pressed it. These were the last words they'd speak to one another before reaching the ground; from now all communication would have to be via hand signals.

'Ready,' confirmed Number Two.

The door opened. The cabin filled with whistling air, buffeting them. With a nod to his companion, Number One sat with his legs dangling into space, gripping an overhead bar for support, and then jumped.

Number Two followed suit. Behind them the door slid shut and the Cessna began banking for the return journey, ready for more thrill seekers.

Seventy-five seconds to deployment. The divers sliced through the air, rolling and spinning, whooping and yelling. Next they spread themselves flat, turning towards one another, meeting with outstretched arms as they interlaced their fingers, each with one eye on the altimeter at their wrist and awash with adrenalin, weightless and free, feeling like gods.

Ten seconds to deployment. Opening altitude: two thousand feet. They broke apart, giving each other space. *Now*. Number One reached to a handle on the side of his rig and pulled, ready for the pilot chute, which would in sequence drag out the main chute.

Counting, *One thousand, two thousand, three thousand. Check.*

Nothing. No chute. He went for his reserve chute handle, located on the opposite side of the rig, and immediately looked above, desperate to see the bright colours explode above him. Still nothing.

He trusted in the AAD. Triggered by pressure, it would engage.

It had to engage.

It didn't.

And instead of slowing to roughly 8 mph, Number One continued falling at 110 mph.

He had just under ten seconds to live.

He looked up. Above him the parachute of Number Two had deployed, a mushroom in the sky. Below him the ground rushed up. He no longer felt like a god. He had never felt more mortal, more fragile.

Not like this, he thought.

But that thought was his last.

CHAPTER 2

Whatever he was doing, wherever he was in the world, Alex Abbott had a rule: never wear anything you can't run or fight in.

On his feet were the same boots he'd worn since basic training – boots that had seen him through Iraq and beyond. Tucked into the right one was his Gerber knife; while in the belt of his sand-coloured cargo pants, which were light, a concession to the Singapore humidity, was a Leatherman all-purpose tool, as well as a tourniquet – the sort with a plastic turning handle – and a vacuum-sealed medipack.

On top he wore a simple black T-shirt. At his wrist was his Omega service watch. He'd had that watch almost as long as the boots.

And right now – as in, at this very moment in time – he was willing to bet that he was the only one at his AA meeting armed with a Gerber knife. *Yup. Concealed weapon here. There's only one winner if it all kicks off at the tea urn.*

They sat in a chair circle. A sparse early-morning meeting of five ex-pats – the British drunks of Singapore – still rubbing sleep from their eyes. It was only the second time he'd attended, but Abbott already knew that the guy opposite would be hurrying off to his job as bank relationship manager and the woman next to him would begin a day of work as a marketing assistant for a dental firm. The other two he wasn't sure about: a young guy who bore a passing resemblance to Rodney from *Only Fools and Horses* – he was the meeting leader – and a much older woman who looked suspiciously like she only came for the tea and misery. Where Rodney or the misery tourist would be going afterwards, Abbott had absolutely no idea. None of them would be spending their day doing what he was doing, that was for sure.

'Have you had a drink today?' he'd been asked on entry.

'No.'

Ding! Truth.

'What about last night?'

'No.'

Bzzt! Lie.

The dental marketing assistant was talking about the time she threw a wine bottle at her husband but didn't remember doing it the next morning. Hubby had threatened to leave if it happened again, and it did, but hubby still didn't take off and she carried on boozing. Until one day he came good on his promise, by which time it was too late to save that particular relationship. She'd ended up taking a company promotion to the Far East, hoping to leave her problems behind, but her problems, being the tenacious sort, came along for the ride. Abbott knew the feeling. He was nodding along to the story, more to himself than anything, when gradually he became aware of the eyes of the meeting upon him.

Uh oh. He stopped nodding, feeling the weight of their expectation, heavy as an iron bar in a backpack. There was no pressure to share, he'd been told, the first time he came. Only there was, really.

He cleared his throat. Come on, Abbott. You served in Northern Ireland. You fought in the Gulf. In two bloody wars. You can't be scared of talking to a few guilt-stricken ex-pats. But then found that his voice shook when he opened his mouth to say, 'My name is Alex and I'm an alcoholic.'

It was the first time he'd ever said it. Oh, he was happy to hold his hands up to being a pisshead. But alcoholic? No. Quite a few people had said it *to* him, of course. His ex, Fiona, had said it a lot. As in, *a lot*. He couldn't remember the first time, just that the insult was like one of those air-fresheners you hang in your car: bright and effective at first, gradually losing its power over time, until after a while you forgot it was even there. The insult seemed to recover its power the first time she used it around Nathan, but even then it soon got old.

Still, though, he'd never said it to himself. He'd never said, 'Abbott, you are an alcoholic,' so saying it now felt like …

Well, nothing, really. No revelation or great through-the-looking-glass moment. Just words. More blah blah in the room, except this time in the dulcet tones of a bloke from the Midlands.

'Hello, Alex,' they murmured back. And maybe they thought that his voice shook with the significance of the moment rather than a bout of stage fright. Either way, they looked at him with sympathetic, encouraging but curious eyes. He looked around the group and forced himself to think of them as saviours not vampires.

'Um,' he started, and then stopped, addressing Rodney instead. 'What do I say, mate?' he asked, knowing the answer. Just stalling for time.

'Well, you can say anything you want to say, Alex,' replied Rodney kindly. 'Why don't you tell the group a little bit about yourself? Why not explore your reasons for being here? Why do you drink, for example?'

Abbott opened his mouth, and for a moment it crossed his mind to talk about mates gunned down or torn apart by IEDs. Reprisal killings in Belfast. The Thai victims of child trafficking, their tongues cut out as a warning to others. Or maybe the women gang-raped in the Congo and then 'sealed' with molten plastic bottles, shunned by their own tribes as a result. Or the bodies in Iraq, their arms and legs hacked off and swapped over in a vile, grotesque parody of a human being.

So many corpses. All of them condemning him with sight-less eyes.

Except, of course, he stopped himself, because at the end of the day he didn't want to be a dick. It wasn't a competition, like my shit is worse than your shit: I drink because life has vomited blood into my face, and you drink because you find it boring doing the housework. That's not how it works. These guys didn't deserve that. Even the possible misery tourist didn't deserve that.

'I was in the army,' he managed instead. 'I was in the army and I find it difficult to put away some of the things I've seen and dealt with, and the booze helps with that. Like the way I see it is if you have all this terrible stuff going on in your head and you could take a pill and make that stuff go away, then wouldn't you take the pill? That's how I feel about booze, I guess. It helps me take a holiday from myself.'

He spoke for a few minutes. Not nearly as much as he'd heard others speak, but long enough, being a man of few words – a man who found the world of touchy-feely group therapy a bit on the weird side, if he was honest with himself. When he'd finished, it was the misery tourist who spoke first. 'Thank you, Alex,' she said.

'I have an observation, though, if I may?' He nodded go ahead. 'You do realise you just spoke about drink in the present tense?'

Oh yeah. So he had. Another thing – and this he thought about as the meeting broke up. When he'd done his 'I'm Alex and I'm an alcoholic' thing, the reason he hadn't felt anything was because deep down he didn't think it was the truth. Or, rather, he knew it was the truth, but he didn't truly *believe* it. Wasn't ready for it yet.

That was something he could have said, he realised later. He could have told them how he often felt outside of himself, watching this man called Alex Abbott slowly destroy himself with drink, waiting to see what would happen next.

Perhaps save that observation for next time, he thought.

If there was one.

CHAPTER 3

Singapore harbour. A horizon speckled with cruisers and yachts. They bobbed and rocked on water that twinkled in a fresh November sun, basking in what was a beautiful day at the tail end of the monsoon season. Later there would be showers, of course, although to call them showers was like calling Hurricane Isidore a light breeze. But for the time being it was calm and pleasant, not too hot, not too cold. A good day to be on the water.

This particular yacht was among the most lavish on the harbour. It belonged to a billionaire London bonds trader by the name of Travis Bryars, and it had dropped anchor yesterday. Having satisfied himself that it was there for the duration, Abbott had spent the afternoon touring the harbour for different angles of observation, eventually settling on a spur used for mooring smaller boats. He'd hired a cabin cruiser for the following day, one with a decent view of Bryars's yacht – a good static position, as they used to say back in the day. And then, to congratulate himself on a day of abstinence and outstanding operational achievement, he'd decided to treat himself to a quick drink at the Big Smile Beach Club, two doors down from his building.

And that, of course, had ended ... not badly, as such. After all, he'd woken up in his own bed, alone, unhurt and with nothing lost or stolen. But not 'well', either, unless your definition of 'well' was elastic enough to include a thumping headache, terrible self-loathing and the crushing knowledge that he had once again failed to get a single day of sobriety under his belt.

It was that kind of well that had prompted him to attend his second-ever AA meeting. *Hey guys, me again. Remember? Army tats and stubble? I sat in silence and declined a Hobnob.*

After the meeting, newly charged with not-wanting-to-drink zeal, he'd returned to the harbour where he'd clambered below decks, dropped his black holdall and set up a binoculars rest in front of a porthole. He upturned a fibreglass storage box and took a seat, screwed a set of Yukon Scout binoculars onto the rest, training them on the yacht, and prepared himself for a long wait.

The whole time he was doing all of that, he didn't think about drinking. No sir. Didn't even think about not-thinking about drinking. And he told himself that getting pissed didn't matter because that was yesterday and today was the big one, and no way was he going to fuck it up.

So all morning he just sat with his hands in his lap – hands that felt useless, that he wished could reach for a drink – and watched Bryars's yacht, the theme tune to *Only Fools and Horses* going round and round in his head, just like the changing of the seasons and the tides of the sea.

Sometime before midday was when things started happening on the yacht. The sound of thumping dance music made its way across the harbour, carried on a light but cooling breeze into the spur where he sat, squished and hot and uncomfortable, and very thirsty.

Pressing his eyes back to the binoculars, he saw figures appear on deck. A champagne bottle was raised, and he heard the pop of a cork. Abbott had no particular love for champagne, but suddenly it looked like the best drink in the world to him. A cheer went up and Abbott adjusted the binoculars to see a small fishing boat approach and two women disembark. Hookers. You could tell. It was the little tell-tale signs like ripped denim hot-pants worn over fishnets.

Something else, too. And Abbott felt his heart harden just a little more. His hatred intensified. The women were clearly underage. Probably trafficked.

Don't think about it. Feelings to one side. Concentrate on the job at hand.

The women were welcomed on deck by three rowdy guys, while not far away stood two other men, watching.

He reached into the holdall, retrieved a wad of papers and checked mugshots. Of the two who stood apart, Travis Bryars was on the left. Smartly dressed, with the sun sparkling off a flute of champagne he held, he wore Ray-Ban aviators and his dark hair was brushed into a neat side parting, looking every inch the trust-fund-kid-turned-late-thirties billionaire that Abbott, thanks to a quick session on Google, knew he was.

Beside Bryars stood another equally smartly dressed guy who Abbott took to be a friend rather than staff. Meanwhile, the other three dudes were security, judging by their build and demeanour.

And boy were they living it up. Watching them manhandle the two women, Abbott got the impression that this was what you might call a staff fun day. Other companies went paintballing. This lot called in the whores and cracked open the bubbly.

Talking of which, more champagne had appeared. The women held their flutes aloft as they danced, and if their intention was to look like every hip-hop music video ever filmed, then they were succeeding admirably.

Watching, Abbott's mind went back to mad nights and dance-floor anthems. And for that reason, and because the sunlight seemed to glint so beautifully off those champagne flutes, and because when yet another bottle was hoisted aloft, he could actually see the condensation on the glass, his thirst increased.

Sod it. He left his post, found a Sheng Siong, bought a bottle of wine and returned. Just the one bottle, mind you. One would be enough – enough to straighten him out but not so much that he was knocking on the door of Mr Fuck-Up.

He used a Thermos mug. They don't hold much, but even so, as he drained it, he felt the alcohol's soft embrace like nimble fingers at his neck and shoulders, relaxing him, chasing away last night's headache, taking all those shit-thoughts that camped out in his head and making them less vivid, drowning out the voices of ghosts.

He put his eyes back to the binoculars. One of the women had disappeared while he was out buying his wine, presumably to start her shift in earnest. The other one was still on deck, doing her best to continue the hip-hop video vibe, even though things had clearly moved on a notch or six. By now, the security guys were practically drooling, all three of them in the kind of rich lather that a mix of booze and prostitutes is likely to produce. Watching her as she was groped by cackling drunks who were even now imagining the various vile and despicable things they intended to do to her, Abbott thought, as he often did, that she was somebody's daughter, and that once upon a time she had been a tiny baby and then an innocent little girl. And now she was a plaything for scumbags.

Abbott watched. She was still pretending to go along with all the high-jinks, but even as she smiled and screamed and played up to it, her eyes told a different story. Her eyes said she was working hard for her money.

They were chasing her around the deck. One of them caught her, roughly pulled off her bikini top then sent her spinning out to the others. She scampered across the deck and right into the arms of Bryars, who indicated that she should wait and then produced a note. She went to take it. Laughing, he held it out of her reach. She tried to jump and grabbed his wrist but this time he took her by the waist, holding her firmly as he stuffed the note into her mouth, much to the general merriment of his buddies.

'Oh, you utter bastard,' hissed Abbott, hating what he saw and feeling terrible for the girl. At the same time he knew that the messier it got on the boat, the more things worked to his advantage. And the earlier he could get the job done, the better.

CHAPTER 4

He sat back, reaching for his Thermos mug and phone. On it was Nathan's text message, received two days ago. *Dad, we need to speak. It's urgent.*

He'd attempted to reply, of course, but had no response. He tried again now. Text and call. Still nothing. He should tell Nathan's mother, he knew, but the problem was that Nathan's mother and his ex-wife, Fi, were one and the same, and Fi was what you might call a firebrand. It had been one of the things that had attracted him to her. After all, a firebrand can be a lot of fun, and two of them together is like napalm.

However, as he'd discovered, a firebrand makes a formidable enemy when things go tits up, which is exactly what happened. Had there been a phone call since then that hadn't ended in a slanging match? Negative.

But Nathan's text bugged him. Scratch that, it *worried* him. And the sensible, responsible thing to do was to talk to Fi about it. Having tanned the wine, he was just drunk enough to do it, too. Seize the day and all that.

He was about to do just that when the phone rang in his hand, caller ID telling him it was his fixer, a guy called Foxhole.

Foxhole was the man behind this job, which had come with the threat that if Abbott fucked it up, then Foxhole was washing his hands of him forever. Why? Because Abbott had made a mess of the last thing he was supposed to do for Foxhole; a simple close-protection gig. He'd got pissed the night before and had failed to turn up, meaning Foxhole had to hastily organise a last-minute replacement.

That had been it for Foxhole. *You're out, Abbott*, he'd said. The fact that Abbott had worked with him since arriving in Singapore buttered no parsnips. It was a one-strike-and-you're-out-deal. Did Foxhole know the reason behind Abbott's no-show? He'd never said, but Abbott figured he'd probably guessed. Meanwhile, Abbott had been in the process of casting his net wider, finding other security companies that worked global markets in the Far East (correction: *thinking* about doing that, during his rare breaks from liquid recreation), when Foxhole had come back on the blower: he needed a specialist and he was prepared to give Abbott a second chance. But cock it up and they were done.

No doubt Abbott would be hearing a repeat of that very threat in the next minute or so. Could be that Foxhole was ringing for that specific purpose, in fact. All Abbott knew was that Foxhole's connection was a company called Hexagon Security operating out of London, who had a reputation for not messing around. No doubt that was another reason Foxhole felt it necessary to keep repeating his threats.

'How's it going?' said the fixer now. He hadn't lost his Chicago drawl, despite ten years in Singapore playing job centre for ex-servicemen who couldn't or wouldn't leave the life behind – guys who called their act of denial 'moving into security' and joined 'The Circuit', as it was known.

'I'm in position. Watching the boat.' Abbott kept it brief, just in case the booze came out in his voice.

'What's going on?'

'Party time.'

'So you move tonight? I can tell Hexagon? Because you know they were hoping to go yesterday, right? But –'

Abbott rolled his eyes. *Dickhead.* They called him Foxhole because that's where he stayed, and back there, safe out of harm's way, he had the luxury of not giving a stuff about unimportant matters such as the need to be as prepared as you can be ahead of possible life-and-death situations.

'I needed a day,' said Abbott.

'So you go tonight? As soon as possible?'

'All things being equal. But yeah, that's the plan. This lot are going to flake out soon, the way they're carrying on. They've been at it since eleven.'

'Don't mess this up, Abbott. You fuck this one up, and you'll be back in the Middle East, tail between your legs, before you can say George W. Bush, got it?'

'Got it.'

'Oh, and need I remind you – no weapons.'

'Sure.'

'Abbott, this is surveillance and tracking, you've no need for artillery, OK?'

'Roger that.'

Not for the first time it crossed Abbott's mind to ask himself why he took this shit from Foxhole, who was to combat what Abbott was to synchronised swimming – i.e. a complete fucking stranger – and he wondered if he should have stayed in Baghdad. Packed away all the shit that went down, stuck it out and made a fortune. Because that's what his old team were doing right now. As far as he knew anyway. They were cleaning up in the security game and he could have been there with them, sharing in the true spoils of war – if he hadn't followed his fleeing conscience. And the answer was that he took this crap from Foxhole because he needed the money. Simple as that.

And at least this way I get to look at myself in the mirror, he thought. *Only just. But still . . .*

He poked a toe at the empty wine bottle. The conversation had gone well, he thought, closing up the phone. If anyone was going to call him out on the being-a-bit-pissed business then it was Foxhole, and he hadn't, which meant that Abbott was absolutely in control. The drunk guy inside was on a tight leash.

Which could only mean it was time for a second bottle.

CHAPTER 5

Singapore's Indian quarter, and in a tiny shop squeezed between the rippling canopies of a food market on one side and the paper lanterns and gaudy clothes of 'Girls Dreamland' on the other was Ray's. No canopies or paper lanterns, just the sign saying 'Ray's' above windows fogged with dirt and age, giving little to no hint of what lay within.

And what lay within was Paxo. It was also Heinz, and Marmite, and jars of rhubarb and custard and Kola Kubes sweets. It was Sun-Pat peanut butter, Hartley's jam, Robertson's marmalade, and Cornflakes. If you were an ex-pat living in Singapore, desperate for a taste of the luxuries back home, unable to go a single extra day without the taste of Irn Bru, then Ray's was where you came. Ray's – proud supplier of Hob Nobs to the ex-pat branch of the local AA group. Either he'd have your heart's desire in stock, or he could get it for a fair price.

Ray wasn't really 'Ray'. He was 'Rey', a Singapore local who'd spotted a gap in the market and exploited it with good humour, business acumen and a perfect command of colloquial English. He was perched on a stool behind a tall counter (Rey had been specific about wanting a tall counter; even he wasn't quite sure why) and looked up as the door opened, admitting the sound of the street outside as well as a tall Caucasian bloke.

'All right, mate?' said Rey.

'Good afternoon,' said the new arrival. He wore a navy mac – very sensible; they were predicting rain for later – and his hair was short. Rey himself was not a man who liked to visit the barbers, which was why he tended to peer out from behind a curtain of lank and greasy hair, but he knew things. He knew that nostalgia and homesickness were all in the mind, which was why only ex-pats ever ate Cornflakes. And he knew a military man when he saw one.

'I'm looking for a guy who loves Branston,' said the well-dressed man.

'Is he in a pickle?' quipped Rey with a big grin.

'You might say that.' The visitor slapped a photocopied image onto the counter: a thin-faced dude with a five o'clock shadow and a haunted look that was unmistakeable.

'Oh, him.' Rey's lip curled and he pushed the page away. 'Yeah, I know him. And yes, he does like Branston. He also likes Gordon's gin and Beefeater gin and Stella Artois, which is probably why he owes me so much money.'

'Where can I find him?'

Rey looked at him, rolled his eyes and spoke slowly, as though addressing someone very old. 'Which is probably why he owes me so much money,' he repeated.

The visitor frowned and reached into his mac.

CHAPTER 6

The shit-thoughts came to Abbott anyway. Like mutating viruses, they had found a way to penetrate alcohol's defence. He tried to banish them but at the same time couldn't help himself returning to them, prodding at them like bruises to see if they were still as painful as they had been before. Thoughts of a footpath along the perimeter of a field on a summer's day, two sets of feet tramping towards a gap in the hedge that led to the riverbank. Of a girl from the past thought lost to him. Of bodies in a village. Of a boy who died in his arms in a battle-scarred street.

'I'm sorry,' he murmured. 'I'm sorry I couldn't help you.' And then, with a gasp, he wrenched himself away, back to the reality of the boat, and a darkness that had slowly crept over the harbour, the sun replaced by a moon that glimmered on grey water, the air heavy and pregnant with the night's expected rainfall.

The two wine bottles shifted on the boards of the deck as he cleared his throat and leaned forward, applying himself to the binoculars, painfully aware of his blurred vison, cursing himself at the same time: *youtwatyoutwat you went and got drunk youtwat.* A vision came to him of Rodney shaking his head sadly. The misery tourist pursing her lips and wagging an admonishing finger. 'You've let yourself down, you've let the school down ...' Even though he knew that was just his drunk brain playing silly buggers.

Right. Concentrate.

Taking deep breaths – lowering his cortisol, increasing his focus – he finally got his head back in the game, his vision settled, and he was able to establish that things on Bryars's yacht had calmed down. In place of cheesy Euro-trance was silence and there was no sign of life on deck. Most likely they were all below, filming themselves doing Christ knows what with the hookers.

All of which meant that it was time.

From his holdall Abbott took his gear, first stripping off his cargo pants and T-shirt and pulling on his dive suit. He strapped on his Glock 17 9mm and then his dive knife on his left leg.

No weapons. Yeah, right, Foxhole. Abbott had a policy: better to be tooled up and not need it, than to be caught short if it goes noisy.

From the holdall he picked a suppressor for the Glock that he dropped into a waterproof comms bag that in turn attached to his chest cache along with a couple of spare mags, vacuum-packed med kit, and a mini emergency air tank which made up his basic ops kit. He threw on the waistcoat-style chest cache and zipped it up the front.

Next he fitted the mouthpiece of his Dräger LAR 5010 rebreather and checked his compass bearing to the target. He went up top, preparing to drop into the water and taking gulps of air from the rebreather at the same time. He knew from past experience that the O_2 from the rebreather would help to clear his head. (Which was the kind of past experience you should, by right, learn from, but don't because you're the species of dickhead who necks two bottles of wine before a crucial job.)

The cold made him gasp as he lowered himself in. Around him the spur was mainly quiet, just the sound of water lapping at the hulls of boats moored there. From further afield came the sound of the harbour at large, the familiar noises of Singapore at night. Lucky for him that Bryars and pals had decided to get the party going early doors.

He took a last visual of the target and then dropped subsurface into the pitch-black, heading on the compass bearing at 3 m depth. His mind worked to overcome the fog of booze in his brain, and he told himself – as in, lied to himself – that being drunk helped sharpen the mind.

Now he was close, and the lights of the target shone through the water like lasers. Abbott hung in the water for a moment or so, feeling for changes in the surrounding environment, then headed slowly to the surface in order to gain visual confirmation of his accuracy.

He was focused now – as focused as he could be in the circumstances. All those shit-thoughts, even his concern for Nathan, were bundled to the margins. His head broke the surface just enough to see the target, approximately 150 m to the front of him. Harbour water traced lines on his goggles, and for a second he felt like he was a little kid again, staring out of the window on a rainy day, watching raindrops race each other down the glass.

Around him, the harbour was almost eerily silent. Music thump-thumped from another yacht, but the sounds of the city behind were a distant background noise. It was as though he had passed from one world into another.

He ducked back beneath the water, executed a roll and dived to a depth of just over 2 m, allowing the inky black water to envelop him. For a moment or so he enjoyed the sensation of the water mixed with that of the alcohol, cocooning him, giving him a womb-like feeling from which he had to shake himself free. His compass took him to the hull of the yacht, and he stayed there for a moment or so, holding onto the hull like a limpet before unzipping a pocket of his dive suit. From it he took the first of the listening devices, placed it and activated it. Next he swam forward and did the same with the second.

From another pocket he drew a small, handheld underwater activation device that he used to conduct a frequency test, alerting land ops that devices one and two were in place and active. Land ops, in this case, being his liaison: guys from Hexagon that he'd never met and probably never would. No doubt Hexagon were being hired by people who wanted to listen in to Bryars's business, presumably in order to get a piece. From what Abbott had seen you could hardly blame them. Whatever game Bryars was playing, he was clearly winning.

He placed the tracking device, switched it to 'go' mode and moved off to the other side of the yacht in order to position listening devices three and four and repeat the frequency test. He fixed the third device. Almost done now. Kicking his legs, he moved to the stern.

And then stopped.

Hanging in the water, suspended from the side of the ship, was a corpse.

CHAPTER 7

In a black Range Rover parked in the shadows on the outskirts of the harbour sat two men, a driver, Chantrell, and his passenger, Tork. They were employees of Hexagon Security, which, in turn, had been hired by a lawyer acting as a go-between for a New York-based financial trader, the name of whom was not known to either Chantrell or Tork. Like Abbott, they were ex-forces and men for hire. And, like Abbott, they understood that discretion and plausible deniability came with the territory.

'Who is this guy anyway?' asked Chantrell. He wore a suede bomber jacket and jeans. Tork called him 'catalogue model' for the way he dressed, which was fine by him, since Tork considered an AC/DC T-shirt the height of sophistication.

Between them on the seat was a receiver, gently blipping away, awaiting the activation of the listening devices.

'A specialist,' replied Tork. Today's T-shirt was a faded *For Those About To Rock* number. 'According to Foxhole, he's ex-SBS. Best in the region.'

There was a pause. The receiver blipped contentedly. 'What's he doing in Singapore, then? Why not be where there's real money to be made?'

'Beats me,' replied Tork. 'Maybe he hates the Middle-Eastern climate. Maybe he's had enough of the place.'

'Be real. It's a proper gold rush out there.'

'I still don't know. Anyway, you might as well ask yourself the same question. How come we're here and not there.'

'Difference is, we go where we're told.' Chantrell shook his head. 'I don't know; there's something iffy about it. I don't like it.'

'You decide that now?'

'I guess so. I mean, I thought there was something iffy about it, but now I'm saying it out loud.'

'Saying it out loud doesn't make it real.'

'Doesn't make it not real. Guy could be a casualty. PTSD case.'

'Look,' sighed Tork, 'give him a chance, would you? He wouldn't be doing the job if he wasn't capable of it, would he? He's special forces. Jesus. What do you want from the guy?'

Chantrell sniffed, conceding the point. After all, they knew the kind of training involved in becoming SF, how the majority never made it past basic (both had, unbeknownst to the other, tried their hand and dropped out), and they each knew that SF were the best. The toughest. The guys who lived in the dark.

The box between them burst into life.

'Devices one and two are in place and active,' confirmed Chantrell, looking down.

Tork reached forward and flipped on the Bluetooth speaker. At the same time, Chantrell picked up, flicked open his phone and began tapping out a text message.

As he did so, two further lights on the receiver between them blinked on.

'That's it,' said Chantrell. 'All four devices are in place.'

CHAPTER 8

Suspended by a length of blue nylon rope tied around her neck, the girl's head lolled at an angle familiar to the hangman. Her eyes were open wide and her mouth formed an O shape, limbs hanging loose, shoulders rounded. Naked.

Abbott hung in the water, looking at her, finally having a reason to be thankful for the two bottles of wine he'd sunk, because at least the booze numbed the shock.

It was her, of course. The hooker from before. The one being chased around the deck. Her hair danced and drifted in the current, and although there was no life in those eyes, it was as though she were watching him. Judging him.

He wondered what it was that lay behind her murder: bad sex, viciousness, sadism, probably some mix of all three.

And he wondered when it had happened, and whether he would have known if he hadn't nodded off, lured into sleep by the siren call of booze. In other words, if he could have done anything to prevent it.

Of course you could. You saw the way it was. The state of them. He thought of Bryars making her eat the money, felt gripped by a fury but did his best to dismiss it, tearing his gaze away from those dead but blame-filled eyes to look down at the activation device in his hand. Signal strength 78 per cent.

Which meant that the job was as good as done. He placed the final listening device and checked the signal again. He had done everything asked of him. He had earned his money. Maybe one day in the future his path would cross that of Mr Travis Bryars and he would get his chance to see justice done, the girl avenged. But not today. Today he just needed to do the job and get paid.

As he turned to swim back, he found that, once again, he had to tear his gaze away from her.

Another corpse, he thought. Another silent rebuke for his failings as a soldier. As a man. He let himself sink to a lower depth, ready to take a reverse bearing back to his small cabin cruiser, already looking forward to the drink he knew would further calm his soul. All that was left was to pat himself on the back for a job completed successfully, collect the money, and try to forget. Try to forget the girl and the look of fear in her eyes. The cackling of the men who tore off her bikini top. The cruelty in Bryars's eyes as he stuffed money into her mouth.

And then he stopped.

Knowing that he couldn't do it. Couldn't just slip away and leave it. Because leaving now meant that these bastards got away scot-free, and he couldn't do that. No way.

What was he going to do?

Didn't know. Making it up as he went along.

He just knew that he had to do *something*, because the opposite of doing something was doing nothing, and right now that wasn't an acceptable option.

He turned and swam back to the ship, removed his rebreather and attached it to the underside of the hull with an anchor suction cup. He used the stern deck to board the yacht and crouched there for a moment or so. Listening.

All was silent. Just the sound of the water kissing the hull. The distant thump of dance music from the other boat, the fuzzy sound of nightlife from the city and his own ragged breathing reminding him that he was out of shape and drunk and not thinking straight, the fuck-it switch well and truly thrown.

But training and instinct kicked in, and he stayed dead quiet, senses on high alert. At the same time, he pulled his Glock, letting the water drain from the barrel. The last thing he needed now was a breach explosion if the shit hit the fan and it got noisy.

He crept forward, gratified by his own noiseless progress, finding a kind of peace within his own efficiency. Then he stopped as something ahead of him resolved itself in his vision. On the deck was a strange, irregular shape that, if Abbott guessed correctly, was …

Yes. A guy asleep on a sun lounger, empty bottle of champagne on its side on the deck beside him.

Abbott approached, steeling himself for the bloke to stir. In the light of the moon he got a better look and saw who it was. The man himself: Mr Money Stuffer, Travis Bryars. He was spark out, arms by his sides, twelve hours of partying having taken their toll. Lightweight.

Abbott holstered his Glock and drew his dive knife, coming closer to the lounger. Bryars stirred and he froze, watching the billionaire's lips vibrate as he let out a gentle snore.

Abbott took up position at the side of the lounger, testing the dive suit for flexibility, knife held ready in his right hand, bouncing on the balls of his feet for a second before he made his move.

And then, in one fluid movement, he swung his left leg over Bryars, dropped down and pinned him to the lounger at the same time as he clamped his left hand over his mouth and brought the tip of the dive knife to the right side of his temple, just below his eye.

Bryars's eyes opened wide with fear and surprise. For a second he bucked and tried to shout beneath Abbott's hand, but Abbott held firm, shaking his head at the same time, silently shushing his prisoner. With a flick of his wrist he opened a nick in the skin just below Bryars's right eye, enough to hurt him, so the warm blood would run down his face and give him the shits about it being so near his eye.

Sure enough, Bryars shut up and stopped bucking. Abbott heard urine spatter to the deck from the underside of the sun lounger and couldn't help but take a certain grim pleasure from the sound.

'Travis Bryars,' said Abbott, his voice a low growl.

Bryars remained still and silent.

'I know it's you,' said Abbott. 'And I know that if you make a sound when I remove my hand, then I'm going to cut your throat – I'll cut your throat for what you lot did to that girl, and then, when your pissed-up buddies come running, I'll kill them, too. Nod your head if you follow.'

Travis nodded, at which Abbott lifted his hand. With a fast movement he swapped his knife from one hand to the other, holding it now to the other side of Bryars's head as he reached for his Glock. 'Not a sound,' he warned. 'You do or say anything, I'll put a round in your bollocks.' He stood and motioned Bryars to do the same. 'Now undress,' he said.

As Bryars began to strip off, his demeanour subtly changed. Where before there was fear, as well as shame at having soiled himself, now there was the beginnings of an anger, maybe even defiance. Perhaps he realised that if Abbott wanted to kill him, then he would have done so already, and that if he was left alive, then he would have his day of reckoning.

It was the little spark telling Abbott that he should put a bullet in Bryars. That by leaving him alive he was storing up trouble for himself. Kill him, though, and the job was a bust. And that, in the short term, was something he literally couldn't afford to do.

What had made him swim back? Was it the booze or the conscience? Whatever. Shouldn't have done it.

'You can leave your pants on,' said Abbott, who had no desire to see Bryars's hairy arse, no matter how much it would humiliate him.

'I'm not wearing any,' replied Bryars. His chin had tilted and he spoke a little louder than Abbott, almost as though daring Abbott to do something.

So Abbott took him up on it. He used the butt of his Glock to break Bryars's nose.

Felt good.

Blood rushed from Bryars's smashed nose at the same time as he opened his mouth to scream and his legs gave away. Before he could sink to the deck, Abbott had stepped smartly forward, clamped his hand over Bryars's mouth once more and was dragging him to the edge of the deck where the line of blue nylon rope ran over the side. Warm blood ran over the back of his hand, icky and unpleasant between his fingers. Bryars mewled in agony.

'Get in,' ordered Abbott. 'You've got a body to bring up.'

Bryars's eyes widened as he turned to Abbott, but whatever he planned to do or say next was lost to the Fates because right then was the moment the shit chose to hit the fan.

CHAPTER 9

From the other end of the deck came a shout. Abbott swung, saw silhouettes emerge and in the same movement, shoved Bryars off the boat and raised his pistol.

Bryars hit the water with a scream and the new arrivals opened fire. Gunshots split the night. Abbott dropped to one knee, held the Glock. The air above him zinged and time seemed to slow down as he found himself in that place he thought of as his combat bubble, a zone that years of training and experience had taught him to locate at will – a place where, despite the noise of battle and threat of imminent death, he found both peace and calm. A place where he felt at his best.

He sighted moving figures and squeezed off two rounds. In reply the shots were haphazard, disorganised, the kind of response you'd expect from men who were being fired upon, who had also spent the day getting pissed.

Not that Abbott could talk, and despite the surge of adrenalin, he almost lost his footing as he took off across the deck in search of cover. Rounds thunked into the woodwork around him and splinters flew as the security guys recovered their composure, found their target and began to trade fire.

Once more, he crouched and squeezed off three more rounds in short succession, keeping the rounds spread. There was nothing to see now, though. The enemy had found cover, and it was he who was out in the open.

He raised the barrel and took out windows, knowing the sound of the smashing glass would help panic the enemy.

He took off again, shots cracking overhead, one of the security blokes calling out his position. Three of them, remember: three drunks against one drunk. Plus, he had the moonlight behind him, backlighting him, picking him out like someone trying to sneak out for a piss at the cinema as he made another dash to the opposite side of the yacht, aware of the sound of gunfire making its way across the harbour and knowing it wouldn't be too long before they dispatched a police cruiser.

Something snagged him and he cried out in pain and took a tumble, having crashed into a champagne stand. This time he paid for it, feeling the sharp pain of a round as it grazed his arm, a tear in the wetsuit already leaking blood.

And that was enough to convince him that there was a time for trading blows and a time for throwing yourself headlong into the inky water, and this was one of those latter times.

Oh Christ, he was thinking as he took a dive off the side of the yacht. *Jesus Christ, mate, you have fucked it this time.*

CHAPTER 10

'Christ. What the fuck is going on out there?'

Chantrell's jaw dropped. The blood draining from his face. With the listening devices activated, he and Tork had fired up the Bluetooth speaker, expecting to hear … well, they weren't quite sure what they were expecting to hear. Some kind of live feed that they could patch back to Hexagon in London, who would in turn provide it to the client.

What they absolutely hadn't expected to hear was the sound of screaming, shouting and . . .

Gunfire.

Chantrell opened the Range Rover door. Sure enough, that same sound could be heard rolling in from the harbour.

'Oh, that's bad,' said Tork, his understatement drawing a glare from Chantrell as they looked from the speaker to each other, trying to work out what was going on. Chantrell leaned over, popped the glove compartment and snatched out a pair of binoculars. The next instant, he was out of the Range Rover, scrambling onto the bonnet and then climbing to the roof, where he stood, training the binoculars across the harbour. 'Muzzle flashes,' he called down to Tork. 'Wait, two sets. Jesus Christ.'

'He's out of the water?'

'Yeah. By the looks of things he's on the bloody deck.'

'*What*? What's he doing out of the water? He was meant to—'

'Yes, for fuck's sake. I know what he was meant to do. Oh, fuck.'

'What now?'

Tork was standing on the door sill of the Range Rover, craning his neck as though that might help him witness what Chantrell could only see with the aid of high-powered binoculars.

'Police cruiser's on its way,' said Chantrell in the desolate tones of a man announcing a death in the family.

'Oh, bloody hell. We've got to call this in. Operation's FUBAR.'

Tork was already reaching to make the call, knowing that the fall-out would be bad. After all, it was they who had employed Foxhole, who in turn had recruited the SF guy, who in turn appeared to be operating in flagrant disregard of every instruction issued to him. This would all come back on them.

Above, Chantrell continued watching. The gun battle was over. Lights on deck had flared on and he saw two armed security guys dart from one end of the yacht to the other.

At the same time, others, including a guy in a towelling bathrobe, were going to the aid of a naked guy who was pulling himself back on deck. The naked guy was Bryars, and Chantrell didn't know why he was naked, or what he had been doing in the water, or why his nose was bleeding and looked suspiciously like it had been busted. Only that whatever had happened, it wasn't good.

As for Abbott. No sign. From the way the gunmen were behaving, he'd gone overboard. Dead? Injured? Lucky escape? Either way, there was nothing else to see, and Chantrell climbed down from the roof of the vehicle just as Tork finished the call. 'You called it in?'

Tork nodded.

'What are our orders?'

Tork looked at him. He made a brisk cut-throat gesture.

Chantrell shook his head in disgust. 'So much for giving him a chance.'

'He blew his chance,' said Tork, wiping the sweat from his face with the hem of his AC/DC T-shirt. 'Soon as he got out that water, he blew his chance.'

CHAPTER 11

Foxhole's office occupied a room at the top of a house that from the outside looked like just another scruffy residence on a narrow street. This one, however, had been divided into other, similar offices. Below Foxhole's security services unit was a money-lender's, below that, a guy who, as far as he knew, and in the absence of any evidence to the contrary, was Singapore's dodgiest landlord. None were businesses who bothered putting their name on the door.

Foxhole sat at his desk now. His blond hair hung damp. Dark stains under his armpits reached almost to the horse insignia of his navy polo shirt, and sweaty, slightly pudgy fingers tapped nervously on his Nokia. He was anxiously awaiting news of the operation. Praying that the news would be good. After all, this job had come through Hexagon Security out of London, and there were two things he knew about Hexagon Security out of London. First, they offered by far the best rates of remuneration this side of the Middle East. Second, for the kind of money they paid they expected exemplary work, and they were not known to take kindly to failure. Which probably amounted to three things, that final one being the most pertinent. OK, four things, if you believed the rumour that Hexagon were not at all averse to using enforcers to tie up loose ends.

Just the thought caused fresh sweat to pop at Foxhole's armpits. The two Hexagon guys, Chantrell and Tork, had insisted on a specialist and it wasn't like Foxhole had books brimming with underwater specialists. Just the one, in fact.

So you gave them Abbott?

I didn't have any fucking choice, he told himself. And besides, Abbott had given him his word. No fuck-ups this time.

The phone rang. Speak of the devil.

'Abbott?' he said, snatching at the word. 'Tell me you're ringing with good news.'

'Yes, mate,' came the reply, 'the listening devices and the tracker are in place. So if you'd be kind enough to transfer the money, I'm sure the manager at Barclays in Burton-on-Trent will be most appreciative.'

But Abbott's breezy tone was forced, and he sounded breathless, as though he were talking on the move.

'What is it?' pressed Foxhole, swallowing, some instinct telling him that something was wrong. Maybe terribly wrong.

'Just transfer the money. We'll talk about it over a beer later.'

He sounded … was he hurt?

'Just tell me what the sweet fuck is going on, Abbott. You know, don't you? You know that I'm going to find out sooner or later, right? So let it be now.'

'OK, all right. I may have been spotted. Shots were fired.'

Foxhole didn't even realise it, but he had stood up. Now he sank back down, his head going into his hands. 'Oh, sweet Jesus. Oh my—'

'Yeah, sorry, mate.'

'You do realise—'

'Yeah, they might come for you. But, look, they'll know that the devices are in place. To all intents and purposes the job is done. It's not a complete balls-up. You can tell them that.'

But Foxhole didn't think Hexagon were going to see it that way. He didn't think that 'to all intents and purposes' was going to be good enough for them. He ended the call, and at the same time rose from the desk, grabbed his windcheater from the back of his chair and swept up his phone, keys and cigarettes, dashing to the door of his office and yanking it open.

In the doorway stood Chantrell.

Just behind him, Tork.

'Hello, Foxhole,' said Chantrell.

'Chantrell,' croaked Foxhole. He cleared his throat, trying to enforce calm upon himself, wondering if he looked as bad as he felt, immediately getting his answer.

'You're looking a bit discombobulated, mate,' said Tork.

'Tork,' he said, hoping they wouldn't pick up on the croak in his voice. 'Chantrell. Good to see you guys. What in the holy mother of ass are you doing here? Everything all right, yeah?' He tried to smile and felt his lips crack as they pulled back over his teeth.

Chantrell shook his head sadly. His hands were clasped in front of him, and if Foxhole had been a fighting man himself, instead of a man who sat behind a desk making unreasonable demands of fighting men, then he would have known that fighting men like to hold their hands clasped in front of them that way because the hands could easily be deployed in either a defensive or offensive manner.

If he'd known that then he might have thought to avoid Chantrell's fist that snaked out fast, catching him in the midriff and doubling him up.

'No, everything is not all right, mate,' said Chantrell, stepping inside with Tork at his heel. 'Everything is not all right at all.'

CHAPTER 12

The man in the raincoat had made his way from Ray's ex-pat shop to the address given, a street in downtown Singapore, lined with tenement buildings on either side, the odd three-storey house squeezed in between them like an afterthought, giving the buildings the look of a row of uneven teeth.

Most were residential and used as homes-for-hire by overseas companies who needed somewhere to put staff, either prior to permanent relocation, or for long-term contracts. As a result, a lot of ex-pats lived there. A lot of British. This, apparently, was where Alex Abbott had made his home for the last eleven months or so.

The raincoat man stopped. This was the one. Number twenty-three. Abbott had the top flat.

Unsurprised by the absence of any security measures, he made his way inside and took the stairs upwards. From behind doors on the landings he heard sounds of life: televisions, music, a couple arguing. Through a window left open traffic noise was borne inside on the cool night-time breeze.

He reached the top, and the door to Abbott's room. There he stood listening for a moment or so before knocking. His clothes were neat, and so was his knock, and when there was no reply he rapped a little louder.

He waited and then with a frown returned to the street. A moment later he was walking into the bar two doors down from number twenty-three: The Big Smile Beach Club.

Rarely had a place been so erroneously named. Not only did it lack anything even remotely suggesting the seaside, but smiles were in short supply. Instead, it was small, and yet at the same time not especially cosy, thanks to decor that back home would be considered more suitable for a café.

That said, it was busy and, as far as he could tell, frequented by a certain type of ex-pat. As in, not the outgoing, sociable kind: copy of the *Daily Express*, memories of Tunbridge Wells and the time that Dirty Den returned to *EastEnders*. But the other kind: the guys who liked to drink either in pairs or alone. Drinking as a means to an end. Punishment drinking.

It figured that Abbott would have found himself a flat just two doors down from a place like this.

Behind the bar sat a Malaysian guy who was far younger and more fresh-faced than any of his grizzled clientele. He was reading a newspaper but looked up as the smartly dressed man approached. 'What can I get you?' he asked cheerily.

'I'm after information,' said the raincoat man.

The bartender pretended to scan the pumps and then the bottles behind him. 'I don't think we have any of that. How about a pint, mate?'

His English was perfect. By the sounds of things he was even adding a touch of Cockney just for comedy value. No doubt when your job was playing nursemaid to a bunch of jaundiced British soaks, you got your laughs any way you could.

'Do you know a guy called Alex Abbott?' asked the rain-coat man.

The smile left the barman's face like smoke dispersing. 'Maybe I do, maybe I don't,' he said.

Which was good enough for the visitor. 'Spend a lot of time in here, does he? Likes a seat at the bar. Not here though,' he ran a hand from left to right, 'not with his back to the door. I bet he sits over there,' he pointed, 'or there.' He indicated the other side where the bar turned a corner, where anybody sitting would have a good view of customers coming and going.

The barman looked at him, intrigued but wary. 'If you're going to ask me where he lives, I don't know.'

'He lives two doors down.'

'Oh, does he?' The barman played it down.

'Yes, and I bet you he's left you his spare door key, hasn't he?' He held up a finger. 'He's left you his door key and he's told you not to give it to anyone but him. Is that right?'

The barman shrugged, giving nothing away.

The visitor leaned forward. He opened his coat. 'But you're going to give that key to me.'

CHAPTER 13

Abbott looked at the phone in his hand. Foxhole had cut him off.

Moments before, he'd pulled himself out of the water and onto the cruiser, cursing and groaning and *owwing* with pain as he slithered across the deck and then took the steps below decks. There, he had pulled himself into a sitting position, still cursing himself *youtwatyoutwatyoutwat*, the words meaningless now but like a mantra and helping to take his mind off the pain in his arm.

He reached for his trousers and retrieved the vacuum-sealed medipack. Pulling his wetsuit off he inspected the wound, cleaned it with solution, patted it dry and then reached for the QuikClot powder.

Next he dressed. Back into his civvies: black V-neck T-shirt with a long-sleeved khaki shirt slung open over the top. The wound wouldn't slow him down. Blood loss was negligible. And so, as he grabbed his holdall and climbed off the boat, heading for his Honda Accord, he called Foxhole.

Who had – not to put too fine a point on it – shit himself.

Abbott's first thought: *Jesus, I'm the one who's supposed to be volatile. Not you.* His second was that, by the sounds of things, he could probably kiss the fee for the job goodbye. And his third? Would Foxhole take the flak, or would he pass the buck? Would he sell Abbott out?

He reached the car. His phone rang, and he got his answer.

'Mr Abbott,' said the caller. 'My name is Chantrell. I work for Hexagon Security. You were doing a job for us this evening.'

'Yup,' replied Abbott. 'All devices operational, I trust.'

'Roger that.'

'So maybe you could authorise transfer of my fee?'

'More than happy to. You able to swing by Foxhole's office right now? We'll have a short debrief and get your fee sorted.'

'Sounds grand. I'll see you there.'

* * *

In Foxhole's office, Chantrell finished the call. 'Abbott says he's coming here,' he said, and Foxhole, who had been slumped dripping in his office chair, hair plastered to his face, gave a start.

'Jesus Christ, he's coming *here*. Do you know who this guy is?'

'You've just told us that he's a hard-assed ex-SBS guy, but that every time you met him you could smell booze on his breath,' said Chantrell. 'So a tough nut who can't shoot straight. I think we can handle that.'

'Not here, though.' Foxhole's usual Chicagoan drawl had risen to a near-screech.

'You can rest your sphincter, mate,' Tork assured him. 'He ain't coming here. He knows there's nothing to be gained from coming here.'

He and Chantrell were already making for the door.

* * *

A hard rain had begun to fall. Having driven pell-mell across the city, Abbott dumped his beaten-up Accord a couple of streets away, grabbed his holdall and then jogged the rest of the distance, getting soaked but thanking the rain for one thing at least. It hid the fact that blood had soaked through his makeshift dressing.

He passed the Big Smile Beach Club, and despite everything – despite the fact that booze was half the reason he was in trouble in the first place – he still had to resist an urge to go in. That was how crazy this shit was. How it was in his brain. Imagine being at the bar: 'How was your day?' 'Oh, you know, getting drunk, staging a covert night-time incursion, finding a dead hooker, getting into a firefight, picking up a flesh wound. How was yours?'

'Yeah, pretty much the same.'

Now he slowed down. Catching himself before he made the mistake of acting out of habit and using the front door, he ducked through a narrow alleyway between his building and the one beside it, reaching a fire escape that he hauled down, clambering up quickly until he reached his window.

He paused on the windowsill, sitting on his haunches, one hand at his wound. From his holdall he dug out his Glock. Next he raised the window and climbed inside, wincing a little with the pain.

He stood there for a moment in the half-light, listening, holding the Glock two-handed by his thigh. Something wasn't right. His sixth sense was trying to tell him something: an internal alarm bell jangling, that somehow managed to pierce the shroud of regret and alcohol he wore.

Then came a voice. 'The barman warned you, didn't he? I told him not to warn you,' and a figure moved out of the shadows.

CHAPTER 14

There's a scene in *Citizen Kane* where one of the characters talks about a girl he once saw on a ferry. It was only a fleeting glimpse, and she hadn't even seen him. But there wasn't a month since when that guy hadn't thought about that girl.

It was a scene that had struck a chord with Abbott, who'd seen *Citizen Kane* one night in Thailand, of all places.

He knew that feeling. It was exactly the way he felt about Tessa.

Only it wasn't every month he thought about her. It wasn't weeks, either. It was days, it was hours. Because wherever he was, whatever he was doing, he thought about Tessa. Sometimes he might go half a day without thinking of her, and on those occasions he'd wonder if he was over her, if the ghost had finally been exorcised. But then he'd be thinking of her again; once more she'd be in his head, accompanied by that ever-present sense of what-might-have-been. No, what-*should*-have-been. Not quite one of the shit-thoughts, but in there keeping them company anyway. Jostling for position.

They'd met at school, back when his whole world was Burton-on-Trent and he already knew it was too small for him. She was his first love and now, he realised, his only. They had lost their virginity to one another and being wild that way found in each other a sexual chemistry that, again, he'd never found with another and could only assume he never would.

Theirs was a tempestuous relationship. Really, they should have just enjoyed each other and made the most of what they had, but they were young and thus had a predilection for introducing unnecessary drama into any given situation, even and most especially situations that did not require it.

Abbott, at the same time, was fighting his own demons. His parents, absent emotionally, too involved with difficulties that would eventually end in divorce, watched helpless as he, a promising student, had drifted towards petty crime, getting into fights, committing minor theft. Acting up. Showing off. He was the original good-kid-turned-bad. Not quite from the wrong side of the tracks but a regular visitor there. He'd even spent time in a remand home for minor arson. A mess, even in those days. The difference being that he didn't know it back then.

Somehow their relationship had survived, and they had stayed together. Back then he took it for granted, being so full of himself, but these days he asked himself why a girl like Tessa would have stayed with a fuck-up like him, and he wondered if it was the whole bad-boy image. Or if maybe she just stayed with him as an act of rebellion at home. Her parents hated Abbott. Her dad *fucking* hated him.

Milestones came thick and fast: exams, part-time jobs, last days of school. The day Abbott passed his driving test he'd picked up Tessa in his mum's Fiat Panda and they'd gone to the cinema, free at last. He was driving that same car when they went to collect their exam results together. She had excelled, of course. He, on the other hand? Well, his time in a remand home had done a lot to help him mend his ways, but he had been too far over into the dark side to turn things around completely. Poor to mediocre was the sad tale of the grades; Tessa, who with her supportive parents and protective older brother (who also *fucking hated* Abbott) knew only stability, absolutely sailed through. She had set her sights on Oxbridge. Abbott, meanwhile, planned on joining the Marines.

So he asked her to marry him. And of course she laughed because nobody got married at eighteen. Nobody in her world anyway, and certainly not Tessa, who thought of her life in stages, like a series of interlocking Lego bricks where marriage was at least two or three bricks away.

Abbott told her that being married need not affect her degree, her career. But she looked at him as though he were insane. He wanted her, that was the thing. He wanted to put her in a little cage.

He knew that now. He knew also that he had frightened her away.

They split up. It was no big deal at the time; they were bound to get back together as they always did. It was the reason their relationship was such a source of fascination for their mates. They were like a living soap: Alex and Tess, on and off like a light switch. During the five years they were a couple, they must have split up and got back together – what? – half a dozen times? Maybe more. And despite the marriage proposal, which was maybe more a gesture of loyalty on Abbott's part than a serious consideration, they would get back together again.

Only this time, things took a turn. During the break, Abbott had a one-night-stand with a girl he met in town one night. A girl called Fiona.

Tess found out. Dumped him. As in, for good this time.

Worse, Fi was pregnant. Not yet eighteen, Abbott was to be a father and had lost the love of his life.

Off she went to Oxford, taking her broken heart with her and leaving him with his. He'd never seen her since. But like the guy in *Citizen Kane*, he thought about her all the time. All. The. Time.

As for him and Fi? For a while they tried to make it as a couple. But the spark was never there. Fi was different to Tessa. Where Tessa was water, Fi was fire. Where Tessa was soft, Fi was hard. Both were determined, but the source of Tessa's determination lay outside the relationship, whereas Fi turned it inwards and onto Abbott, onto their marriage.

And the biggest bone of contention? That would be his long absences as a serving Marine. While he was away, she would complain that he was never there. When he was at home, she would remind him that he was never there. His drinking didn't help, of course, and became a bigger factor in their relationship the more time went on. It meant that Abbott could never win any argument. Whatever the dispute; whoever was in the wrong, it always came back to that. Drink was as much her weapon of choice as it was his.

Their son, Nathan, was the glue that held them together. For a while. For a long time, actually. But in the end it wasn't enough. Nath was ten years old when they split. Not long later, Fi had met another guy, a pen pusher from the Ministry of Defence, part of the MOD's 'defence diplomacy' division.

Needless to say, and in accordance with every rule of divorce, the new guy and Abbott had never got on. They were different animals. And while there was no romantic rivalry over Fi, Abbott resented his replacement fathering Nathan.

Abbott would snipe, making no secret of his derision for 'defence diplomacy', while the other guy would make barbs about Abbott's parental absence. For his part, Abbott made the most of the fact that his SF bearing and air of unpredictability intimidated the other guy whom he had named 'Cuckoo'.

In short, the two were, if not outright enemies, then rivals.

Which made it all the more surprising that Cuckoo was standing in his one-room apartment in Singapore.

CHAPTER 15

'All right, Cuckoo?' said Abbott.

Cuckoo sighed. 'Can't you for once use my actual name, Abbott?'

Abbott looked at him, seeing the Cuckoo he knew of old: a man who was born to mow the lawn into neat straight lines and then settle down for Sunday lunch. A solid guy. Everything Abbott wasn't and didn't want to be – but somehow envied anyway.

'You can't remember my real name, can you?' said Cuckoo, icily.

'Is it Clive something?'

'No, not Clive.'

'Ian.'

'No.'

'Alan.'

'Yes, it's Alan.'

'Well … Cuckoo. How about you tell me what you're doing in my apartment?' asked Abbott. As he spoke, he pushed the Glock into the waistband of his cargo pants, went to the centre of the room, brushed aside a threadbare circular rug and reached to crack open one of the floorboards. He began decanting his diving gear and assault rifle into the void beneath, reluctantly giving up his Glock and his knife, too, replacing the floorboard.

'We need to talk,' said Cuckoo.

'Couldn't you have called?'

'I didn't think you'd take the call.'

'And why wouldn't I?'

'You know why.'

Abbott replaced the floorboard and then moved to a chest of drawers, yanked open a drawer and began rummaging.

'What are you doing?' asked Cuckoo, as Abbott began tossing socks and pants onto the bed before moving quickly to the wardrobe, grabbing a couple of shirts and adding them to the pile.

'I'm putting up Christmas decorations, what does it look like? Hate to break it to your ego but you weren't the reason I was coming through the window.'

'You're leaving? Where are you—?'

Abbott reached into the top of a cupboard, located and popped a small panel that he'd rigged up and retrieved his passports and his old military ID. Like most operators in his game, he had two passports, a 'clean' one and a 'dirty' one. The 'clean' one was, literally, clean. The kind of passport that barely received a second look at passport control. The dirty one, on the other hand, was covered in visas and stamps, mostly for Middle Eastern countries. Say you were going to the States, which passport would you present? Exactly.

'Where am I going?' he said now, slipping both passports into his trousers. 'Anywhere but Singapore, mate.' He began stuffing the holdall. He had found a couple of door wedges that he tossed into the bag and Cuckoo seemed about to ask him about them when something else occurred to him.

'You know that your arm is bleeding, right?'

'Bullet graze,' said Abbott, enjoying how Cuckoo paled a little.

'And would that bullet graze have anything to do with you needing to leave Singapore all of a sudden?'

Abbott rolled his eyes. 'No, it's just a coincidence.'

He shoved his laptop into the holdall, zipped the bag shut.

'Look, we need to talk,' repeated Cuckoo.

'OK, talk.' And then Abbott stopped. Finally, the penny had dropped. 'Is this about Nath?'

At the same time, the door shuddered. Somebody had put their shoulder to it. It happened again, only with even more force, and this time it seemed to bow around the Yale.

Abbott reacted first. Putting a finger to his lips, he motioned Cuckoo to stay where he was in the centre of the room. In the same instant he dived to the side of the door, flattening himself to the wall just as another kick came, and then another, before the Yale finally gave, the door flew open, and in came the two men from Hexagon: Chantrell and Tork, guns in their fists.

They stopped at the sight of Cuckoo. Both staring at him, feeling suddenly unsure of themselves. They'd never actually met Abbott, but thanks to Foxhole they knew what he looked like, and they didn't think he was the guy who stood in the middle of the room. But then again, maybe with a haircut, a shave, a healthy clothing allowance and a change of outlook, perhaps it was …

'Abbott …' began Chantrell. A question. A challenge. A greeting.

'It's not Abbott,' said Tork.

Their hesitation was all the invitation that the real Abbott needed. Coming from behind, outside of their peripheral vision, he grabbed Chantrell's gun arm and at the same time moved across them both, spun and rammed his elbow hard into Tork's face.

The movement ended with Abbott holding Chantrell's arm across his chest. It took a split-second. Chantrell's eyes widened as he saw what Abbott was about to do, and in the next moment he was screaming as Abbott snapped his arm.

Chantrell sunk to his knees, mewling in pain, out of the battle. Hurt, blinded and with his nose streaming blood, Tork tried to bring his gun to bear, but Abbott moved in for the kill, this time using his head on the bridge of Tork's nose – his nose that quickly went from merely broken to permanently damaged beyond repair.

As Tork fell, consciousness making an exit, Cuckoo came forward to grab his gun, stopping him from accidentally discharging his weapon.

Now Tork was out of it, Chantrell groaning on the floor as Abbott and Cuckoo made their escape through the window and down the fire escape.

'I didn't think you'd be any good in a fight,' said Abbott as they rattled down the steps towards the street. As Cuckoo preened he added, 'I still don't think you'd be any good in a fight.'

CHAPTER 16

It was still chucking it down with rain as Abbott and Cuckoo jumped into Cuckoo's hired Lexus. As they moved off, Abbott caught a glimpse of something in the wing mirror and twisted to get a better look, squinting through the rain-sluiced rear window.

A hire car had drawn into the street. Abbott saw an outline of the driver and a mop of white hair, almost brilliant white, as though lit from within. The car stopped outside number twenty-three and White Hair got out. Heedless of the downpour, or seemingly so, at least, he looked up at the building.

And then, almost as though he could sense the nearby presence of Abbott, he looked to his right – directly at the fleeing Lexus.

Now they were turning out on to the street and Abbott saw the white-haired guy hurrying back to his car.

Shit.

'Could be that we have another visitor; don't hang about,' he told Cuckoo. 'And while you're doing that, how about you tell me the reason why you're in Singapore.'

'The way you were back there—' said Cuckoo, sounding like he hadn't heard the question.

'What do you mean?' asked Abbott.

'Taking those two guys out.'

'Yeah? What about it?'

'I've never seen you like that before.'

'Well, it's never been take-your-love-rival-to-work-day before.'

'So that's it, is it? Just another day at the office for you?'

'Yup. We even have a sweepstake for the Grand National.'

'It was impressive.'

Abbott rolled his eyes. 'Yeah, well, I'm not completely fucking useless, you know, despite what you might be hearing elsewhere.'

'But you are drinking? I mean, I can smell it on you.'

'Anything else?'

'Yes. How come you ended up here? Why did you leave Baghdad a year ago?'

'None of your fucking business. Look, I'm not drunk in a gutter. I'm assuming I meet whatever standard of competency you have. And if I don't, then tough shit. Tell me what you're doing here. What does Nathan have to do with it?'

Cuckoo's voice was flat in reply. 'Nathan's missing.'

Abbott took a deep breath and turned his head to stare at the rain-streaked city passing by. 'Yes,' was all he said.

'You knew?'

'Let's just say it's not a complete surprise. What do you know?'

'OK, well, um, I don't know if you were aware or not, but Nathan was with the Marines, stationed with the British contingent at the Turkish air base at Incirlik …'

Fair play, Cuckoo had tried to keep his voice neutral, but still the news hit Abbott in a series of gut punches. Two years ago he'd argued with Nathan about joining the army, trying every trick in the book. Like, Nathan was really into trainers so Abbott had said, 'There's no point in having the best clobber if your legs have been blown off,' which was a bit below the belt, literally and figuratively.

'Do you really want to end up like me?' he'd added, 'Probably fucked up from PTSD? Is that what you want?' Which was the only time he had ever invoked his own drinking as a negative, and certainly the only time he'd ever prescribed himself PTSD.

Not that any of it helped. Nathan was dead-set. The trouble was that Abbott had long since promoted the idea that the army had been the making of him (which it had been). That it had kept him on the straight and narrow (which it had). If the army was in Nathan's DNA, then that was because Abbott had put it there, and no amount of retro-fitting deterrents was going to put him off. Nathan saw through it all.

What's more, of course, he'd inherited his mother's determination, and although she hadn't wanted him to join up either – she and Abbott couldn't agree on what day it was, but they'd agreed on that – it was one battle she couldn't win.

And so, yes, Abbott knew that Nathan had joined the North Staffordshire Regiment. He knew that Nathan had undergone thirty-two weeks of Commando training in order to become a Marine. Abbott had gone to Nathan's pass-out at Lympstone, the Royal Marine's Commando Training Centre. Was that the last time he'd seen Fi? Yes. Was that the last time he'd seen Nathan? Also yes.

Which was why Abbott didn't know that Nath had been sent to Turkey, so close to Iraq. That came as news to him.

'Take a left here,' he said distractedly. His hand was in his lap, his fingers slightly curled, and it seemed like only yesterday that Nathan had been a tiny baby, lying along his forearm, his head in Abbott's palm. 'Imagine being so small that your whole head can fit in someone's hand,' Fi had said at the time. They'd been close then. She'd put a hand out to Abbott. 'It must be like having your own personal giant to protect you.'

Abbott had chuckled. *Don't get used to it, kid*, he'd thought. *It never gets this good again.*

'As far as we know he took leave to Baghdad,' continued Cuckoo, eyes never leaving the road as he took a left, negotiating city traffic.

'Baghdad?' snorted Abbott. 'Not exactly where I'd choose to spend my leave.' He reached for his holdall, pulled off his shirt and set to work repairing his dressing.

'Exactly,' said Cuckoo. 'The thing is that Fi kept him on a tight leash. You know what she's like – a bit of a mother hen. When he went out to Turkey she made him promise to Skype her every other day minimum. Absolute minimum. So she was pissed off when he missed his slot.

'Well, at first she was. And then she moved on to worried, and it's been a bit of a sliding scale since then. Do they go upwards, sliding scales? I dunno. Anyway. He hasn't responded to email, texts – nothing.'

'You contacted the base?'

'No, we didn't think of that. Yes, of course we contacted the base.'

'Leave the sarcasm to me. What did they say?'

'Well, that was when we found out that he'd taken leave and gone to Baghdad.'

Abbott shook his head. 'Taken leave of his fucking senses, if he's gone to Baghdad,' thinking, *Baghdad of all places*. Saddam had been caught and was awaiting trial, his old palace being used as a base for the coalition. The city itself was a war zone:

bombed-out, plagued by water and food shortages, lawless and chaotic, a powderkeg of insurgency, revenge killings and ethnic division, a civil war waiting to happen. Earlier that month a US Army Chinook on its way to the city had been shot down over Fallujah. Plans to accelerate passing over control of the country to the Iraqis had only added to the fevered atmosphere in the region.

Cuckoo continued. The army had said that Nathan was on leave when they voiced their worries and refused to elaborate further. When two more days had passed with still no word from Nathan, Fi insisted something be done and Cuckoo was her choice of man to do it, being nearest. There's no worry like the worry of a mother with a kid in a war zone.

Nor that of a father, thought Abbott, but he knew he was in no position to lay claim to feelings of parental concern, which were always going to be eclipsed by those of the mother anyway. Fi, in tears down the phone, had accused him of pressurising the boy into joining up, but nothing could have been further from the truth and that's what Abbott had told her, even though they both knew that it wasn't about anything Abbott did or didn't say to Nathan. It was more about his status as father in the boy's life, absent and yet a constant presence. Other kids had actors and rock stars on whom to fixate and project, Nathan had Abbott.

So not because of him – not in the sense that Abbott was ever at his shoulder, urging, 'Join the army, it'll make a man of you, blah, blah,' but just because Abbott was there. He was Dad. He was the protective giant.

Around the time that Nathan joined up, things were turning shit in Abbott's life – he'd taken up drinking as a career choice. He sent a card on Nathan's next birthday. The birthday after that, he managed a text. Iraq had happened and he heard from Fi that Nathan wasn't involved. But he didn't hear it from Nathan. Gradually, the two of them had moved from 'not speaking very much' to 'estranged'.

The way Fi always told it, Abbott was some kind of monster and never a true father to his son. She was wrong in the diagnosis – he wasn't a monster – but she was right to flag up the symptoms. And when she told him that it was better that he stayed away from Nathan for good, she was probably right about that, too.

'You see, I was tempted to think of Fi's concern as maybe being a bit misplaced,' said Cuckoo now, drawing Abbott from his thoughts. 'But now I'm not so sure.'

Abbott was remembering the text message of the other night, trying to weigh up his own concerns and those of Fiona. 'There's something else, isn't there?' he said. 'Fi's a bit of a mother hen, like you say, but she knows the score. She's not one to go pressing the panic button unnecessarily.'

Cuckoo nodded. 'Yes. Two nights ago, she had a call from Nathan. She heard weird noises and then the line went dead.'

Abbott liked nothing about that sentence. 'What sort of weird noises?'

'She couldn't really say.'

'Oh, come on. Like shouting? A party? Put it this way: what conclusion did Fi reach based on what she heard?'

'Well, she thought it was as though someone had snatched the phone out of his hand.'

Fiona, for all her faults, wasn't a flaky type. She wasn't given to flights of fancy. On the one hand, if she thought that it was the sound of Nathan having the phone snatched out of his hand, then Abbott was tempted to believe her. On the other hand, she didn't know the sort of stupid shit that young squaddies got up to, and someone could easily have grabbed his phone and dialled 'Mum', before Nathan had the chance to snatch it back.

'Did she tell the base about this call?'

'They pretty much said that he was either drunk or playing some kind of trick. Still putting her back in her box. More important things to do, et cetera.'

Abbott twisted to look behind them. There was nobody following. No sign of the white-haired guy. 'And back in her box is Fi's least-favourite place, yeah?' he said to Cuckoo, who gave him a rueful look in return. For a moment they grinned at one another and then Abbott pulled his shirt back on, dropped the stuff back into his holdall. He turned his head to look out of the window once more, seeing the lights of the city flash by. He tried to conjure the face of his son and found he couldn't. *Where are you, Nathan?* he thought, which set off an aching worry in the pit of his stomach.

For a while the only sound in the car was the metronomic swish of the windscreen wipers, until Abbott said, 'So you've been dispatched by home ops. OK. So why come to me? Why Singapore and not straight to Baghdad?'

'Because you'd never forgive me if I didn't come to you; because she asked me to; because you're still his father; and because you know Iraq.'

'Again, you could have called.'

'She wanted me to see you, Abbott. She needed to check on you.'

'To see if I'm up to the task of tracking down my own son?'

'That's about the size of it.'

'Oh, I see. So it *was* an interview. And if I hadn't passed your test?'

'Who says you have? But if you hadn't, well, then she picks up the phone to someone else.'

'Like who – who the fuck does Fi know who can …?' He stopped, realising that he already knew the answer: one of his old team: Burton, Stone or Mowles. And if it had come to that? Would they have been prepared to help? He wasn't sure of the answer.

Abbott sat back. 'It would be Iraq,' he sighed, closing his eyes against the sudden invasion of unwelcome images: the bodies. Dismembered bodies. Thinking of Nathan's text message, feeling the worry gnawing away and knowing he must return there. 'I'm leaving right away, you realise,' he said.

'*We* leave, Abbott.'

'No. I go alone.'

'Uh-uh.' Cuckoo shook his head.

'OK, then. Fair enough. You tag along and then I'll give you the slip when we reach Baghdad. How do you fancy your chances in Iraq by yourself, eh? Think about your answer but remember that playing *Medal of Honour* doesn't count.'

'I can handle myself.'

'Yeah, yeah, sure you can. Look, there's no such thing as "defence diplomacy" in Baghdad, Cuckoo. You might as well try to stick daisies down the barrels of their AKs. Sorry, but you either do this the easy way and wave me goodbye at the airport or you can do it the hard way and find yourself ankle-deep in a shallow grave.'

'I made a promise to Fiona,' replied Cuckoo, resolutely. 'I'm coming.'

They passed a huge billboard advertising Lucky Strikes. Beneath it a road sign for the airport.

'I know where we're going, you know,' said Cuckoo. 'I've known since we left your apartment. My stuff's in the boot, passport in my pocket ...'

CHAPTER 17

Abbott checked behind once again, and again saw nothing.

He turned back quickly. 'OK, we've got a tail,' he said. 'Here, take this road,' and then reached across to wrench the wheel of the Lexus.

As the car swerved with a small screech of tyres on the warm road, Abbott was thrown into Cuckoo, almost making the situation worse.

'Christ, be careful,' protested Cuckoo, shouldering his passenger away. 'Jesus, man, you nearly took us off the road. Are you sure you're in any fit state?'

They missed the turn. Abbott had twisted to look behind again. 'Ah, no,' he said, 'my mistake. They've turned off. They weren't following.'

They made it to the airport and left the car parked illegally outside the terminal as they hurried inside. At the airline counter Abbott went first, buying tickets for the ten-hour flight from Singapore to Jordan, which was due to leave in an hour's time. He moved away and slung his holdall over his shoulder, as though to wait for Cuckoo who stepped up to the counter and asked for the same again, relaying his details to the customer services guy.

'Passport, sir?' asked the assistant.

Cuckoo nodded, reached through the buttons of his mac to the inside pocket. Felt nothing.

He tapped his coat, then unbuttoned it. No passport and suddenly, it hit him. Realisation dawned. In the car, when Abbott had reached across to wrench the wheel from him, it wasn't a drunken lurch at all, it was—

Christ. He wheeled around.

Sure enough, there was no sign of Abbott.

He grabbed his phone, flipped it open and dialled Abbott, who answered on the second ring.

'Abbott—' started Cuckoo.

'I'm sorry, mate,' said Abbott, sounding as though he was on the move, no doubt towards departures.

'I'm coming with you,' said Cuckoo.

'Oh, come on. Whatever Fi says, you and I both know you're better off out of it. You'd only slow me down in Baghdad. No offence, but you'd be a deadweight. Look, I appreciate that you stepped up back there in the flat. You showed proper bollocks. But that shit is nothing compared to what is going down in Iraq.'

'I promised Fi.'

'You promised, but it was me who made you break that promise. Just Abbott, being a bastard once again. Come on, Fi thinks I'm a big enough villain as it is. She'll understand. She'll probably love it that you've had a bit of the old Alex Abbott disappearing act. "Told you so," she can say.'

'So what now? I'm fucking stranded, aren't I?'

'I'll post back your passport when I reach Jordan. Scout's honour. In the meantime, you can still be a help if you want.'

Cuckoo sighed. 'Go on, then. How?'

'I'll need some kind of ops. For example: first thing you can do is get me a last-known address for Nathan in Baghdad.'

'All right, I'll work on it,' replied Cuckoo.

'I'm sorry, Cuckoo, but it had to be done. It's best this way.'

'Yeah,' agreed Cuckoo. 'Yeah, I understand.'

He knew that Abbott spoke the truth. They both did. Abbott could practically feel his relief halfway across the airport. Chances were that Fi would know it, too. This was a job for him and him alone. As he made his way to the gate, he put in another call. 'Potter,' he said when the guy answered. 'I need a favour or two. I'm on my way to Jordan – yes, mate. I'm coming back to Iraq.'

CHAPTER 18

During the flight, Abbott charmed the stewardess into leaving him with more than his rightful drinks allowance, letting his Royal Marines tattoo do half the work and a winning smile the rest. 'Thank you for your service,' she'd said, leaving him with a selection that brought him envious glances from nearby passengers.

He checked his wound in the toilet and came to the conclusion that it would be fine. He'd been lucky. Another lucky escape to add to the list. Back at his seat, he watched a film, *Bad Santa*, about a boozy department store Santa, which only made his thirst worse.

He wanted to ask for more drink, but at the same time didn't want to be *that guy* – didn't want to see the look in the stewardess's eyes change as her perception of him moved from 'deserving hero' to 'scrounging old soak'.

Instead he reached for his precious iPod, cueing up an album by LTJ Bukem which he found helped keep the shit-thoughts at bay.

And it did. In a way. Instead came thoughts of Tessa.

* * *

For some reason, and despite the fact that he thought of her so often, it had only belatedly occurred to him to plug her name into a search engine. Had she married but not changed her surname? Either way, she was there, top result, which took him to the homepage of the law firm Fitzpatrick & Sims. There she was, in the section marked 'our colleagues'.

All those years. People change. They become unrecognisable facsimiles of themselves. But not Tess.

She was older, of course. It was there in the eyes. But her face had not widened and fattened out the way faces do when time has its say. And because it hadn't widened, her lips – which were always one of her most precious assets – remained unchanged.

'You've got the mouth of Debbie Harry,' he used to tell her.

'I wish I had the rest of Debbie Harry.'

'You and me both. Oof!'

Something else about her remained unchanged. She had always worn her fringe straight and just a little too long so that it almost covered her eyes. It made her look as though she were constantly peering out from beneath it, something that Abbott had found unbearably sexy at the time. Likewise, it meant that she often had to tilt her chin a little in order to see, which gave her a haughty look that, again, he found irresistible. When she was cross or upset, her chin dipped and her fringe protected her from the world.

'It's my trademark,' she had said at the time, and it turned out that as with everything else about Tess she had been true to her word. There she was on the Fitzpatrick & Sims website, peering out from behind that very fringe. Not quite exactly the same. But almost. Enough. Also visible was a high-necked white cotton shirt, while round her neck was a necklace and …

He leaned forward.

A pendant.

And not just any old pendant, either, but a pendant that he'd bought her. The last present he'd ever given her, in fact, and maybe the first one that you'd ever call a proper, grown-up gift. It was for her birthday, the one before they finally split up; he'd been working at the local Kwik Save at the time and had saved hard for this pendant that she'd seen in the window of a jeweller's shop in Burton-on-Trent. A round thing in hammered silver, it was, about the size of a ten-pence piece.

It didn't mean anything, of course. He knew that Tessa wasn't wearing that pendant because she pined for him or was somehow sending him a message. She was wearing it because she liked it and because she was practical that way. Simple as.

Even so. And while he was careful not to read too much into it, he did take something from it. He took it that maybe she didn't still hate him, and that perhaps she still remembered him – in a good way.

So he sent her an email to say howdy from the past and that he still thought of her, and that he hoped she could forgive him for the hurt he had caused. And he told himself that he was only doing it in order to achieve closure and by doing so get over her.

A day later her reply came, and in it she said that it was lovely to hear from him. That she, too, thought about him often. On reading that particular bit, Abbott had tensed, wondering whether the 'him' of back then was worth recalling and then relaxing when her next words were 'always fondly'.

She mentioned no significant others, nor children. She made no reference to her and Abbott's shared past nor their ugly ending. She wound up her note by saying how lovely it would be to catch up properly. And in brackets she left her phone number.

Christ, he'd mulled over the inclusion of that phone number. Just a few little digits, but God …

After all, she hadn't specifically requested that he ring her. Ring her for what anyway? What did 'catch up properly' even mean? Continue the email correspondence? Meet over coffee or for a drink? Or talk on the phone?

And he knew that she would not have agonised over her wording as much as he did, because that wasn't really her – her being more comfortable that way. More comfortable in her own skin.

But hey, she'd included her phone number. So, in the end, he'd made a decision.

CHAPTER 19

'Hello,' she'd said. The way people do when they answer the phone.

Only, not quite. Because it wasn't a cautious hello. It wasn't a hello-who-is-this-stranger? sort of hello. It was a hello that said, 'Thanks for calling me, whoever you are,' and it shot him right back in time, reminding him of how she'd always sounded: open and warm and generous with herself, a charm that made her a hit with mums and dads, great with old people, and even – and maybe even especially – bad lads who'd done a spell in remand school, who thought they were at war with the world.

In short, she'd had an aura. And like her fringe it had survived the years.

'Hi, Tess, it's Alex.' He wondered how he sounded to her. As worn as he felt, perhaps.

She paused. He thought he heard a short intake of breath, but if that was true then she composed herself quickly. 'I knew you'd be in touch one day,' she said. His mouth opened to ask how she knew that, but she was already ploughing on, asking, 'How did you get my email? Oh, wait, of course. You were the guy who rang reception about the school reunion? There isn't – of course there isn't – any school reunion. That was you.'

He found himself blushing. It was one thing deciding to email her, he knew. Quite another going to so much effort procuring her email address. But, yes, no getting around the fact.

'And you knew I worked here because …? Was it the website?'

'Yes.'

'Of course. The website.'

'I saw the pendant,' he said.

'Right,' she said. 'I always liked that pendant.'

'It looks really – you know – um … nice on you.'

Nice. He'd used the word 'nice'. He flashed back to a teacher in primary school who had banned the whole class from using the word 'nice' in their stories.

'Well, you always had good taste,' she said.

She didn't remember, then, that it had been her choice.

'So, you … um. Well, you're still in the army?' she asked brightly.

'Recently ex of the army, actually.'

'I see. You, oh God, what's the word? Demobbed?'

He chuckled. 'They don't call it that, but something along those lines, yes.'

'Where are you, then?'

'I'm in Baghdad,' he told her. He'd dropped it like *boof*, expecting a reaction and for that reaction to be concern. A show of care. Instead she said, 'Well, it's quite a good line, considering you're in the middle of a war zone.'

It should have occurred to him earlier, really. The reason she'd been happy to speak to him, giving him her phone number, inviting him to call. It wasn't because she felt a sense of unfinished business or had ghosts she wanted to lay to rest or thought that she and Abbott might have a second shot. None of that. Quite the opposite. She was fully reconciled to it. Confident that they could be just good friends. It was there in her tone of voice, at first. And then in the knowledge, almost casually dropped, that she had a husband, Phil, and two kids, Joshua and Emily.

'And what about you?' she asked. 'Did it work out with – um ...'

No, he had told her, choosing his word carefully. It 'hadn't quite worked out' between him and, um, but they had an amazing boy, Nathan, to show for their efforts.

He didn't mention the estrangement. How he and Nathan had not spoken since the great army announcement. One of many things he chose not to mention at that particular point in time. Like how getting off with Fiona that night in Burton-on-Trent, when he and Tess were 'on a break' (and oh, how he laughed at *that* particular episode of *Friends*), was probably the biggest mistake of his life.

'So when are you back from Baghdad?' she asked him.

He didn't know. At that point, of course, he had no idea that his immediate future lay in Singapore. What he did know, though, was that he would love to see Tessa at some point. And that's what he told her.

There was a pause. It was the first time since the call began that she'd seemed at all unsure of herself. Up until that point he might as well have been an old pal calling up to shoot the breeze. 'Well, that would be nice,' she said, 'I'm just not sure. I mean, Phil's not the jealous type, but—'

Abbott had already formed a mental image of her husband, this 'Phil'. It was a mental image with the caption 'perfect guy'. He didn't drink, or not too much anyway. There were no skeletons in his closet, no demons keeping him awake at night, no anger-management issues or unresolved shit with his family. He was probably skilled in something more marketable and humanitarian than the most effective means of killing people.

What's more, this perfect Phil, although not the jealous type, was the reason that Tess was hesitant about meeting him.

'Of course,' said Abbott quickly, wanting to swiftly paper over the awkward moment, 'of course. Look, it's just great to speak to you, to hear that you're OK, and that ...'

Another pause.

And a pause.

And still a pause.

'That what, Alex?' she prompted at last.

'That there are no hard feelings, I guess.'

She laughed like, *How could there be?* 'No, Alex, there are no hard feelings. Look, stay in touch. It's good to hear from you, it really is. Drop me a line when you have a moment. But let's just talk, though, before we go thinking about meeting up. Things are different for me now, and I dare say they're different for you, too. You understand that, I'm sure?'

And that was it. That had been the end of the conversation.

During his months in Singapore, he'd emailed her a couple of times. Within these emails he was probably guilty of giving her the impression that he was a good deal more prosperous than he was in reality, painting a slightly photoshopped version of himself, but hell, he was hardly the first person to do that, and nothing he said was an outright lie, just a slight varnishing of the truth.

Why? Why not tell the truth: I'm a fuck-up? The whole time he knew that he was sowing the seeds, laying the groundwork, preparing for some mythical night out in the future when he and Tessa would meet up and he would be able to tell her his troubles so that she could save him from them. Just as she always had.

Her replies were always sweet and encouraging. Friendly, if a touch formal. She never took the bait when he gave her the chance to open up. She kept it on a friends' footing.

Until one day, when she mentioned that husband 'perfect man' Phil was out of the country on business. One of the kids was on a school trip, the other was staying with friends. She had a spare three days and didn't know what to do with herself.

In his reply he had said, 'What a coincidence, I'm back from Singapore then, in London. Perhaps we could meet up?'

Thinking, could he scrape together the money for the airfare in time? For two days he had waited, checking his email over and over again until the reply came.

'Are you really in London that day?' she had asked.

'I am,' he replied.

This time the reply came back straight away. 'Then I'd like that. How about Friday night after work?'

He'd checked. The potential meet-up was in five days' time.

CHAPTER 20

Abbott was worried about Nathan, and the thought of going back to Baghdad filled him with dread. There was, however, a silver lining, a kernel of pleasure to be found in the otherwise wholly unpleasant business. It gave him the opportunity to revisit one of his favourite places on the planet: the InterContinental hotel in Amman.

He'd never used the spa at the InterContinental, but he loved the fact that it had one; he wasn't that bothered about the magnificent views, but he grooved on the fact that it had magnificent views. Mainly, he just loved its luxury, and what it represented to men like him. How it was the one place you could get to live in peace and relative safety before the sleepless nights and mayhem of Baghdad.

It was always that way going back to Iraq. The InterContinental was your marker point. Beyond it lay the road to Baghdad where there might as well have been a sign saying, 'Abandon hope all ye who enter here,' and for that reason the hotel almost seemed to taunt you with its promise of comfort and safety. Tearing yourself away from it took an effort of will, and the more you knew about Baghdad, and what lay in store, the greater the test.

As ever, it was a test Abbott was more than willing to take.

He settled into his room, decanting all his gear from the holdall and placing the empty bag to one side. He checked his wound, which was healing nicely. Next, picking up his phone, he made arrangements with Potter, who told him that the next morning he could join a convoy to Baghdad in exchange for riding shotgun. Perfect. Potter on point as ever. *You beauty, mate. You fucking beauty.* What's more, he wasn't going to have time to get too used to the luxury of the hotel and its crisp, laundered bed sheets. A mixed blessing, for sure. His convoy left tomorrow when it would take the well-trodden route east favoured by members of The Circuit and journalists travelling into Iraq, guys who would shack up either in the InterContinental or Grand Hyatt in Amman for a few days before trying to cobble together a convoy or join one in order to take them into Baghdad.

Why a convoy? Safety in numbers. That's why. His job was to provide the muscle.

He grabbed his empty holdall and took a trip to the below-ground parking garage, down one floor, and then the next, and then the next, to where the air was thin and warm, and every noise seemed to echo off the unpainted grey concrete surrounding him, a sharp contrast to the luxury of the hotel above.

The further down you went, the older the cars – or so it seemed. The occasional one was freshly parked but here in the subterranean depths, the majority of vehicles were either covered in dust or protected by huge sheets, and most had been here not days or weeks but months or years.

It was here that he located his car, an old BMW. He looked at it for a moment or so, giving it the once-over for any tell-tale signs of tampering, even getting down onto all fours and shining a small pen-torch beneath it before he was satisfied. He stood and brushed himself off, lifted the sheet and retrieved the key from the wheel arch. Opening the boot, he took a look around to check that he was alone and then removed some of the contents, placing them into his holdall. He zipped the bag shut, locked the car up, stowed the key and returned to his room.

There he sat on his bed and spent a moment admiring the view of Amman from the window. *Back in the Middle East. Back*. How could one place seem at once so much like home and yet so alien? He'd never get his head around it.

He reached for the holdall, unzipped it and took from it an M4 assault rifle almost identical to the one he'd left behind in Singapore, as well as a Glock nine, boxes of ammo and a Gerber knife.

He laid it all out on the bed, the familiar trappings of his rig, remembering how, when he'd stowed this lot in the BMW, he'd vowed that he was doing it for the last time. He'd told himself that he was never returning to Baghdad.

And yet he'd still stowed the gear. Just in case. Because it was one thing making that pledge. Another thing seeing it through.

After he'd cleaned the weapons he decided it was time for a drink. In the bar, he spotted a couple of journalists – one American, the other English – and listened in on their conversation before joining them. 'Are you part of tomorrow's convoy?' he asked.

They both nodded, both looking a little pale around the gills. They knew the stories. How bandits carrying AK-47s had made the road a favourite striking spot. The bandits took cash, satellite telephones, laptops, anything of value. Rumours were that the Iraqi drivers worked with them, tipping them off about the gear journalists were carrying.

Abbott introduced himself as the security consultant for the convoy. He saw their eyes go to the rum and coke he held. It didn't matter, though, he told himself. He was only planning on having one drink.

But it was one thing making that pledge. Another seeing it through.

CHAPTER 21

The convoy of five white GMCs formed up just before four the next morning. They were all the same model so that they could all travel at the same speed, which, Abbott knew of old, would be ninety miles an hour all the way along the two-lane highway that lay ahead.

Abbott would be passenger in the lead car, and he checked in on his driver, Ali, an Arab who looked him up and down, paying particular attention to the M4.

There were several reasons that the M4 was Abbott's favourite weapon. One of them was that it was great for this kind of job: air-cooled, gas-operated, magazine-fed, but short and light, easy to handle in the cab of the GMC. Another reason was that it looked the part. People saw you were carrying an M4 and they knew you meant business. Sure enough, Ali nodded, seemingly satisfied that man and weapon were both up to the job.

Abbott acknowledged him with a grin. He didn't blame Ali for appraising him. After all, they had a fifteen-hour journey ahead of them. Most likely it would go off without incident, but if they were attacked, then Ali had every right to expect some degree of competency from his security. Another thing: the more interest the driver paid to Abbott's ability to protect him, the less likely he was to be in the pay of the bandits.

Abbott introduced himself to the two journos in the back of his GMC: a blonde woman with dark circles under her eyes, and her cameraman, who was already pulling a filthy bucket hat down over his eyes in order to sleep.

Abbott turned away, wiped a layer of sweat from his forehead and let the AR hang on its strap as he walked the rest of the convoy, checking in on each of the vehicles, each of them rammed with sweating journalists and cameramen, a mix of men and women who all seemed to blur into one as far as Abbott was concerned. Some were friendly and chatty, some reserved. All of them were hopped up on nerves and excitement and that odd mix of adrenalin and fear unique to four in the morning.

In the final car sat the two reporters he'd met in the bar the previous evening, and as with the rest of the passengers, he leaned forward to shake their hands, delivering a strong, forceful handshake.

Their eyes, however, slid away awkwardly. They knew what Abbott knew: that last night he'd had more than just the one. It had been more like 'several' – five or six – rum and cokes before he'd retired to bed. He wasn't drunk, he'd told himself – then and now – and having had four hours' sleep he knew he was fine to shotgun the convoy.

Question was, would those guys feel the same? Would they tell their pals that he'd been knocking them back in the bar? Would that information then be relayed to the rest of the journalists on the convoy, perhaps make its way back to Ali and ultimately to Potter? If so, it wasn't exactly a great start. He needed Potter on his side for what was to come in Baghdad.

At just after the hour, the convoy began its journey. Ali set the pace, his foot to the floor, an intensity to his gaze which alternated between staring straight ahead and flicking to the rear-view to check on the GMCs behind.

The two in the back of the lead car both slept, but they could afford to relax. They were, after all, still in Jordan. This was the easy bit.

At the truck stop in the town of Safawi, still in Jordan, they stopped to refuel and the GMC drivers stocked up on bread from an open storefront while journalists took pictures, filling their boots, knowing that the bright lights and modernity of Amman were far behind them now.

This was what they'd come for. This was the Middle East that played well back home.

On they drove. At around noon, they reached the border, marked by two archways. Abbott could remember when a picture of Saddam Hussein had adorned that very border, but now the spot was empty. There instead was a US Bradley fighting vehicle, various grunts hanging around. A turret gunner, his eyes hidden by Aviators, chewed gum and watched impassively as officials checked passports.

Passing through, it was as if a collective sense of anxiety descended over the entire convoy. All senses on high alert now.

They were in Iraq.

Still, at least the route was better-maintained. One thing you had to say about Saddam, he kept his roads in good order. The surface was flat and steady, and safety rails ran either side. The GMCs, once white but now beige from a constant cloud of sand and dirt, trundled on. Ahead of them was a bridge, bombed into a tangle of metal and concrete, blown out by American forces.

They took the long way around, journalists snapping away at the bomb-damaged bridge, as they made their way to a temporary structure further along the river.

Forty miles outside of Fallujah they stopped once more, taking on water and fuel. Before they set off again, Abbott turned to the two journalists behind. 'Right, it gets really hairy from here. Any roadblocks, we plough through. Any vehicle gets too close we treat it as hostile and open fire. Is that clear?'

They looked at him, nodding mutely. 'Good.' Abbott got out to deliver the same message along the line.

The drivers, all of them old hands, showed no emotion, practically yawning as he delivered his little pep talk; the effect on their passengers was markedly different.

Funny, thought Abbott, as he jogged back to the lead car, the M4 thumping against his thigh. In the space of fewer than forty-eight hours he had rejoined The Circuit and was back in action. Like the Middle East itself, the feeling was horrific and yet also as though he was right back in his comfort zone. Back where he had always belonged.

In formation, they drove on, skirting Fallujah and Ramadi. And then Abbott saw them in the rear-view: two large Mercedes, almost diplomatic-looking, which had appeared on the road behind them, clouds of dust in their wake. They were approaching fast.

'Ali,' was all Abbott needed to say for the driver's eyes to flick to the mirror, seeing what Abbott saw. The driver's right leg shifted, the GMC finding a little extra speed.

Behind, the two Mercedes were gaining. Now they were close enough for Abbott to see that four men were inside each. Anywhere in the world you went, four men in a car was bad news. In Iraq, it was *fucking* bad news.

OK. Abbott knew the drill: they'd attack the front GMC and use it to block the others. He looked left and right. Christ, he hated those barriers. In this part of the world they were nothing more than a helping hand for bandits, stopping vehicles from leaving the road and going onto the open desert beyond. Preventing escape, in other words.

Sure enough, Abbott watched as the front car hauled up to the left of the convoy and came racing up the inside at the same time as the second one fell in beside the last GMC.

The next thing he saw was the snouts of AK-47s, appearing from the windows of both Mercedes. It wasn't like he'd ever doubted they were bandits, but even so there was something about seeing the guns that sealed the deal for him, marking the moment that he went from on-high-alert to knowing this was a contact situation. At the same time, almost as though summoned, the peace came upon him, washing all before it like a tidal wave that rid him of all the shit-thoughts and all the last vestiges of hangover, leaving only the soldier behind.

Beside him, Ali was muttering something as Abbott eased the M4 onto his lap. 'Steady, mate, keep it steady,' he said, one eye on the mirror, praying that he could rely on Ali to remain calm. The Mercedes grew bigger in the wing mirror. The barrel that poked from the passenger window extended as the bandit inside waited for his moment to open fire.

Abbott clicked off the M4's carry strap, eased off the safety. *Easy now. Easy does it.*

The Mercedes drew up alongside. Squinting along the barrel of the AK-47 was a bandit, and for the first time, Abbott got a good look at him. He was just a kid, and in another time that might have given Abbott pause for thought, but not now. He'd seen them younger, and kid or not, he was a gunman with Abbott in his sights.

He raised the M4. The kid saw it. His eyes widened, but he had no time to react, and at that distance Abbott couldn't miss.

He squeezed the trigger. The kid disappeared in a mist of blood. The windscreen shattered and the Mercedes veered off, ploughing into the guard rail, busting through and spinning out in the sand. At the same time, Abbott flung himself at the window to see the second Merc. Rather than stop and go to the aid of their companions, they were coming after him, wanting either payback or to finish the job, or most likely both. He saw a muzzle flash and heard two rounds zing in the air above his head before he opened fire in reply, one grouping into the front grill of the Mercedes, into the engine, the other, into the windscreen.

In the next instant the second Mercedes had swerved, its windscreen a spider's web, tendrils of smoke already appearing from the bonnet as it ground to a halt.

Abbott stayed half in and half out of his own window, carbine held steady, watching as the two beached Mercs became specs in the distance.

Then he pulled himself back into his seat and settled back with a mix of relief and elation, a sense of having got the job done.

Ali looked across at him. Sweat gleamed on his forehead, but he nodded. 'Good work,' he said.

CHAPTER 22

Despite being the Singapore branch of a renowned security firm with a global reach, the Hexagon offices were decidedly low-rent. In the middle of the single room were two large desks that had been pushed together in order to form one larger work area, and it was here that Hexagon's two men in Singapore, Chantrell and Tork, would sit on the rare occasions they found it necessary to use the office.

They were there now, with Chantrell nursing a broken arm, recently set at the hospital and newly plastered, and Tork, his nose now sporting a bandage, staring glumly and silently into space. Neither had slept and the bottle of whiskey they shared was having little effect on their jangled nerves.

Reason? The job was a bust. While at the hospital, they had relayed their bad news to Hexagon in London, who had asked them to return to the office and await further instructions. Someone would contact them, they were told, and so they waited, assuming that a call would come as they drowned their sorrows.

There was a knock at the door.

With a look at Chantrell, who shook his head like, *Will you look at the state of me?* and reached for the bottle of whiskey with his good arm, Tork sighed and stood, treading carefully across office detritus (a gym bag, old computer, a pile of lever arch files, several VHS cassettes) to the door.

'Hello?' he said, warily.

The voice in reply was plummy English. 'My name is Kind.'

Tork took a deep breath. This was it, then. The process of contrition was about to begin.

He opened the door to a tall guy with a shock of very blond, almost white, hair. Tork looked him up and down and then turned his back on him and regained his seat at the desk, leaving the visitor to close the door behind him.

'What did you say your name was?' asked Tork, settling back. Because of the broken nose the word 'name' came out like 'bame' and 'what' like 'bot'.

Their guest stood with his legs planted a foot or so apart, wearing a bomber jacket, unzipped, his hands clasped in front of him. Whoever he was, he wasn't one of Hexagon's admin types. This guy looked like he'd spent time in the field. He had that watchful air about him.

'My name is Mr Kind,' he repeated.

'First name "Too"?' said Chantrell, and then looked surprised when the visitor agreed with him.

'Inevitably, that's what they call me, yes. They call me Too Kind. Or sometimes Toothkind.'

'"Toothkind", repeated Tork. 'Like the Ribena?'

'Mr Kind to you.'

Chantrell and Tork shared a look and Tork rolled his eyes – *We've got a right one here* – both knowing that this was the game they'd have to play, wondering if their crummy jobs were worth playing arse-licker to this Aryan-looking motherfucker.

In the corner of the office was an old, battered leather armchair. Kind moved over to it, picked up a sheaf of papers, dropped them to the floor and sat down. As he did so, his bomber jacket opened, revealing the shoulder holster beneath. Tork and Chantrell traded another look with their eyes. Despite the fact that Kind now sat sunk into the armchair, his knees almost at the level of his forearms and looking faintly ridiculous, neither felt inclined to laugh.

'You were at number twenty-three yesterday,' said Kind.

Chantrell nodded. Tork looked confused. 'How do you …?'

'I know because you were after Abbott. Snap. So was I.'

'You know about Abbott?' Tork even more confused now.

'Boo bow about Babbott,' mimicked Kind, and Tork bristled. 'In the sense that I have learned about Babbott since arriving here, yes. Your pal Foxhole was most helpful.' He crossed one leg over the other. He wore boat shoes and the kind of jeans that looked as though they had been ironed carefully by his mother, complete with crease.

'You should have made yourself known, Mr Kind,' said Tork. 'We could have done with the help.'

Kind chortled. 'I can see. Now, who was the man that Abbott was with?'

'Bo idea,' said Tork.

'Lucky for me, I have an idea. The licence plate of his hire car. It was left at the airport.'

'Uh huh. So they both skipped out?' said Tork.

Kind shook his head. 'Abbott did. The second individual never travelled, for whatever reason.'

'So you find him and you can find Abbott?'

'Yes, there is that. Or you could sit around in your shitty

office drinking and licking your wounds.' Mr Kind smiled. 'One of the two.'

'So bot happens now?' asked Tork, curling a lip.

'Well, I know what happens now,' said Kind. 'Question is, do you know what happens now?'

'If I knew what happens now, I wouldn't have to ask you, would I? What has Hexagon told you to do next? How about that?'

'Hexagon?' Kind look upwards, as though thinking. 'Hexagon? Oh yes. The firm you work for.'

Tork, feeling a little uneasy now, said, 'Well, don't you work for Hexagon? Isn't that what you're doing here?'

Slowly, Kind shook his head. His right hand rested along the arm of the leather chair.

'What?' pressed Tork. On the other side of the desk, Chantrell had straightened. 'You work for the guys in New York?'

Kind smiled thinly. 'I see. So it's "guys in New York" who employed Hexagon to track and bug Bryars's boat, is it? What else can you tell me about them? A name, perhaps? I need a name.'

Belatedly, Tork realised that he had made a grave error. An assumption, you might say. He placed his glass of whiskey back on the desk and laid his hand beside it, trying to look casual. His Sig felt heavy at his hip. To Kind he said, 'You work for Bryars, don't you?'

'I do,' said Kind, pleasantly. 'Mr Bryars has employed me to find out who wished to spy on him. He is also keen that our friend Abbott should know of his displeasure. And any others who might be peripherally involved.'

The moment hung in the room.

Tork's eyes flicked to Chantrell, who also wore a Glock.

'Well, my colleague and I here are both armed, Mr Kind, so ...'

'As am I.'

'I suggest you get out of here before weapons are drawn and you find yourself outgunned. Looks like you've found out everything we know anyway. We were not told the identity of the client. Just that he was based in New York. As for you, you might as well get out while the going's good.'

'Can't do that,' said Kind apologetically.

'We're not Foxhole, Mr Kind,' said Tork. As he spoke he moved his hand at the same time, bringing it closer to the edge of the desk, decreasing the distance between his hand and the butt of his Glock. 'We don't scare that easily.'

'You're not listening to me. Mr Bryars is very, very angry. Quite apart from nursing a broken nose, he now knows that one of his competitors has declared war on him, just not which competitor. He wishes to make it understood that he intends to win that war. "Scaring you"? Scaring you is not on the menu, I'm afraid.'

Tork's hand dropped. At the same time, Chantrell let go of his whiskey glass and reached for his own gun.

Kind was quicker. The hand that had lain across the arm of the armchair snaked inside his jacket reappeared holding a Sig Sauer. The report sounded impossibly loud in the small room. Tork, whose gun had only just cleared leather was jerked off his seat, the hole in his throat already fountaining blood. Chantrell took a double tap to the chest, still fumbling with his own sidearm.

Kind stood, moving over to where Tork writhed, a puddle of sticky blood forming around him. Dispassionately, he looked down upon his AC/DC T-shirt already black with blood. *For those about to rock.*

'We salute you,' said Kind. He knelt, placed the barrel of the gun to Tork's kneecap. He didn't have long. Tork was losing blood fast. 'Who hired Hexagon?' he asked.

Tork gurgled, hands at his throat.

'Who hired Hexagon?' repeated Kind, but Tork didn't know and, anyway, was just moments from death.

Instead, Kind stood, and the gun thumped as he put a second bullet in Tork to finish him. He moved to where Chantrell lay still, squatted to check for a pulse and, satisfied, holstered his weapon.

He pulled out his phone, took pictures of the two bodies and then left the office.

CHAPTER 23

Baghdad was the sound of a broken machine that was still grinding on despite itself – a war machine, with a soundtrack of helicopters clattering overhead, the distinctive growling of Humvees trundling across bullet-strewn, bomb-damaged streets, and the occasional rattle of gunfire, a jarring contradiction to the regular sound of the call to prayer.

In other words, Baghdad was just as Abbott remembered it – only more so.

He'd split at a time when the coalition forces were struggling, to say the least. Back home, their respective governments had told their people that securing Iraq was a simple business. On the ground, it was anything but simple; it was bloody and deadly and gruelling and soul-destroying. But the governments didn't want to admit that; instead they supplemented their military presence with commercial security operators, which was where The Circuit and the likes of Abbott entered stage left. Guys who'd fought in the war and now wanted to share in the spoils. These guys were the coalition's guilty secret. *Can't do without you. Don't want to admit you exist.*

As the military presence was stretched ever more thinly, increasing numbers of jobs were handed out to private security.

The guarding of compounds, embassies and diplomatic staff became the job of The Circuit, who were also called upon to help train local cops and security personnel. Moving in at the same time were firms hoping to cash in on the US $18.4 billion reconstruction fund being offered by the coalition. Suddenly, journalists weren't the only Western civilians who needed babysitting in Baghdad. The staff of the various construction companies needed guarding, too: engineers, architects, accountants, you name it. Most of these guys had never seen a real-life gun in their lives, lived in a constant state of trouser-browning fear, and were more than happy to pay through the nose for expert protection. By the time that Abbott had left, PSCs, as in, the commercial security companies who made up The Circuit, who employed guys like him and his fireteam, were the second largest foreign armed force in Iraq behind the US military.

So, yes, if he'd hoped that things might have calmed down in the meantime, then tough shit, they hadn't. If anything, the Wild West atmosphere of the city seemed to have got even more feverish.

And where did that leave the city? Like purgatory. Like hell on earth. Abbott moved through what he saw were burned-out vehicles, charred and twisted metal, a constant counterpoint to the sun-blasted sandstone elsewhere. But most of all, he saw frightened people, the Iraqis themselves, caught in the middle. These were the people most devastated by the war. Driven by hunger and paranoia and fractured loyalties, they jostled, carrying hampers of food, pushing wheelbarrows, dealing with grotty children and crossing checkpoints under the jittery and watchful gaze of GIs whose Ray-Bans robbed them of expression yet also somehow failed to hide the fear that Abbott knew lay in their hearts.

To the US grunts, every single Iraqi citizen could be an insurgent; one false move might trigger an IED – the busiest coalition unit was bomb disposal – and every article of local clothing might hide a suicide vest. You could have all the Humvees and Bradleys in the world, millions upon millions of dollars' worth of deadly, high-tech equipment, but they were bugger-all use against an enemy who hid in plain sight, who despised them and would stop at nothing to hurt them.

Abbott saw it all. He saw the occupying force, the resentful citizens, the journalists from CNN and Sky who scurried around faithfully recording events for the folks back home to take in during their morning coffee. He saw the security guys, all muscles, shades and earpieces, knowing that half of the job was a show of force. He felt the heat, the very air dark with the threat of snipers, IEDs and kidnapping, the whole city a testament to the fact that America's attempt to bolt on democracy was – so far, at least – an almost total failure.

Was Nathan here somewhere? Abbott found himself scanning the crowds as though in hope of catching sight of him. *'Hey, son, fancy meeting you here. Gotta say, you've been causing a fair few people a whole lotta worry.'* Still clinging onto that hope that it was all a case of crossed wires. Of worried parents jumping to conclusions.

At the same time, he felt unnerved and jangled within himself. He found himself having to take deep breaths and began to wonder if he was hyperventilating. Thinking. There's never a brown paper bag around when you need one, knowing that this was as much the delayed fallout from the attack on the convoy as it was the sensory assault of Baghdad.

And something else, too. Memories of the city haunting him.

One event in particular. The reason he left.

He reached into his holdall, finding a half-bottle of vodka which he surreptitiously upended into his mouth. Get a grip, Abbott, he thought, waiting for the booze to work its mojo. Otherwise what was the point in being here?

He did, at last, the booze doing what it was paid to do, and he called Potter.

Apart from having said goodbye to Ali at the convoy, wishing the various journalists well during their Baghdad stay – and the pair who had avoided his eye earlier were the most generous with their handshakes – Potter was the first person he had spoken to on entering Baghdad.

'Abbott,' drawled the fixer, answering the phone. Abbott knew and liked Potter of old. Back at the beginning of the year, he had been a useful go-between on the odd occasion that Abbott and his teams had needed one. He was to Baghdad what Foxhole was to Singapore, only way more accomplished and trustworthy. A cool-as-a-cucumber black dude, he never did anything quickly and that included all forms of communication. 'Something tells me that you're in Baghdad right now. How did your transfer go?'

Abbott filled him in, omitting the unnecessary details, finishing by saying, 'Did you manage to sort me out, mate?'

'Got you a room at the Al Mansour.'

'And the other thing?'

'All done.'

Abbott grinned. 'Great,' he said, and the pair of them agreed to meet later as Abbott made his way to the Al Mansour hotel near Sinak Bridge.

A tall brown building that, thanks to its size and shape, to say nothing of its rows and rows of inset windows, looked not unlike a waffle balanced on one end, the Al Mansour was a hotel with which Abbott was familiar.

There the similarity with Amman's InterContinental ended. The Al Mansour certainly wasn't a bad hotel as such – hey, it had a pool and air-conditioning – but it had a drawback, and that drawback was the fact that it was situated in Baghdad, and in Baghdad, everything, up to and including standards of luxury, was relative.

Abbott stepped off the hot and teeming streets and into reception, which was like a cool oasis of calm. He checked in, giving the receptionist a big smile on loan from the vodka. Once in his room, he dumped his bag on the bed, unzipped it and took the door wedges from it. He stood with his back to the door, kicking the wedges tightly beneath it.

Next he went back to the bed and reached underneath. There, where he knew it would be, was a backpack left for him by Potter.

He drew it onto the bed. Inside it was a car key. Also, an MP5 Kurz and bungee sling, a Sig Sauer 9mm pistol, plenty of rounds, a DOD contractor ID, low-profile body armour and a phone.

Excellent. Everything he needed. A sub-machine gun rather than a rifle, the Kurz was smaller than the M4A, and way more easily concealed, which made it perfect for use in Baghdad. He'd wear the low-profile body armour with the Kurz on its improvised bungee sling criss-crossed in a figure of eight across his back. Over that he would wear a shirt that was two sizes too big. A trained eye would see he was tooled up, but that was about it, which was good enough for coalition soldiers. Security personnel were allowed to carry arms. Just keep it discreet was the best MO.

Meanwhile, the bungee sling was key. Not only did it keep the Kurz resting snugly under his armpit, but it also acted almost like a stock, creating tension when the arm was fully extended, steadying the weapon during use. A small lead weight was sewn into the bottom seam of the shirt below the weapon which allowed clear access to the Kurz when the weapon was drawn, the last thing you wanted was a trigger-guard full of shirt.

He spent time checking over the weapons, making the pistol and Kurz ready with a full magazine and slipping the Sig down the back of his shirt. He checked his escape route. From the small balcony on the adjoining room a ladder led to the roof of the hotel which he knew as both a great means of escape and the route that somebody wanting to come after him would choose – a bit of a double-edged sword, that one. Still, it would have to do.

When that was done, he made a call to Cuckoo.

'How's Singapore?' he asked.

'You mean how is the English consulate in Singapore?' replied Cuckoo icily. 'Because that's where I've mainly been, trying to sort out a new bloody passport.'

'I said I'd send it to you.'

'And exactly how long is that going to take? What is the postal service between Baghdad and Singapore like these days?'

Abbott bit down on a chuckle. 'OK, point taken. Yeah, you might be better off sorting out a new one.'

'Anyway, I've used the time profitably,' sighed Cuckoo. 'I've got an address for you. Nathan's last known lodgings in Baghdad.'

'Thank God. And where did that come from?'

'It came through the base. Not through any official channels, mind you. A mate of Nathan's.'

'And this mate, did he know anything about what Nathan was doing in Baghdad in the first place?'

A stag night. Visiting a buddy. Something innocent. Please let it be that.

'Only that Nathan was a bit guarded about it. This guy reckoned that Nathan maybe had a job of some kind, perhaps earning a bit of extra money on the QT.'

OK, maybe that. I'll settle for that.

This was it. This was the beginning of the trail.

Abbott took a deep breath. 'OK,' he said, 'Let's be having that address, then.'

CHAPTER 24

The car keys left for him by Potter had fit a Mercedes left in an off-street garage not far from the Al Mansour. Thanks to his association with Potter, Abbott knew the garage of old. He knew the car, too. Well, the type of car – it was one of Potter's specialities: an old armoured Merc that had once made a part of Saddam's fleet. It was also to be Abbott's transport during his Baghdad stay.

First, though, he needed to make a simple addition. With him he'd brought a Union Jack sticker that he stuck to the sun visor. Approaching checkpoints he'd flip the sun visor down and then show them his military ID. It was his old one that he'd kept after leaving the army, and it bore a picture of him with short hair and in uniform, a far cry from the scruffy mess he was now. But he knew from experience what it told grunts at checkpoints. Flashing the ID looking the way he looked? It said he was special forces. Factor in the Union Jack on the sun visor and sure enough, nine times out of ten they'd wave him right through.

Now to take a drive. His destination? Nathan's last known address.

He stood on the street, looking up at what was a squat, four-storey building. Flat-fronted, sun-scorched and typical of the neighbourhood, which was mostly residential and – surprisingly – mostly local.

Definitely the right place. According to the information given to him by Cuckoo it was 'lodgings', whatever that meant: a B & B? A temporary room to rent? God knows. What it wasn't, though, was a hotel. A normal, run-of-the-mill 'here's your key, sir, enjoy your stay, breakfast is seven till ten' sort of place.

So why hadn't Nathan taken a room in a hotel? Because surely he can't have known Baghdad well enough to source this place himself? Which meant that somebody had put him up here. Question was, who? And why? And did his being here lend more credence to the theory that Nathan had been out here on a job?

Or perhaps lured here with the promise of a job.

The front door to the building was open. In he went. On the wall was a cluster of cubby holes for post, but the one for Nathan's room was empty. With the building silent around him he climbed up to Nathan's door. From his waistband he drew his pistol.

And knocked.

If only Nath would open the door, bleary-eyed, maybe a little shame-faced. And who'd care if a hooker lay in bed behind him? Certainly not Abbott. It would still be the Carlsberg of father-son reunions. Right before Abbott got to bollocking him, that was.

But there was no answer to his knock. And if the whole Nathan-missing thing was a question of gradually fading hopes, from a starting position of 'it's probably nothing, a false alarm' to 'it's something – it's definitely something', then a little more of that hope faded at that point.

On a whim, Abbott pulled his phone from his pocket and tried Nathan's number for what must have been the hundredth time since getting the text message in Singapore.

This time, however, he heard something. A phone ringing from behind the apartment door. 'Nathan,' he shouted now, hammering on the door. 'Nathan, mate, are you in there? Nath!'

There was no movement, no reply. Just the ringing.

And then it stopped and went to voicemail, just as it had for days. By now he was reaching into his cargo-pants pocket and pulling out a little wallet of lock-picks. Moments later the tumblers fell into place and Abbott crouched to one side of the door as it swung inwards, his Glock held two-handed.

The room was empty.

'Nathan,' he said again, and when there was no reply he straightened, went inside and closed the door behind him.

The room was small and shabby and had an unoccupied air. Stale and warm, the air-con shut off. What struck Abbott hardest, however, was that some kind of struggle had taken place here. Twisted bedsheets, a curtain pulled halfway off the rail. The wardrobe door hung open and clothes spilled out, as though somebody had blundered into it, flailing.

Wait, though. Was this really the sign of a struggle, or was it somebody who had turned over the room, looking for something?

He looked and saw no sign of Nathan's phone, rang it again and then located it on the floor beside the bed where it was plugged in, which told him that this struggle had happened sometime after Nathan had gone to bed for the night. He checked the door and there was no sign of a forced entry, which meant that either Nathan's attacker was a dab hand with the lock-pick or that Nathan had let him in.

Also under the bed was a laptop which Abbott pulled out and dropped on the bed with the phone, looking at them, biting his lip and feeling his sense of alertness subside and his heart sink.

The last hope that Nathan would be alive and well, with nothing more painful than a sore head and maybe a dose of something itchy to show for his temporary departure from the grid was fading. Correction: *had faded*.

Because this – this was real. This was Fi's maternal worry made concrete and his own worst fears confirmed.

And yet …

Looking around, there was also something staged about it, almost as if the room had been dressed to look like the scene of an invasion. Or was that just his natural old-git cynicism and suspicion coming into play. And did it matter anyway, because, either way, the net result was that Nathan was in trouble.

But if it had been staged, then what it meant was that Abbott was being led by the nose. He was being played.

And if that was true, then …

The whole thing was a set-up. It was a trap.

Just off the bedroom was a small bathroom. A washbag had been left. A toothbrush, too. None of it disturbed.

Abbott returned to the bedroom, deciding that he had seen enough. He collected the phone and laptop and left, closing the door gently behind him.

He was preoccupied as he reached the Mercedes and climbed in.

And for that reason he failed to see the pair of eyes that watched him from the shadows.

CHAPTER 25

Back at the Al Mansour, Abbott investigated Nathan's phone. Aside from over a hundred missed calls and about half as many messages, the last activity was a text message that came from a number not in his contacts.

The message was brief, with no clue as to the identity of the sender, just a line of digits and on the line below, a number: 1200. Or midday. Abbott played a hunch, checked on his laptop, and sure enough the numbers corresponded to a grid reference in the city.

As for the sender? Abbott looked at the number long and hard. He cross-referenced his own contacts for the number. He googled it. Nothing.

Now he opened Nathan's laptop. It was password protected, of course, but he thought back to a time when they'd bought Nathan his first computer and how he had helped to set it up, which included creating an email address. 'You have to remember this password,' he'd told Nathan at the time. 'Because if you're anything like me, you'll use the same one for everything.' (And in Abbott's defence, Internet security wasn't really a thing back then. And even if it had been a thing, then it probably still wouldn't have been an Abbott thing.)

They had a cat in those days. It was collected from a rescue centre when Nathan was six or seven because Fi thought that a boy should have a pet. She was right about that. Nathan doted on the cat, which was a cute black thing called Pudding. As in, 'black pudding'.

Abbott keyed it into the challenge box: *Pudding.* The laptop obediently flicked to the home screen, and he felt his heart break a little. As yet, there had being nothing about his discoveries that had screamed *Nathan*, but here it was. A link with the past, a link with a past that Abbott had been a part of. One he had helped to form.

Feeling like a snoop but knowing he had no choice, he opened emails. The most recent were the usual collection of junk, marketing, banter with mates. The last few were all from Fi. 'Catching up' was the subject line of one. After that 'Hello?' was in the subject line and following that, 'Getting worried now'.

Prior to those …

Abbott scrolled down and one particular email jumped out at him. Though the subject line was blank it was the sender that set off a buzzer. It had come from somebody whose email address began with the word 'Fingers'.

Abbott swallowed, looking at it for some moments. Above his head the room's air-conditioning clicked on. He opened the email, wondering if it had come from the same place as the text message. Maybe so, because once again it was the very soul of brevity. Just a phone number, in fact.

He picked up Nathan's Nokia. Same phone number.

Now he reached for his own phone, scrawled to his own contact for 'Fingers'. The number was different. His finger hovered over the call button.

Stone. Guy Stone. Essex-born, but because of the way he spoke he got called Cockney. For a while. That was before he got the tip of his middle finger shot off in a contact and they called him Fingers.

Taking a deep breath, Abbott pressed the call button.

The phone rang. And rang. He let it go to an automated voicemail.

He clicked off the call and sat wondering why Stone had been in touch with Nathan. And whether this was all connected to the reason Abbott had left Baghdad eleven months ago, desperately hoping that it wasn't. Knowing that it probably was.

His mind went back now – back to the team: him, Stone, Mowles and Burton. The four of them had served as a fireteam in the SBS. After the fall of Baghdad, they fell into business together. There was never any agreement nor any handshake. Nothing formal. Just the shared desire to earn some proper wedge. They'd seen others going it alone, coining it in as a result and, not to put too fine a point on it, they wanted a piece of the pie, because the pie was A, a big pie, and B, a delicious pie.

They remained together. The idea was they came as a team, unaffiliated to any commercial security firm in particular. If you employed them, then not only did you avoid commission, but you also got all four, so you could be assured that there were no weak links, no team vulnerabilities. They liked to think that theirs was something of a blue-chip, bespoke experience. Something like that anyway.

All of which suggests they'd been best buddies. Not really. They were more like the Premiership sides made up of players who all spoke different languages: absolute dynamite on the pitch, pretty much strangers off it. Or like the Rolling Stones. Turning it on for the audience, barely speaking backstage.

Well, that was how it seemed from Abbott's perspective anyway. He'd never really got the whole 'brothers in arms' thing. How you didn't fight for your unit or your country, you fought for the man beside you. To him, his time in the military had been a job, the man beside him a workmate. Yeah, they were 'mates', but they weren't really *mates*. He had preferred to reserve himself for his family.

Bzzt.

Bullshit alert. Bullshit detected on aisle three.

OK, fine. Of course he hadn't really and truly reserved himself for his family. He was just as neglectful with them as he was with his friends. More so. The bad dad of Baghdad, that was him.

Not that he knew it then but looking back now he could see that his whole time in the army was spent sinking deeper into himself. The only good friend he was making was the bottle. He would often say that the army had been the making of him, that it had saved him from a life of prison, and that was true, but there had definitely been a trade-off. Not quite a deal with the devil, but there or thereabouts.

For a while, this not-really-a-band of not-quite-brothers had rubbed along together OK, making good dosh for minimal work, and on those occasions that they had a drink together they'd have a round of mutual backslapping, as successful men like to do, and they'd put their efficiency down to the fact that each had equal authority in the group. They were a democracy.

That was the idea. In actual fact, however, a hierarchy of sorts had begun to form. Special Forces attract alphas, and all four of them were that, and each of them coped in different ways.

There was Burton. Simon 'Biscuits' Burton. He was a big guy – he'd spent time in Australia as a kid and had never lost the accent or the attitude. True, he was sometimes a little too plain-talking for his own good, but he was just as quick with a smile, and he was always the one with the right tools to break whatever ice might have been forming. With Burton you got the sense that wherever he went, whatever he was doing, he'd have mates. He'd win people over.

Next there was Gerald 'Badger' Mowles, a Scot who was a bit of a closed book. Great with comms and maps. Of them all, Mowles was the quietest, the most content to collect the pay cheque, and let top-dog status fall elsewhere.

And lastly there was Guy Stone, aka Fingers, one of those guys who was always tightly wound. He was a bloody good soldier. Tough, decisive, committed. But he was one of those who had a brooding side. As though he was constantly working up a chip on his shoulder. He was the one most given to pessimism; the one who'd go off on a local, start giving lip to a coalition soldier.

The longer they had stayed in the army, the more Stone seemed to resent the military life. He hated the poor pay and the fact that they were commanded by men who didn't have a fraction of their skills or expertise. This was stuff that the rest of them absorbed and resented, too, but they accepted it as a fact of life, just one of those things. Not Stone. He had seemed to simmer with it, both before they left the military and then again afterwards.

He and Abbott, meanwhile, were the two alphas among alphas. Occasionally they butted heads. Nothing serious, but it was there. That little bit of needle between them that was always going to come bubbling to the surface one day.

It took the businessman Mahomet Mahlouthi to speed up that particular process.

A big, expansive Iraqi with a taste for wearing tailored suits at all times, Mahlouthi was a legend in Baghdad, and his villa in the centre of the city was something of a local landmark. Thanks to a network of underground irrigation beneath the complex, lush vines covered most of the walls, inside and out. While every other building in the area – actually, the whole of the city – was the same colour of bleached-out beige, Mahlouthi's place was an oasis of climbing green. Not only that, but his home had escaped the bombing; it still looked as good as the day the builders had left. Wonder why, and you'd be told that Mahlouthi's network of spies and contacts made him the most informed man in the region. And because knowledge is power, and always will be, he tended to be left alone. Sure, he was regarded with suspicion by all sides – especially the coalition – but mainly he was tolerated and left alone, his usefulness outweighing other concerns.

Yet although he had an air about him, as though bullets would always bend around him, Mahlouthi was not above feeling vulnerable. It was for this reason that he employed the services of Abbott, Stone, Mowles and Burton. At first they were brought in to provide close protection for when he and his retinue were out and about. After all, Mahlouthi was a proud polygamist and, thanks to a series of backhanders, had judicial permission to take multiple wives. There were three of them at one point, and Mahlouthi was fiercely protective of them.

Meanwhile, the big Arab found that he liked having Abbott and co. around. It was understandable: as a team, they were impressive. They were efficient and well-drilled, battle-hardened and sinewy. All four of them like sharpened blades. They looked the part and they could walk it just as well as they talked it. And while Mahlouthi liked the security aspect, of course – the peace of mind for himself, his staff and his wives – he also liked the status it afforded him. The fact that he employed an entire ex-SF fireteam as close protection. He felt that it sent a message to all sides.

And so he proposed keeping them on a retainer, the idea being that they would be resident at the villa, providing him with full-time personal security, as well as acting as go-betweens, keeping coalition forces off his back and fostering good relations in that regard.

In practice this had meant ensuring that the coalition turned a blind eye to Mahlouthi's lifestyle, his nefarious business dealings, a process that involved managing kickbacks, practising good diplomacy, oiling the wheels in the Green Zone and handling intelligence.

For this – this mix of bodyguard, PA and bagman – the four of them were paid well. What's more, they were able to live in resplendent comfort. Since Saddam's presidential palace had become the main operations centre for the coalition, Mahlouthi's villa was probably the most well-appointed home in Baghdad, and he was as generous with his villa's wine cellar as he was with his money.

After a while, however, Abbott had grown tired of being Mahlouthi's personal attack dog. He wasn't greedy, and the wage was enough, but even so Abbott was wondering whether better money could be made elsewhere. He worried that the pampered lifestyle was making them soft. Privately, he was also concerned that the pampered lifestyle was helping to make him a full-blown alcoholic. Nobody was a more frequent visitor to the wine cellar than he was.

Stone, though, was making plans. He, too, wanted to earn more cash but had a different aim and made no secret of the fact that he intended to operate his own PSC. Executive Alliance Group, he planned to call it. For him, Mahlouthi's villa was the ideal base in which to hatch his corporate plans. Abbott, Mowles and Burton would be on board, he would tell them over drinks. But there was no question who'd be EAG CEO. That would be Stone.

At first they'd gone along with the idea, buoyed by Stone's enthusiasm, as well as the sneaking feeling that the idea would probably never reach fruition anyway.

But gradually, as it moved from pie in the sky to a pie nearer ground level, it dawned on them that it was really going to happen and, slowly, the cracks had begun to appear. Those little niggles that had always threatened to bubble their way to the surface? Now they did.

CHAPTER 26

Abbott rang Cuckoo, and hating having to say it, told him about Nathan's room, about the laptop and the phone and the text message. An account of everything he knew so far. He didn't mention his suspicion that it had been staged, figuring that might be a level of paranoia too far.

'What should I tell Fiona?' asked Cuckoo when he was done.

'Not the whole truth, is my advice. Tell her I'm still looking. Tell her I've got the feelers out. Tell her that I know what I'm doing and not to panic.'

'She already knows that, Abbott.'

Any pride or admiration that Fiona had for Abbott she'd kept well-hidden, both during their relationship and most especially since. Abbott knew full well that Fiona wouldn't be sitting at home glowing with confidence in Abbott and knowing that the search for her little boy was in safe hands. She'd be fretting that Abbott would be drunk in a ditch, and no doubt furious with him for having jettisoned Cuckoo at Singapore airport.

So Cuckoo was blowing smoke up his arse. Which was good of him, really. Didn't have to do that.

'So,' said Cuckoo. 'What do you think it all means?'

'I don't know.'

Don't dare to think.

'Well, all right, then. How about this?' said Cuckoo. 'Nathan going missing is something to do with you.'

That was bold from Cuckoo. Abbott said nothing.

'Well?'

'I don't know. Perhaps.'

'OK, what if—?' began Cuckoo, and then stopped.

'What if what?'

'What if Stone was somehow using Nathan to get your attention, send you a message? Perhaps he actively wanted you to travel to Baghdad. Why might he want you in Iraq, Abbott?'

'No idea, mate, no idea,' said Abbott. His mind was still kicking out a tickertape of answers that unsettled him. 'Look, either way, I need to get in touch with him.'

'Stone? It might not be that easy. The MOD may have a last-known address, but the chances are it'll be a family home. You knew him well. Don't you have that?'

'We were on the same team, we weren't sending each other Christmas cards. I've got a mobile for him but there was no answer. I'll keep trying it.'

Cuckoo gave a short, dry laugh. The irony of more unanswered calls was not lost on either of them. And then he said, 'You never got around to telling me why you left Baghdad.'

'No, I never did.'

'Didn't seem too important before, but maybe it is now.'

'Leave it, will you?'

Abbott was letting his tone of voice tell Cuckoo that he was sailing close to the wind, only Cuckoo didn't seem to be getting the message. 'Was it anything to do with this guy, Stone?' he pressed.

Abbott ignored the question. 'Could you find out where he is now?'

Maybe, at the other end of the line, Cuckoo wondered whether to press for an answer to his previous query but decided against. 'I could find out, I suppose. But, I mean, he was in *your* team, Abbott. Strikes me that you'd be the best person to go looking for him. Just try another bloke on the team. Somebody will know.'

'Call it a two-pronged approach. You still got contacts. Some-one'll know where he is.'

'Could be that he's still with Mahlouthi. Why not try him?'

'I refer you to my previous answer. Look, just do your best, mate. Do what you can.'

'OK, on one condition.'

'What is it?'

'You stop calling me Cuckoo.'

CHAPTER 27

A little while later and it was getting dark. Abbott was standing on the street, opening and closing his eyes, breathing hard.

He was at the grid reference given in the text message. The place where Nathan had been sent, surely not by coincidence. It was a street in the Kadhimiya district, running alongside the infamous Kadhimiya women's prison. In the shadow of the walls of the jail were the stalls that in the daytime sold produce, empty now. On the other side of the street were bombed-out and boarded-up shops and apartments.

It looked the same as it had before. The same as he remembered it.

And this was where Nathan had been sent. He'd been sent here by Stone. And of course that meant something.

The prison blocked out what little moonlight there was. The street kept its secrets. Abbott decided to return the following day at midday, and he'd reached the car when there came a call from Cuckoo.

'Cuckoo,' he said as he got in.

'You said you weren't going to call me Cuckoo.'

'Sorry, mate.' Abbott shook his head. 'Won't happen again.'

'OK, I did some checking,' said Cuckoo, sounding guarded.

'And?' he said. He looked out at the prison, wondering whether he should just come clean with Cuckoo. Tell him everything.

'And … how close were you to Stone?'

'Oh, you know …' Abbott started and tailed off.

'OK. Well, I'm sorry to tell you that he's dead. He drowned in a swimming accident two days ago.'

Abbott felt disquiet shift at the pit of his stomach. 'Where?' he asked.

'Apparently, he was taking some R & R in the Kurdish mountains.'

'The pools are beautiful there,' said Abbott thoughtfully.

'Is that so?'

'But that's not right,' added Abbott. 'That's not right at all. Drowned? Fucking hell, Stone was the strongest swimmer of us all. Drowned doing what?'

'Just swimming, apparently. Relaxing.'

'No evidence of foul play?'

'None that I know of.'

'Sounds wrong.'

'I'm telling you what I know, Abbott. Which is that the man you suspect of contacting Nathan has since died.'

'Yeah, in good old *mysterious circumstances*,' mused Abbott. 'Look, mate, you're making yourself useful here. How about we continue in that vein? Are you down with that? I need to know the current whereabouts of Burton and Mowles.'

'Burton I know about. That came up during the search for Stone. He's still in Baghdad somewhere. Mowles I don't know about. Why do you want to know where they are?'

'Fingers didn't drown. He wasn't the drowning sort. So someone killed him and bothered to make it look like an accident.'

'You're reaching.'

'We'll see.'

Abbott ended the call and made his way back to the Al Mansour to freshen up. That evening he had an appointment with Potter. And thank fuck it was at a bar.

Unbidden, an image had come to him: a body in this very street.

You didn't help him.

CHAPTER 28

Later, Abbott was heading for the Green Zone. He flicked down his sun visor on approaching the checkpoint and watched as the grunt's eyes ranged over the ID and then over him, grinning, feeling just a little jazzed by the booze (just enough, not too much, always a bit of a numbers game) and knowing full well that he looked the part. Sure enough, the grunt waved him through and was already turning away as Abbott drove into the zone.

Still the same, he thought, looking around. Like a town within a town. Physically, it looked similar to the outside but there were far fewer locals, of course, and a more relaxed atmosphere about the place. Again, this was Baghdad. Everything was relative. Compared to the outside, the Green Zone was an oasis of calm.

He made his way to the Baghdad Country Club, the favoured watering hole for those in the zone. Modelled on a traditional golf club, the Country Club was rightly proud of its slogan, 'It takes real balls to play here'. Abbott checked in, surrendering his Kurz and his Sig to the guy on the front desk, who would stow them in the safe for the duration of his stay. There at the front was the famous sign: 'No guns, no ammunition, no grenades, no flash bang, no knives, no exception.'

It was said that the owner of the Baghdad Country Club, a guy called James, would don body armour and mechanics' overalls in order to go on liquor runs, smuggling the booze through the backstreets and into the club. Abbott was on nodding terms with James and could well believe it. The guy was a character.

Meanwhile, feeling lighter without his weapons and a little more vulnerable as well, Abbott continued into the busy bar area. Right away he saw Potter, seated at a corner table, looking just as Abbott remembered him. Quick-eyed but at the same time laidback to the point of horizontal with it, he wore a black cotton shirt, open at the neck, and black cargo pants, effortlessly managing to look smarter and cooler than everybody else around him: foreign correspondents, off-duty Circuit guys, contractors.

As Abbott approached, Potter stood up and the two shook hands. Abbott took a seat opposite, then decided he didn't like sitting with his back to the room and shifted around so that he was seated beside Potter.

Potter looked at him. Like a man whose personal space was being invaded and, rather than sit side-by-side, moved around himself, rolling his eyes at the game of musical chairs.

'You got in OK, then?' he asked Abbott when they were both settled.

Abbott eyed the glass of beer on the table in front of Potter, feeling an almost indecent rush of anticipation at getting one of his own. No doubt about it, the fires inside were well and truly lit tonight. 'The ID did the trick,' he told Potter. 'They didn't check more than that.' He raised his hand to call for his own beer, twirling his finger in the internationally recognised signal for 'two more here, please'.

Potter nodded. 'They'll be checking more thoroughly in the days to come.'

'Oh yes?'

'Word is that Condoleezza Rice is paying a secret visit. Security's tightening. Place is in a state of panic and you can bet there's a bit of housecleaning going on.'

'Noted,' replied Abbott, thinking, *Better have a shave, then.*

'I was about to ask how you are, but ...' Potter gestured as though Abbott told his own story, 'I guess "not good" is the answer.'

'Why? You don't think I'm catwalk ready?' said Abbott, wondering how long it would take the beers to come. 'It's the eyebrows, isn't it? I haven't had them threaded in at least a fortnight.'

'Nah, you just look ... a bit shit, really.'

From most people, it might have been considered a personal comment, but not from Potter. He and Abbott went back to when Potter had been a fixer for Hercules, a security company that had employed Abbott and his team on a couple of occasions before they took the Lone Ranger route, and Potter had been their liaison.

He'd gone freelance not long after that. He and Abbott had stayed in touch, Potter constantly trying to tempt Abbott back onto the market.

Point being, he knew Abbott.

'Might have something to do with the fact that I've not long flown in from Singapore and haven't stopped since.'

'Yeah, it might be that,' said Potter, looking meaningfully at the drink that was placed in front of Abbott. His own drink went untouched and he watched as Abbott lifted the glass of amber liquid to his lips and drained half of it in one go. 'Might also be that.'

'This?' Abbott took another greedy gulp and then wiped suds from his chin with the back of his hand, not really caring how he looked doing it. 'I've got a handle on it. I'm a bit hung-over now, but that's all. A bit hung-over. Very tired. Back in Baghdad and I haven't even told you what I've found out since I've returned.' He banged the glass back on the table and held Potter in a long, challenging glare.

Potter sat back, hands up. 'OK, OK. Point taken. You got the stuff OK?'

'I got the stuff.'

'Car OK?'

Abbott gave a chef's finger-kiss. 'You the man.'

'Cool, well, I put my ear to the ground like you asked,' said Potter.

By now Abbott had drained the last of his drink and had already raised his hand and made the twirling motion for a second time. 'And?'

'Nothing. No sign of Nathan,' said Potter, holding up a finger to signal that only one extra beer was needed. 'No kidnapping reports that fit the bill. You know, Abbott, it's not exactly uncommon for squaddies to go off the grid.'

'We're not pushing the panic button without good reason, Potts. There are other extenuating factors. Do you remember Stone on my team?'

Potter's eyes dropped and he nodded slowly. 'Funny you should say that. I heard something of Stone today, in fact. Something I wanted to ask you about.'

'You mean the fact that he's dead?'

Potter nodded slowly, eyes steady.

A burst of laughter came from a nearby table. Abbott waited for it to die down. 'Did you hear how?'

'An accident. What was it? Car?'

'Uh-uh. Drowned. Best swimmer in my team. Drowned.'

'Sounds like you don't buy it?'

'I'm saying it feels unlikely.'

'Good swimmers drown, Abbott.'

'Or maybe *are* drowned.'

Potter pulled a face like he was considering the possibility. 'Stone had enemies. Plenty of people would have wanted that fucker dead. Put it this way, I can't say I was crying into my coffee when I learned that he'd shuffled off this mortal coil.' Potter looked at him with slightly challenging eyes. As well he might; your teammates were like your mum and dad: It was one thing slagging off your own, quite another when an outsider did it. Abbott didn't bite, though, no doubt confirming Potter's suspicion that he and Stone had long ago fallen out.

Instead he said, 'Go on. What do you mean?'

'Well, you know he was doing really well, right?'

Abbott shrugged. 'He was definitely heading in that general direction when I left, yeah.'

'And you didn't have the option of joining him on his trip along the road paved with gold?'

'I preferred to slum it in Singapore.'

Potter leaned forward. His face was pleasant. His words were not. 'You know, a man could get pissed off giving so much help to a guy who's holding out on him.'

Abbott sighed and sat back in his seat. It was one thing taking the high hand with Cuckoo, he realised, quite another doing it with an old head like Potter. 'Oh, come on, Potts. It's just stuff, you know? Stuff I don't want to talk about. Maybe not ever, but certainly not now. You want me breaking down? A full-on PTSD episode here and now?' He was laying it on thick but hey, you had to do what you had to do.

'All right, mate, all right,' said Potter, dropping it.

'Sorry. And thank you. And don't ever think that I take any of the stuff you do for me for granted, because I really don't, you know.'

'Fine. All right. Stop before I burst out crying.'

'OK, moving on. Tell me about Stone.'

'Well, he formed his own firm, called—'

'Executive Alliance Group.'

'You knew.'

'That's the direction I was talking about. Went well, then, I assume.'

'Just a fucking bit. He stole a huge contract off Hercules.'

'Go on, what contract?'

'Farlowe Global.'

Ouch, thought Abbott, pulling a face. Of all the industrial contractors operating in Iraq, Farlowe were the biggest, and currently in the process of developing a vast portfolio of industrial and residential projects, as well as moving into energy services, primarily oil and gas, but renewable energy sources, too. As such, they had a huge complex in the Green Zone, second in size only to Saddam's palace, as well as a bunch of satellite offices, both inside the zone and out, as well as further afield in Iraq.

Abbott had no idea how many Farlowe personnel were deployed in the whole of the country, but it was enough to populate a small town, maybe even a big town, which meant that they needed a fuckload of security personnel. The contract, therefore, was immense.

'Yeah. Exactly.'

'How much?'

'I don't know. I'm not privy to that kind of information.'

'Ballpark.'

'Oh, God, fuck, you know, a big six figures.'

'Fuck me.'

'Fuck you? Fuck me. I was out on my ear.'

'Come again? Hercules fired *you* because Executive Alliance Group stole a contract?'

'Yeah,' said Potter. 'Bear with me. We'll get there.'

'OK, but how did Executive Alliance Group even have the resources to fulfil a contract like that?' asked Abbott. Last he knew of it, EAG was but a glint in Stone's eye, an idea born at a large kitchen table inside Mahlouthi's villa. Suddenly it had the capability to fulfil a security contract with Farlowe Global.

'Well, this is the clever bit,' explained Potter. 'EAG swiped the contract out from under the nose of Hercules, which was suddenly a firm without a portfolio. In Iraq, at least. As you know, they'd been doing stuff in Somalia, but in Iraq it was pretty much Farlowe only. Without Farlowe, Hercules was left high and dry. No way could they win anything big enough to support the kind of infrastructure they had. What's more, they – by which I mean "we", because I was still there then – leased our Green Zone HQ from Farlowe, who wanted it back. And guess who they gave it to?'

Abbott looked at him. 'No. Surely not.'

'Yup. EAG moved in, took over the whole shooting match. A bunch of senior personnel left but otherwise it was business as usual. All they changed was the sign above the door. OK, they changed a bit more than that, but you know what I mean.'

'And this was just Stone, was it? What about Biscuits and Badger? At one time there was talk that we'd all be involved.'

'But you bowed out?'

'Events overtook me.'

'Well, I don't know. Stone was CEO. He was the public-facing figure. That's all I knew, because of course it wasn't long after that that I was packing my own cardboard box and heading for the exit.'

'Being senior personnel?'

'Yeah. And thus associated with the previous regime. Maybe. A bit of that. Also a bit too much wondering aloud and to the wrong people how a pissant start-up like EAG can completely muscle in on a huge operation like Hercules.' He indicated his glass. 'Too many of these in here one night. Too much of just saying what everybody fucking thinks anyway. And on that note I happen to know that EAG is also under investigation by the CIA and UK military intelligence. But they're keeping it on the down low.'

'Oh yes. And what is the general thrust of their investigation?'

'Well, if it was me, I'd be thinking about kickbacks and insider information. Maybe something even more damaging than that. Anyway, to come back to my original point, you can't do any of that without making enemies. Which means that Stone had plenty of people who wanted him dead.'

Abbott felt himself slipping into the alcohol, knowing he shouldn't but unable to resist. He squeezed the bridge of his nose in order to summon rational thought. 'None of which helps me get close to knowing where Nathan is,' he said. 'A guy contacts Nathan. A guy dies. And I'm none the wiser.'

'You carry on with the spadework,' said Potter. 'Less of this.' He mimed drinking. 'And more of this.' He mimed digging. 'In the meantime, I'll make some inquiries of my own.'

Abbott's shoulders slumped. 'It could be that this is all about me, Potts,' he said, wanting to test on Potter what Cuckoo had suggested. A fear that he barely dared give voice to.

'Well, if Stone's been in touch with Nathan, then quite possibly,' said Potter.

'And that maybe Nathan's being used in some way. Used as bait.'

Potter pulled a non-committal face. Instead, the thought simply settled over Abbott like a cloak and he took an unhappy pull of his beer, saying a silent sorry to his son, missing, doing God knows what, God knows where. Paying, as he always had, for Abbott's shortcomings.

'So what now?' asked Potter. 'I can make some inquiries on your behalf, but what will you be doing in the meantime?' he spoke with a meaningful look at Abbott's glass.

'Nathan's missing,' hissed Abbott. 'I won't be spending my time getting bladdered, all right? Can you get me an interpreter? Ask him to meet me tomorrow?'

Potter agreed and Abbott gave him the address of the street in Kadhimiya. The two drank some more, making what amounted to small talk for a while, until Potter, with a wide yawn, announced it was time to go.

He meant them both, of course, and grimaced when Abbott announced that he planned to have one more for the road. Shaking his head but too drunk himself to raise much concern, Potter left with promises to do his best, and Abbott waited until he'd gone before availing himself of the Country Club's famous take-outs – two bottles of red – in order to continue the night's drinking back at the Al Mansour, telling himself that he'd drink one bottle.

Which he did, as he opened Nathan's laptop and began another, ultimately fruitless search of its contents.

And then he started on a second bottle. He was on his third glass and beginning to find it difficult to focus on the laptop screen when there came a knock at the door. His Sig was on the tabletop beside the computer. He snatched it up, stood and swallowed, gathering himself as though under scrutiny before walking steadily – correction: *trying* to walk steadily – to the door.

'Who is it?' he asked, the words only just identifiable as proper words. He stood by the side of the door, in case anybody on the other side put a round through it. At the same time, his Sig was raised, pointing at the window and the fire escape. The window was open, allowing in a cool November-night breeze. The cream linen curtain rippled slightly. He pictured killers on the fire escape outside, assassins in the corridor outside his room.

And then came a small voice. 'It's me, mister.'

Abbott put his eye to the peephole. Outside, the corridor was empty apart from a little Arabic boy, just nine or ten, so he took the chance, opened the door, peering quickly up and down the hall at the same time. The boy stood with his hands behind his back and his chin raised, waiting for Abbott's attention.

'Yes?' said Abbott. He heard the slur in his voice but took heart from the fact that the kid was young and probably wouldn't twig that he was drunk.

'Are you drunk, mister?' said the kid.

Abbott frowned at him. 'Always, mate.'

The kid looked pleased about that. He spoke in a polite voice. 'Mr Mahlouthi wonders if you would join him at his residence. He would very much like to talk to you.'

Mahlouthi. Mahlouthi and a body in the street.

'No,' croaked Abbott.

'Mr Mahlouthi would very much like to see you, mister,' repeated the boy insistently.

'Well, then, Mr Mahlouthi is fresh out of good-luck tokens, then, isn't he? Because I'm not going anywhere.'

'Mister—' started the boy.

'Do you know what fuck off is?' snapped Abbott. He was swaying in the doorway now. A guy who was drunk and in charge of a gun and yet somehow, pathetically, also failing to intimidate a little kid.

'I'll tell him you said no.' The little kid smiled, then dashed away down the corridor, out of sight.

Abbott closed the door, went back to his boozing.

CHAPTER 29

It had been the end of June when it had happened. Abbott was still at Mahlouthi's then. He and Fi were long divorced, of course, and it was already well over a year since he'd last had any contact with Nathan.

Meantime, the maintenance was killing him. Abbott, never good with money at the best of times, was struggling. He was one of those guys who spent what he made and was having no difficulty spending it just because he was in Baghdad. The whole team were doing their fair share of drinking and drugging.

Of course, he didn't realise it at the time, but the drink and the drugs were his way of coping with the situation and with other people. It was the crew at the ex-pats' AA in Singapore that had led him to thinking that. It hit him like a bolt of lightning at the first meeting. One of them – it might even have been Rodney out of *Only Fools and Horses* – had talked about drinking to 'self-medicate'. It was the first time Abbott had heard that particular expression, the first time he'd thought of drink as an actual medicine. Something you took to ease the pain. It struck a chord.

So that was it, looking back. That was one of the reasons he drank and still did. To take himself out of life and away from himself. To ease the pain. To 'self-medicate'. Funny how knowing that didn't seem to help him stop, but it was a bit of comfort at least.

But there was another reason. Or perhaps another way of putting it would be to say that the medicine had another side-effect to which Abbott was partial. It made him feel normal. So while the sober version of him made the right noises about comradeship, the band of brothers and all that jazz, he never really felt it on the inside. Drunk, he did. He actually briefly felt at one with the team. He felt like he'd happily die for these guys.

Waking up sober, of course, he'd realise it was just a trick of the alcohol but during the night-time, he was just one of the lads. And if anybody noticed that he usually kept himself to himself during the daytime, well, they didn't say so, putting it down to 'just Abbott'. He was a good soldier, he knew. A good man to have at your side during a contact, and being a good soldier trumped every other consideration. You could be any weirdo you wanted, as long as you were a good soldier. As long as you held up your end in the field.

Was that the reason that Mahlouthi had called him into the office that day – his distance from the others? Either way he was asked to report. Abbott's quarters and those of the three other guys were across the villa from Mahlouthi's area, which was like a house within itself. To get to it meant traversing almost the entire length of the complex, then crossing a pool area to the portico that marked the entrance to Mahlouthi's inner sanctum, an area that he shared with his three wives.

It used to be the case that the pool area was open, but the first thing that Abbott and co. had done was insist that it was covered. Some people looked at the pool and saw a lovely sun trap, a place to relax with a drink and a J.K. Rowling novel. The four ex-SBS blokes saw the perfect entry point for an assault, complete with abseil ropes.

He made his way across, nodding at one of the wives who sat by the pool. She frowned at him as though she blamed him personally for the glass that now comprised the ceiling of the pool. Them's the breaks, he thought, and climbed the steps to enter Mahlouthi's quarters. Unlike the rest of the villa his area seemed to be swathed in linen, which swayed gently in the air-conditioning. Walking through to Mahlouthi's office and knocking gently on the door, he felt like he was inside a 1980s pop video. Half expected Simon Le Bon to appear.

'Come.'

In the office he was directed to a seat opposite Mahlouthi, who sat at his desk, reclining in a leather upholstered swivel chair, the arms of his pinstripe suit crossed across his large chest, regarding Abbott from behind fashionable spectacles and a thick black beard.

'You wanted to see me,' said Abbott.

'Yes. I have a business proposition for you.' Abbott looked at him and then nodded for him to go ahead before Mahlouthi continued. 'I am in possession of a rumour. This rumour has in turn become a suspicion, and if this suspicion proves correct, then that suspicion in turn becomes information – information I should very much like to pass on to the coalition, all in the name of our continued good relationship.'

'Yeah? And?' said Abbott.

'I would like you to confirm whether or not this rumour, as in, this suspicion, is correct.'

Abbott tested the waters. 'OK, we'll get onto it straight away. Let me know what you have and I'll get Badger to run some checks …'

Mahlouthi smiled, revealing rows of good teeth. 'I think you understand, given that I have called you here in secret, that I would rather this be kept between you and me for now.'

Abbott shook his head. 'Uh-uh. No way. We work as a team. You know that better than anyone.'

Mahlouthi made a disbelieving noise. 'You each have jobs you do away from the group.'

'Not really, but even if we do, we don't keep them secret from the others.'

Mahlouthi had been leaning forward, but now he reclined again. 'Are you sure about that?'

He smiled, and Abbott wondered what Mahlouthi knew of Stone and his plans for Executive Alliance Group. Did he think Stone was operating alone? Come to think of it, Stone might as well be operating alone, since the rest of them were very much at the humouring-him stage.

He decided not to go there, wherever 'there' was. 'If the others in the team are doing it, then that's on their conscience. I'm not going to.'

Now Mahlouthi leaned towards him. He reached for a block of Post-it notes, wrote down a figure, tore off the note and slapped it down in front of Abbott.

Abbott looked at it, then back up to Mahlouthi. It was a big number.

'That's a big number.'

'It's on top of what I already pay you.'

'Well, yeah, I gathered that.'

As Mahlouthi took a deep breath, his forearms crossed across his chest, and rocked, as though buffeted on stormy seas. 'Do you want the job or not?'

Everyone has a price. And Abbott's was some way south of the figure scrawled on the Post-it. It was too much to turn down. Simple as that.

'All right,' he said. 'No promises. Just tell me what it is you think you know.'

'In the safe knowledge that nothing I tell you here goes any further?'

'Nothing said in this room leaves this room.'

Mahlouthi's smile again revealed his perfect dentistry. 'There's a Foreign Office worker. Based here in Baghdad in the Green Zone who I believe is passing information to the Russians.' He passed across a fuzzy photocopied picture of a young man. 'This gentleman here,' he said, tapping the photograph. 'Confirm that he is indeed passing information to the Russians. And if he is, then find out his identity. That's all. That's all you have to do.'

'And you need *me* to do that?'

'Snatching a quick photograph is one thing. I need someone with greater access to the Green Zone in order to learn his identity.'

Abbott plucked the Post-it from the tabletop. He held it up like it was the winning betting slip, his guarantee. 'OK,' he said.

* * *

Abbott found a spot in an office building opposite the Foreign Office and begin keeping watch. On the first day, he saw the kid. Not much older than Nathan. Smart-but-casually dressed in what looked like Gap's Middle Eastern War Zone range, and yet somehow without that wet-behind-the-ears look you might have expected from a man of his youth.

However, there was something wary and closed about him, and Abbott soon clocked why, because from what he observed, it did indeed look a lot like the kid was up to no good.

Abbott kept watch six or seven hours a day. Mostly, the kid spent all morning in the FO building. The next time he showed his face was to leave for lunch, which was probably contrary to official guidelines but Abbott could understand it: in the Green Zone, guys like him felt almost safe. Insurgents would launch the odd mortar attack; there had been suicide-bomb attacks, too, but these were rare, and it was by far the safest area of the city, surrounded as it was by walls and barbed-wire fences, controlled by just a handful of checkpoints. Civilians felt safe there; they could almost imagine they were back home. The business was of war – sorry, 'keeping the peace' – but it was still a business. And business required bureaucrats.

And so, the kid behaved just like any other office drone going about their daily business.

Almost.

On the first day, as he left for lunch, he reached for his phone, looked at it briefly then replaced it in his pocket. His face betraying no emotion.

Abbott checked the time. It was 13.17.

It happened again, the second day – again at 13.17. And when the same thing happened on the third day, Abbott began to think that Mahlouthi's intelligence was good.

On the fourth day, he saw the kid leave the FO, receive his 13.17 text and then return to the office, only to emerge a few minutes later, this time holding an envelope.

Moments later, as he made his way along a crowded street, he passed two men in civvies who walked on either side of him, one of them talking on the phone, the other making a great show of staring off into the middle distance.

After the pass was made, the kid was no longer holding the envelope.

You're a spy, thought Abbott. He felt somehow disappointed in the boy, having formed a favourable impression of him otherwise. He wished that Mahlouthi's intelligence had been wrong.

Later that same day, he followed the kid from the Foreign Office to a gated apartment complex that he clearly called home. As luck would have it, he knew the guy on sentry duty and was able to get inside and find out where the kid was staying. The next morning, he checked that the kid had gone to work and then paid a visit to his apartment and let himself in.

Inside, the apartment was neat and smelled slightly of last night's dinner. Quickly, Abbott made a tidy search, careful not to leave any evidence of the break-in. He wanted some idea of why this kid might have got himself involved with a foreign power but had no joy on that score. He had to be satisfied with simply learning the kid's identity. His name was Jeremy Robinson. He was twenty-two years old.

Abbott had returned to the villa and reported his findings to Mahlouthi who nodded, satisfied. 'Excellent. This is the proof we need,' as though the matter was closed. But Abbott, in the meantime, had been thinking about Robinson. Thinking: what would be his punishment? Stopped, for sure. But exposed and arrested? That was a whole different kettle of metal, because being arrested meant being taken by the Yanks, and we all knew what they did to suspected spies in captivity. Clue: dehydration wasn't an issue. And Robinson was just a kid. And if he was spying for the Russians, then no doubt it was only because they had something on him. Anyway, Baghdad was full of spies. Robinson was just one of many.

In short, standing in Mahlouthi's office, he had what you might call a change of heart, and said, 'No, it isn't proof. Not enough proof, anyway.'

'I think it is. I think it's sufficient.' Mahlouthi was already reaching for his phone.

'Wait,' pressed Abbott. 'Even if you think that, then wouldn't the information be more valuable if I could identify the contact, whoever it is the two Arabs are giving those envelopes to?'

'It might.' Mahlouthi looked thoughtful, perhaps thinking of the price he could command. Then, in the next instant, he grew wary. 'This is not some kind of military solidarity you're displaying here, is it Abbott?'

'Do you see any solidarity so far?'

'No, but who's to say you haven't grown a conscience in the meantime.'

Abbott felt as though Mahlouthi could see right through him. 'If the guy's passing military secrets to Russians, then that goes against my interests, too. I need to be sure. Just leave it with me.'

In the meantime, Abbott had an idea, and the next day he left a note under the door of Robinson's lodgings.

That evening he received a phone call, the voice wary. 'Who is this? What do you want?'

'One at a time. Do you want me to say who I am, or what I want?'

'Start with who you are.'

Abbott couldn't help but smile. Kid had balls.

'OK, let's just say I'm a friend. You're maybe not going to think so, but I am.'

'I don't know what the hell you mean.'

'I mean, if you want, I could talk about what happens at thirteen seventeen every day. About two gentlemen in dish-dashas and the odd brown A-four envelope. I could talk about that, if you like.'

'I don't know what you're on about.'

'Good, fine, that's what I'll tell my employer.'

'Who is your employer?'

Yup. Had to hand it to the kid. He was not to be intimidated.

'My employer is a man who would love to give you up to the coalition. He is someone to whom you are nothing more than goodwill and a payday. Unfortunately for him he's employed a wishy-washy wet liberal to spy on you and that wishy-washy wet liberal wants to give you the chance to get out while the going's good.'

'Well, I don't know what you're talking about,' said Robinson, 'but either way I wish you a good day.'

'No,' said Abbott quickly, before Robinson could cut the call. 'It's not that easy. You don't understand. I have to give something to my employer. I'm giving you the chance to make that something not you. You give up your contacts and that's the information I'll pass on. You hold out on me, then I'm giving you up. Your call.'

'OK, then,' sighed Robinson. 'We'd better meet. Where?'

That night, Abbott made his way on foot to the agreed meet point, the Kadhimiya women's prison.

Under his shirt, he carried his MP5 Kurz, ready to use it, mindful of the dogs on the streets. They had grown fat feasting on corpses during the war and now roamed the city in packs with a taste for human flesh. They were not the only aspect of

Baghdad that became more forbidding after nightfall. It was not as though the bomb-damaged and rusting car wrecks disappeared during the day, just that when the streets were filled with traffic and pedestrians, they seemed to fade into the background. You could tune them out like visual static. At night, however, they stuck out as jagged outlines against the night sky. Stark, charred and jagged reminders of war.

He reached the prison just in time to hear something that struck him as odd. There were sounds of a struggle, and he rounded the corner to see two men standing over a figure on the ground. He saw the blade that one of them held. And in the half-light he saw blood leak from it, onto the prone body below.

'*Hey*,' he shouted, and reached around the Kurz in one fluid, practised movement, extending his arms, pulling the Kurz on its bungee sling at the same time as he called, 'Stop right there, you two.'

But they had no intention of doing that, and perhaps knowing how unlikely it was that Abbott would fire on them, they moved away, taking two steps backwards each, as though testing him and then, when he didn't open fire, turning to run.

They clattered off down the empty street, turned the corner. Abbott let the rifle drop then ran, skidding to the guy on the ground, twisting him round.

The face that looked up at him, pale in the watery moon light, was Jeremy Robinson's. He was wearing a Nirvana T-shirt, blood spreading quickly across the picture of the baby reaching for the dollar bill, the fabric torn by one, two, three stab wounds.

Robinson coughed, blowing a little fountain of blood that pattered on Abbott's forehead and cheeks. His eyes were crazy, spinning. One hand, clawed, rose as though to grab Abbott but instead hung in the air, his fingers moving weakly, the life leaving him in front of Abbott's very eyes.

He'd seen men die before, of course. But never like this, never so close, where it was as though he was witnessing the soul depart, the life force leaving behind just an empty vessel made of flesh and bone.

In the next second Robinson's eyes focused. Finally, the clawing hand found purchase, reaching to touch Abbott's cheek, and as he died he said one final heart-breaking word. 'Dad.'

CHAPTER 30

'You fucking cunt.'

'I don't know what you're—' Mahlouthi was saying. His eyes were flicking to the door. Abbott was shouting. Anybody in the vicinity would have heard.

'You absolute fucking cunt,' said Abbott. 'You told them.'

'Who?'

Abbott's mind was racing. *Not the coalition, no, but ...* 'Somebody. I don't fucking know. But you told *somebody*, and you told them what we'd agreed *not* to fucking tell them, didn't you?'

Mahlouthi was standing, palms planted on his desk, shaking his head, eyes closed behind the spectacles. 'No, no, no, I did no such thing.' His voice was a harsh whisper. 'I abided by the terms of our agreement. You were to pass on to me a more valuable name. That is what we agreed.'

Abbott wondered if Mahlouthi was telling the truth and realised that he didn't know. After all, if Mahlouthi had had his suspicions about Jeremy Robinson, then others would have them, too. The murder might simply have been the tragic consequence of spying. It might have had nothing to do with Mahlouthi.

Nothing to do with Mahlouthi and all to do with you, because it was you who wanted to meet, wasn't it? It was you who inadvertently brought him outside the safety of the Green Zone.

It was not quite daybreak when Abbott, riddled with guilt, assailed by demons from the past and sick of Baghdad – no, sick *with* Baghdad; knowing the place was slowly killing him – chucked his belongings into his bag, made major inroads into a bottle of rum and left behind the foliage-covered walls of Mahlouthi's villa, the place that had been his mink-lined prison for two months.

Just a few hours after that, he blagged his way onto a convoy from Baghdad back to Jordan – back to the InterContinental hotel – and from there on to Singapore.

CHAPTER 31

In Singapore, Cuckoo took a seat at a table outside a café. 'So you're the guy they call Foxhole?' he said.

'Yes, that's me.'

Foxhole was American. That was the first surprise. For some reason, Cuckoo hadn't expected that. He'd also assumed that he would be a little more prepossessing. This guy was a wreck. For a start, it looked like he hadn't slept for a week. Plus he was sweating profusely. He sat with his hands on the table. They lay either side of a cup of coffee that appeared to have been standing untouched for a while. His forehead shone, his eyes moving quickly. It struck Cuckoo that he looked like that guy in *Dracula*. The one who ate bugs and gibbered in a cell. What was his name? Airwick, or something.

'Are you all right, mate?' he asked across the table, concerned more for himself than Foxhole's welfare. At the same time, he looked around. It was a bright day, and there were plenty of people both in the café area and in the sun-dappled square beyond: eating, drinking, sitting on the wall of the fountain and enjoying the weather. But if any one of them was watching Cuckoo and Foxhole, it was impossible to tell. And if this was a set-up, then a set-up for what?

'Yeah, I'm all right,' managed Foxhole, doing little to put Cuckoo's mind at rest.

Foxhole had reached him through his hotel, requesting to meet him, and because he had to all intents and purposes been Abbott's employer, Cuckoo thought it best to go along. Now, however – *just look at the guy* – he was way less certain.

Renfield! That was the guy in Dracula.

'I wanted to check on Abbott,' said Foxhole. He was unconvincing. His voice shook. Fresh beads of sweat popped on an already oil-slicked forehead. Everything about this was wrong.

'How did you know to contact me?' asked Cuckoo.

'You're Abbott's friend. I knew you were in Singapore.'

'How?'

'Abbott told me.'

Cuckoo doubted that but decided it wasn't worth pursuing. 'OK, well, Abbott is fine,' he said warily.

'There was a job that went wrong …' started Foxhole, swallowing.

'Yes, he told me about that. He told me that you wouldn't be happy. But if you're hoping that I can help you with anything there, then I'm afraid you're very much mistaken. I know nothing about that job and as for him, he's got bigger fish to fry now.'

That ought to shut him down, thought Cuckoo. Put that in your pipe and smoke it.

'There are some people after him,' said Foxhole.

'Oh yes?' said Cuckoo warily. 'Why is that?'

'Because the job went wrong.'

Cuckoo shrugged. 'Well, uh, I know he fucked up, but surely there's a risk factor built into any job?'

Foxhole shook his head slowly. There was something about the way he shook his head. As though he had an egg balanced on it. His hands still hadn't moved from either side of the coffee cup and his teeth were bared as though biting down on his own distress. For the first time, Cuckoo noticed something else. Foxhole was wearing a badge at his lapel. A simple button badge, with no slogan, just a red button badge, the sort of thing that schoolkids wore to denote their house.

'No,' said Foxhole tightly, 'Abbott didn't just mess up. He went the whole extra nine yards. He put himself on two big hit lists.'

'Oh, Jesus Christ, honestly, good luck to them. Let's just say they're going to have a hard time finding him.'

'Where is he?'

'Like I'm going to tell you.'

At that, Foxhole leaned carefully back in his chair, raised his chin slightly and shook his head from side to side, clearly signalling somebody.

Seeing it, Cuckoo tensed, his head jerking left and right, then up to the windows of surrounding buildings.

At the same time, his phone chirruped. Without taking his eyes off Foxhole he pulled it from the pocket of his mac. Number not known. 'Hello?' he answered, watching Foxhole, who, apart from giving the signal, had not moved a muscle. 'Who is this?'

'You don't know me,' came the voice, 'my name is Mr Kind.'

'Yes?'

'You're Alan Roberts? Abbott's friend.'

This was bad. Again, that thought: what would Abbott do? He'd play for time. He'd stall and assess the situation. Look for an opening.

'OK, Mr Kind. Sounds like you want to talk. How about you show yourself?' said Cuckoo, gratified to hear that his voice was steady.

'No, I don't think I'll do that, Mr Roberts. I think I prefer it where I am.'

'And where is that?'

'Oh, don't worry. I'm within range.'

Cuckoo froze. Slowly, he made to get to his feet.

'No, I wouldn't do that if I were you, please, Mr Roberts. Let me show you why. Do you see the badge that Mr Foxhole is wearing?'

'I do.'

'Look closer.'

Cuckoo leaned forward. Sure enough, he noticed something about the badge. Disguised by the red of it was the pinprick of a laser sight.

'You see that?' said the voice in his ear.

'I see it.'

'Good. Now, if you do anything other than something I've asked you to do, I'll kill him and then you. Do you follow that?'

'Yes,' said Cuckoo. His face was wet against the phone.

'Good. Now listen, do you know who hired Hexagon Security to bug Travis Bryars?'

Cuckoo's mouth opened and closed. 'Um … um … I don't even know what you're talking about.'

'No,' sighed Kind, 'I've been hearing that a lot, including from our friend Foxhole. Oh well, couldn't hurt to ask. Now where were we?'

The thought came to Cuckoo that he didn't want to die. He was not a coward but nor was he especially brave, and nothing like this had ever happened to him before.

'Yes, that's right,' continued Kind, 'I need to know, where is our friend Abbott? Wait – before you answer, one thing. I'll check your answer. I'll check your answer here and now, and if it's the wrong one, then I'll kill somebody. Do you see that woman at the table next door?'

There was a family beside them. They were probably on holiday, boisterous and enjoying themselves. 'Yes,' said Cuckoo. He saw the red dot dance on her back. 'I thought you were going to start with Foxhole?'

'I've changed my mind,' said Mr Kind.

'So you'd kill her, too, would you? A complete innocent?'

'How about I haven't decided who I'm going to kill? How about that, Mr Roberts? Keep you on your toes. Now. Give me your answer, make it the correct one, and we can avoid me having to decide which of you to shoot first.'

Cuckoo knew it was a bluff. After all, Abbott was in Baghdad. How the hell could Kind check his whereabouts? Answer: he couldn't. Could he?

Except that Cuckoo knew how woefully under-equipped he was for situations such as this, because the honest answer was that although logic told him Kind was bluffing, he had no real idea how these people worked. For all he knew, Kind could easily confirm whether or not Abbott was in Baghdad. And, of course, Kind knew that.

Across the table from him, Foxhole was urging him with his eyes, whispering, 'Tell him. Tell him what he wants to know. Please just fucking tell him, man.' The laser sight was back on him, dancing slightly on the red button badge. Cuckoo thought of Kind asking who had hired Hexagon and wondered what tortures Foxhole had already had to endure.

'Foxhole whispers the truth, Roberts, old fruit,' said Kind in his ear, laying on the Britishness thick, enjoying himself. 'Heed his wise words.'

Cuckoo's thoughts were wild. He didn't have the training or the temperament of an Abbott. Cool in a crisis was not in his vocabulary. His brain had fixed on one thing and one thing only. If he told a lie, then he was dead. If he told the truth, then Abbott was dead.

Then again, and on second thoughts, was he dead? Was he really? After all, Cuckoo could warn Abbott. Plus, Abbott was SF, for fuck's sake. He was already in the most dangerous place on earth. He would take it in his stride.

From somewhere Cuckoo summoned a little steel. 'For your own safety I shouldn't tell you where he is.'

At the other end of the line, Kind gave a dry chuckle. 'You let me be the judge of that. Where is he?'

'Baghdad,' said Cuckoo.

'Baghdad? Is that so? And what is he doing in Baghdad?'

Cuckoo ignored the question. 'You can't check it, can you?' he said.

'Careful, I might find I want to scratch my itchy trigger finger. What's he doing in Baghdad?'

'He's looking for his son, and may I recommend you don't get in his way.'

'Strong words, sweaty man.'

'You don't know who you're dealing with.'

'Nor do you. But of course you have my name. And you can tell that to Abbott when you warn him, can't you?'

Cuckoo said nothing.

'And I can't let you do that.'

Cuckoo opened his mouth to say something when Foxhole stood up.

'Go,' he shouted. Faces of other customers turned their way. 'There's a gun,' Foxhole yelled at the top of his voice, directing himself at Cuckoo. 'Run!'

And then his head jerked, a hole in his forehead opened and the back of his skull exploded in a shower of blood and brain matter. There was no bang – Kind must have been using a suppressor – but even so, the people around them knew what was happening and a sense of general pandemonium began to spread across the café terrace and then into the square like a shockwave.

Instinctively, Cuckoo ducked as another round ricocheted off the table, hitting a nearby diner in the shoulder, her scream further adding to the panic. A third round thunked into the table, smashing a coffee cup and missing Cuckoo by inches as he turned to run. Then more bullets, this time on automatic fire. Another customer span and fell. Others panicked, overturning chairs and tables, crockery flying. Inside the restaurant the realisation spread and customers dived for cover, while around them in the square a scream went up and the serenity of the day was shattered as customers and sun worshippers scattered.

Cuckoo joined them.

He felt like a sitting duck as he ran. He heard a bullet ping off the ground behind him. More shots came, the lack of a corresponding gunshot sound adding a surreal edge to the general terror. And then Cuckoo felt a pain – a bright, agonising pain that flared – and in the next instant he was falling, pitching headlong forward.

And then there was blackness.

CHAPTER 32

Abbott awoke on his bed at the Al Mansour hotel fully dressed.

He awoke with a start, partly as a result of last night's booze, which lay upon him like an oil slick, and partly as a result of a dream, a vision of the Robinson boy's dying face that had morphed into something else: another boy, much younger, though, a boy who called his name: 'Alex ... Alex ...'

'We know you couldn't save him, Alex. We know you did your best.'

But I didn't save him. It was on me.

He thought of Nathan as a tiny baby. Whenever he was home, Fi had used the opportunity to insist he did the night-time feeds, which meant getting up at 3 a.m. The way she played it, it was like she did it to punish him, a means of saying, 'Look what I have to put up with.' But the fact was, he loved the alone time with Nathan. He'd fix himself a drink, just the one, and with the warmed bottle of milk in one hand, and his drink in the other, he'd rouse the tiny Nathan from his slumber, taking a seat in a leather armchair to begin the feed, and just watch. Suffused with love, as though it were an actual present entity in the warm, darkened room, he'd watch Nathan. The way his tiny hands grasped the bottle. The way that he watched Abbott as he fed. Occasionally, he would fall asleep and Abbott would have to gently rouse him (Fi insisted that he took the whole bottle on pain of death – Abbott's death). Sometimes, if the bottle was secure, he'd reach up one hand to grasp Abbott's finger in a tiny, chubby fist. During those moments Abbott felt truly bonded with his son, and he'd pledge to be home more, to do more. His own father had been remote and cold, as loveless in fatherhood as he seemed to be in marriage. He didn't want that for Nathan. He told himself he'd break the cycle.

But of course he broke that promise every time. And every time he left Fi on the doorstep holding Nathan and every time he returned with booze on his breath and more blood on his hands, and little Nathan would cling more tightly to his mother, who would give Abbott eyes over the boy's shoulder, the gap between them getting wider and wider.

But not this time, Nath, because it's not too late, it's never too late to be the father you deserve. The hero you want. I'm coming for you.

And then came a voice in his head. A voice from the past saying, 'We know you couldn't save him, Alex. We know you did your best,' and he reached for his iPod, like a toddler clutching at a comforter. Faces. Corpses. Thoughts of Tessa. Over on the desk the curtain shifted in the morning breeze. Sunlight dropped through a gap in the curtain and pointed the way to a bottle of wine on the desk, remnants of last night, giving the bottle a green shine.

Just one nip of that. One little slug will set you straight.

But one's too much and ten's not enough.

Just a nip will silence the voices.

We know you couldn't save him, Alex.

Only who were they talking about? Were they talking about a figure from years ago? Were they talking about Jeremy Robinson?

Were they talking about Nathan?

From somewhere he found a surge of strength. He pulled himself from the bed, tearing off his iPod headphones at the same time. The next thing he knew, he had swiped the half-empty bottle from the desktop. But instead of upending it into his mouth, he took it to the bathroom. He poured it down the sink, telling himself he'd taken his last drink, that his days of waking up feeling this way were at an end.

A voice inside reminded him that he had been here before. But it was a lot easier to pour away your booze when there was still so much in your bloodstream. The real test would come later. In the meantime, he sank back to his bed, trying to work out his next move but guiltily knowing that lying here, hungover, wasn't helping him find his son.

He tried poking away at Nathan's laptop again but turned up nothing new and ended up closing the lid with a small cry of frustration. He wished there were somebody with him now.

No, not somebody. Her. Tessa. He wished she were here to tell him that everything was going to be OK. That he wasn't going to make a mess of things this time.

CHAPTER 33

He had met her in London. Two months ago. Only two short months ago.

There were times when Abbott couldn't quite believe what he had done in offering to meet her. Telling her that he had a meeting in London. What a fucking idiot.

And why had he done it? Well, that would be the booze talking. Mostly, booze made you do stupid stuff. Sometimes it made you do the things you otherwise wouldn't have done. Things you ended up thanking it for. Christ, there were so many marks in the minus column, there had to be some upside, right?

The whole stuff with Tessa. The writing to her, pretending he needed to be in London the very night that her husband was away and her children elsewhere – he lived in Singapore, for fuck's sake – was all down to the booze.

Yet instead of inventing an excuse and pretending that his London business had been cancelled, Abbott found himself going through with it. Why? Because it never occurred to him to do anything different. Because Tessa was in his head night and day, and he told himself that he wanted to expel her from his thoughts, or at least get the idealised seen-through-rose-coloured specs version of her out of his head, and what better way to do that than meet the current version of her.

After all, in his mind, Tessa remained in her twenties. But she was older now. She had a couple of kids. That changes you. It takes away some of what you once were. Life did that. Would she be different? Would *he* be different? Answers on a postcard, please, addressed to 'Of Course You'll Both Be Different, You Arsehole Competition, PO Box 555', and that was why he wanted to meet her. To replace the romantic, idealised version with the reality.

Or that's what he told himself, anyway.

The restaurant she chose was Kettner's, a famous old London landmark on Romilly Street in Soho.

He remembered that she had used to talk about going there, that it was an ambition she had held, something to do with it being her dad's favourite place, and he guessed that she'd long since fulfilled that ambition, and choosing Kettner's was a way of stating it, of saying, 'Look how far I've come, with my degree in law and my familiarity with restaurants that long ago seemed so distant and out of reach.' And among the many things that he wondered and worried about ahead of the meal was just that: was she meeting him to show him that she'd moved on, and therefore to rub his face in what he was missing, what he'd given up?

If so, well, who could blame her? She had every right to be that way, of course. He had hurt her badly. And if so, if that was the way it went, then he would take it on the chin. He would accept it as nothing less than he deserved.

He bought a new shirt and spent an age getting ready, accompanied by a couple of tins of lager, just for Dutch courage, and nothing too strong, either. Cooking lager, nothing over five per cent.

And it was funny, again, looking back, but booze wasn't a problem that night. He drank, of course, and certainly he drank too much. But it wasn't an issue, not the way it always had the potential to be at other times.

It's funny. How that night he was a version of himself that he really, truly liked.

He'd arrived before her, in all his glory, such as it was. He sat at their table with his hands on the tabletop in front of him, feeling like a first-time suitor, a guy on a blind date, the fluttering of nerves in his stomach adding to the whole nostalgic feel of the trip. There's a lot to be said for nostalgia, he realised then. It took you away from yourself – back to a distant and better time.

Then she came. And as he stood to greet her, he realised straight away that she hadn't gone to anything like the same effort as he had. She was smart, of course. But smart in a day-of-business way, complete with sombre grey trouser suit and a small leather briefcase that she plonked down heavily with a sigh, as though it represented more than just a physical weight.

That sigh. Everything about her seemed to suggest that she was bogged down with work, and instantly he knew that whereas all he'd thought about all day was Tessa, it was work that had occupied her thoughts. Seeing her looking almost preoccupied, still decompressing from her day, he actually found himself relieved that she'd turned up at all.

'Sorry I'm late,' she said, leaning to give him a quick air kiss, the kind of London air kiss that he didn't understand, like whether you were supposed to go for both cheeks or just the one. Twist or stick, that was the thing. And this was one of those occasions that he got it wrong, going for the other cheek when she was already turning her head to find her seat.

Gathering herself she beamed at him, and everything about the smile was genuine. No nerves, no agenda that he could see. Just pleased to see him. When was the last time anybody had been pleased to see him? 'Ever the gentleman,' she said.

'I beg your pardon?' he replied, surprised to hear the words in his mouth, 'I beg your pardon' not being an expression he was accustomed to hearing himself use. *You what? Come again?* yes, but *I beg your pardon?* – where had that come from?

'You stood for me,' she explained. 'It's not a criticism. It's nice. I like it. It suits the surroundings.' She waved a hand at the old-school-yet-upmarket fittings around them. 'You always were a gentleman,' she added, and he was delighted that she remembered that side of him. Not his bouts of temper, his wayward ways.

But, God, it was good to see her. She had always been attractive, but what made her better than just good-looking and actually beautiful was that sheer radiance from within. The way she had of making you feel like you were the only one in the room. In that moment, Abbott thought Tessa was everything.

And then he came back down to earth with a bump.

'I can't stay long,' she said.

'I beg your pardon?' he said, really getting some mileage out of his brand-new expression.

She pulled a face. 'It's just that I have a lot of work to get through for tomorrow. I mean, it's amazing to see you and I'm so sorry and everything, but you know how it is?'

He nodded. Yes, he agreed, he knew exactly how it was.

'Oh, you're a sweetheart,' she said, reminding him of how she used to deploy that word, 'sweetheart', always using it to disarm friends and old people. And perhaps she didn't remember – best that she didn't, really – but he'd once asked her never to use it for him because he hated those exact connotations.

'No, sure,' he said. 'That's fine. I mean, it's great that you should be able to carve out time to see me.' That had sounded sarcastic, he knew, so immediately he tried to wind it back. 'I mean, you know. I know how busy you are.'

'It's all good. It's brilliant,' she said, and thank God, because their attention went to the waiter who appeared at their table.

They ordered drinks and perused menus. Peeking over the top of his menu at her, Abbott felt a sense of great euphoria. He wished he could bottle this moment. It was not about 'London ways', or being in the military or living in a war zone, carrying guns. It was just about sitting here, opposite the best person he had ever known.

'I sort of wondered if you'd ever be in touch,' she said, when drinks had arrived and the pizzas were on their way.

A smile drifted about her lips. Her eyes shone. He felt somehow played with and yet didn't feel offended by the idea. 'Why?' he asked. 'Because of ...'

'The pendant. You saw the pendant, didn't you? Wasn't that what you said on the phone?'

'Yes, I did.'

She grinned now. 'I wore it that day for the pictures. I wore it just in case you ever came to the page.'

He was flummoxed. She hadn't said *that* on the phone. 'You really did?'

'Yes,' she said, as though it was the most natural thing in the world, which to her it probably was.

'But how did you know I'd even go there?'

'Oh, come on. Everybody googles their exes, don't they? If there's a picture of you going up online you're always going to think, "Maybe my ex'll see this." God knows I've got enough of them.'

Pictures? Or exes? He thought he knew which but decided not to interrogate the idea, not wanting to think about the men she'd known in between.

'But why?' he asked. 'I mean, if you did it knowing I might see it, then why?'

'I don't know. I guess because I wanted you to see that I was successful and happy and reconciled to how things were between us. I don't know.'

'So ... what? Were you wearing things as signs to other exes?'

She looked taken aback. 'No. Gosh, this got heavy real quick. I wore it because you were the one I knew before I became the person I am now. Pretty much. Mainly you. And you were the one I wanted to speak to, to say, "Look where I got. I got where I wanted to go." But not in any kind of *told you so* way. And the pendant represented that. I guess it said "thank you".'

He gave a little shrug. 'You did everything you did despite me, not because of me.'

She screwed up her face, pretending to give the matter serious thought. 'Well, yes, I guess you're right. Yes, I did really, didn't I? OK, in that case, what it said was, "I don't bear a grudge. There are no hard feelings." Oh, I don't know, do I? I just saw the pendant and thought I'd wear it. And I'm beginning to wish I hadn't.' She sounded peeved but was smiling, still being playful, enjoying herself.

'Yeah, sorry, I shouldn't have brought it up,' he said, leaning into the joke. 'Actually, it was you who brought it up.'

'OK. Yes. Look, let's start again shall we?'

And so they did. They caught up. He told her that things hadn't worked out between him and Fi, and they managed to negotiate that minefield with the minimum of discomfort, which was either good because it could have been awkward or bad because she didn't give a shit anymore, he couldn't decide, and she mentioned her husband, and he thought that he'd ask her a bit more about him – 'Phil' was the name—

'How is Nathan?' she'd asked.

These, of course, were the days when Nathan had merely been estranged, not missing. 'I haven't seen him for a while. We're not really talking at the moment. Yours are still kids, right? It's when they get to be adults, that's when the problems really start.'

'So I've heard.'

They talked, and they ate, and her insistence that she was only going to have one course before leaving to prepare for her following day's work seemed to go by the wayside.

Pizza was eaten, and then dessert – a 'cheeky dessert', according to Tessa, who made noises about watching her weight, though of course she looked fantastic – and more wine was brought.

She talked about her husband at last, and Abbott couldn't sense any particular swing either way. She didn't sound unhappy in the relationship, but then again, neither did she eulogise it. If she wanted to subtly put Abbott off, then, frankly, it was too subtle. He couldn't work it out. Was it simply that she had no agenda, and therefore no feelings left for him? He wasn't sure. She seemed intrigued about his work – he kept it light – interested in his divorce from Fi and concerned about his estrangement from Nathan, but not excessively so.

And as they talked, he wondered if he was simply being schmoozed, charmed and flattered, as she must have done with her clients. He felt quite a profound hurt at the thought. She'd got more drunk, though, and a little more expansive, and it dawned on him that there wasn't a guard to go down. There wasn't a guard at all. When she talked about the past, she seemed to do it as though the past for her was not full of skeletons and demons and dark memories the way it was for him. She talked about it in positive, glowing terms, a past remembered with affection, a past that edited out some of the worst bits, including, thankfully, the very worst of him. The hurt he had caused was never mentioned, not directly nor obliquely. As though it did not exist.

There were just good times and fun memories. Smiles and wine knocked back with relish until, suddenly, it was there, as though she had reached down, retrieved it from the depths of that leather briefcase and plonked it on the table: 'You really hurt me, you know.'

The words had changed her face, which had dropped a little. Her eyes shone and he knew that it was more than just the wine. And while part of him already mourned the great time they'd been having, another part of him felt relief that it was in there, at least – that things ran deep with her. In a way it was what he had wanted, what he had come here for, and now here it was.

'I know,' he said.

'It took me a while to get over it.'

She looked thoughtful. Was chewing her lip.

But you did get over it, he thought, which is more than I was ever able to do.

And then, somehow, they had ended up in a taxi, and they were going back to his hotel.

CHAPTER 34

It was the fountain.

Cuckoo had the fountain to thank for being alive. For just as Kind's bullets had rained down around him, one of them clipping the back of his leg, he had tripped over the fountain's low retaining wall and dropped back into the water.

For a moment or so – probably no more than a second – he blacked out. By the time he had recovered his senses, the shooting seemed to have stopped, although the screaming and pandemonium was still in full flow.

Cuckoo had left the scene before any emergency services arrived, wanting to avoid an investigation but mostly wanting to avoid a repeat encounter with Mr Kind. No doubt they would catch up with him at his hotel sooner or later. Questions would be asked, especially if they had CCTV that put him at the same table as Foxhole.

For now, however, his instinct was to take himself away from the epicentre of the activity.

On his way back, he checked in with Fiona, who asked him if he'd been anywhere near the terrible shooting incident she'd seen on the news. They were saying it was a likely terrorist attack. Or maybe some nut job.

No, he said, denying all knowledge of what, by a comfortable distance, had been the most terrifying experience of his life. 'Oh, thank God,' she said, and then moved swiftly on. 'And have you heard from Alex?'

'No,' he told her, he hadn't heard from Alex. All he knew was that Alex was still in Baghdad, still putting the feelers out in search of Nathan. He didn't tell her about the death of Abbott's team member, Stone, or 'Fingers', or whatever his name was. Didn't see the point in worrying her.

Arriving back at the hotel, he had cleaned himself up, washed and dressed his cut and put on the news. Foxhole had been killed, two others injured. Other casualties were mostly like him, cuts and bruises, and most of those incurred in the panic.

He had been very lucky, he knew. Luckier than Foxhole. He chucked his suitcase on the bed and began neatly folding things into it.

Next, he opened his laptop, checked his emails.

Oh fuck.

With a sharp intake of breath, he reached for his phone.

CHAPTER 35

'Hello?' Abbott had been making his way across Baghdad on foot. He was on his way to the Kadhimiya address that Nathan had been given, intending to arrive there at midday in order to meet the translator provided by Potter.

Why?

Why not? He was swiftly running out of leads. And, after all, this was something he could actually *do* while he waited for info, either from Potter or from Cuckoo.

And then the phone had rung.

'Abbott?'

'Cuckoo.'

'Alan.'

'Sorry. Alan. Tell me you have something for me,' said Abbott. 'Some information. Something. Any fucking thing.'

'Well, did you hear about the shooting in Singapore yesterday?'

'Um …' Abbott screwed his eyes shut momentarily. He had a vague splintered memory of seeing something on the television, and that in itself was a reminder that every minute, every second he spent in blackout was more time spent failing his loved ones. 'No … I heard something. Why? Was that …?'

'It was Foxhole,' continued Cuckoo, going on to tell Abbott the whole story, finishing by saying, 'you left quite a mess behind you, Abbott.'

'Mess is my middle name. This guy. The one who phoned you at the table. Kind, did you say?' He thought of the white-haired guy he'd seen on the street in Singapore. Him, maybe?

'Kind in name if not in action.'

'Very good, mate.'

'Thank you.'

'Well, look, obviously he was planning on tagging you at the same time. You'd better watch out. Leave that hotel, find another one. See if you can get accommodation with the consulate. Anywhere that he can't find you is the important thing.'

'I'm way ahead of you. I'm leaving now.'

'I'm sorry, mate,' said Abbott. 'I'm sorry all this shit is on you. Look, let me know if—'

'I've got something for you.'

'Something else, apart from you nearly dying and there being a killer after me?'

'You know you seem remarkably relaxed about that.'

'I'm in Baghdad, Cuckoo.'

'Alan.'

'I'm in Baghdad, Alan. My son is missing and one of my ex-teammates has just died in mysterious circs. So the guy trying to kill me will just have to take his place at the bottom of my in-tray.'

'He's a dangerous guy.'

'Dangerous? This geezer who opened fire in the middle of Singapore. You don't say. Look, let's get on with it. What have you got to tell me?'

'You asked me to look out for Burton and Mowles. I put the feelers out. Burton—'

'Most likely still in Baghdad, yes. I heard from Potter. Mowles?'

'Dead.'

Abbott stopped. He was close to the prison. 'Mowles is dead?' he said. 'Mowles and Stone *both* dead.'

'How did it happen?'

'Skydiving accident. Two weeks ago.'

'Before Stone.'

'Yup.'

'And another accident,' said Abbott, more to himself. He was reeling now. Feeling wrong that his thoughts were not for Mowles, whom he had never known well, and nor for his family – a wife and two boys – but for the current implications of his death.

'Yup. This one in Mexico, where they've ruled it as death by misadventure. Not enough attention paid to the equipment. You know what this means, Abbott, don't you?'

'I know what I think it might mean,' replied Abbott, making his way along the street. 'How about you tell me what you think it means.'

'OK, how about this? How about somebody is killing members of your team one by one. Maybe.'

'It's a theory. Why do you think they might be doing that?'

'Reprisals, perhaps.'

'Reprisals? As in revenge? As in for something we did back in the day? Some terrible deed that we're now paying for?'

'Well, maybe.'

'It's a good thought. It'd make a nice story to tell my biographer. The trouble is, there is no terrible deed. We were just a bunch of squaddies serving our country and trying to make a bit of dough.'

Which wasn't *quite* the truth, he thought, but still. It would have to do for the time being.

'Fact remains, Abbott,' pressed Cuckoo, 'two of your team are dead in weird accidents. I mean, I'm guessing that Mowles wasn't in the habit of jumping out of planes without triple-checking his equipment?'

'It's hardwired, mate,' agreed Abbott.

'There you go. Anyway, a motive is in the eye of the beholder. All we know right now is that two guys are dead, and Nathan is missing. And that means that you could be walking into a trap.'

'Fine trap. If you know it's laid.'

'But what if the trap is one you can't avoid?'

'Like what if your son is the bait?'

'Exactly. What do you do then?'

'Ain't nothing you can do, mate, apart from keep your wits about you.'

'What do we do in the meantime?' asked Cuckoo.

'You're OK, are you?' checked Abbott. 'You're not so wounded that you can't do a little bit more digging for me?'

Cuckoo sighed. 'No, I'm not that wounded, no. Let me know where X marks the spot and I'll keep on doing your digging for you.'

'OK, where Burton is. We need to find out. Could it be that he's still working for Mahlouthi in some capacity?'

Something came to Abbott, a memory that flitted in and out of his head as silvery as an eel, so that, for a second, he thought it might slip away as quickly as it had arrived. It was a little kid with a cheeky grin and ...

Oh, Christ. The envoy from Mahlouthi. The one he'd told to piss off. With a cringe of guilt and shame, Abbott knew that he'd missed a golden opportunity. At the same time, the mere thought of Mahlouthi hardened his heart a little.

'OK, I'll do my best,' Cuckoo was saying.

'And another thing, while you're on the case. Find out who Mowles was jumping with that day.'

'Sure.'

'And one more thing. I need a recent picture of Nathan. Are you able to send me one right away? Something I can just show on my phone.'

There was a moment of awkward silence that Abbott didn't have a recent photograph of his own son.

'Sure. Would you like that in civvies or uniform?'

'How about both, just to be on the safe side? And Alan—'

'Yeah?'

'Thank you, mate.'

Shortly afterwards, the pictures arrived with a ping.

Abbott let them marinade on his phone a while, and when at last he came to open them he did so with a mounting sense of trepidation. Why? Because from baby to toddler to kid to teenager, Nathan had been a handsome, happy lad with an open face and a mop of unruly fair hair. As Abbott knew, though, the army had a habit of smoothing off those rough edges. In his own case, that was for the better. He was far better off without those rough edges. Would have been in prison otherwise. But if you were a kid like Nathan? 'The army will change him,' he'd said to Fi during the time of the great Army Arguments.

'Yeah, well, let's hope it changes his mind,' she'd shot back.

But it hadn't. Or not yet, at least, for it was still early days. And Abbott felt his heart sink to his boots as he looked at the pictures. Gone were the nearly blond curls. Gone was the ready smile. In its place, the same shaven-headed, number-two-all-over, tough-guy look sported by every other squaddie, every other grunt. Give him the shades, plop a helmet on his head, and you couldn't pick him out of a line-up; he'd look like every other coalition soldier on the streets of Baghdad.

Funny, thought Abbott, looking at the pictures. He wanted to find Nathan, but he also wanted to reclaim him from a life that would likely corrupt him unless he bailed out now. Corrupt him in the way it had corrupted Abbott.

Because that's what good fathers did. They saved their sons.

CHAPTER 36

Once again, Abbott found himself back on the street with the walls of the prison scowling down upon him. However, there was a marked difference between now and last night. Then, he'd been practically the only person on the street. Now, he was one of many – the area was teeming with activity – and yet he was the only Westerner around.

Even so, the Iraqis who passed or manned the stalls in the shadows of the prison walls paid him little mind, no doubt bracketing him with every other member of the occupying forces: American grunts keeping the peace, British squaddies passing through Baghdad on their way to help provide stability in other, further-flung regions of the country, members of the security forces – it didn't matter to them. They were all the same.

Abbott found himself scanning faces around him, looking for something. What? Anything. Anything that might give him a clue as to why Nathan had been summoned here.

And then he saw something – a shock of white hair, a glimpse of a Western face in the crowd. A guy wearing smart jeans – jeans like they'd been ironed – and a suede jacket.

And then it was gone, leaving him wondering if he'd imagined it. It had been a day since Cuckoo's contact in Singapore, more than enough time for the white-haired guy – this 'Mr Kind', presumably? – to have made his way to Baghdad. Well, Cuckoo was right about one thing. Whoever he was, he didn't worry Abbott. Just one more thing to add to the list. *Take a place at the back of the queue, mate.* And either way, when Abbott looked again, he had gone. Perhaps a figment of his imagination. Then again, he wasn't sure his imagination could conjure such a figure.

Who on earth irons their fucking jeans?

'Mr Abbott?'

He turned. Standing before him was a guy of around his own age with a close-cropped beard. He wore a light-coloured linen suit and looked as cool as the other side of the pillow, practically the Arab version of Potter.

'My name is Ibrahim. I understand you need some help with translation?' he said.

'I do,' said Abbott. He explained his mission and the two of them wandered over to the stalls that lined the street, going to the first one, where a woman was trying to keep the dust from her crisp linen.

Ibrahim gave a short bow. Next, he held up Abbott's phone in order to display first one picture of Nathan and then another, asking the woman whether she had been here the day that Nathan was due to be here. Whether she had seen Nathan.

She looked from Ibrahim, her gaze warm and friendly and not at all suspicious, to Abbott, whereupon a cloud passed over her features. Not so much 'passed' as stayed there, threatening rain.

She shook her head. No. She knew nothing. Ibrahim thanked her. They moved on. At the next stall, Ibrahim had a longer conversation and when they moved off after another strike-out, he said to Abbott, 'You may find this is a bit of wasted exercise, Mr Abbott. The people of Baghdad are used to watching without seeing. And they're used to seeing without talking.'

Abbott came to a halt and held out a hand for Ibrahim to do the same. 'Stop. Wait. If that's the case, then you need to reassure them that this is not a military matter.'

'Me?'

'Yes. You.'

'I am here as a favour to Mr Potter.'

'Right, so do him the fucking favour and do right by me. Be clear to these people that it's a personal matter. Nothing to do with the coalition. They're not going to get picked up. Hoods dragged over their faces. None of that. All right, Ibrahim? Can you do that?'

Ibrahim looked at him coolly. 'I see,' he said. They moved onto the next stall but were waved away before Ibrahim had even had a chance to make his introductions. Abbott felt something rise within him: a mixture of panic and irritation, his hangover sawing away in his head. Aside from various assurances from Potter and Cuckoo that they would investigate on his behalf, he had nothing, literally nothing, to go on, and what was the fucking point of even being in Baghdad if he was helpless, unable to control the situation, at the mercy of a bunch of people whose language he didn't even understand?

The news of Mowles had added yet another dimension. He was no nearer the truth – and yet somehow it was as though the truth was approaching him, ready to overwhelm him.

At the next stall, a rickety structure selling various oils in earthenware jars, it seemed like they were going to flame out once again.

This time, however, there was something more guarded about the woman's response, something that made Abbott think that she knew more than she was letting on. Ibrahim had been holding the phone, but he snatched it away, holding it up close to the woman's face. 'This man. Have you seen this man?' he barked. 'It's my son. It's my boy.' As Ibrahim tried to simultaneously translate, calm Abbott and reassure the woman, Abbott pointed a finger, moving it between the photo and his own face as though to highlight the family resemblance. 'It's my son. He's missing.'

Right up in the woman's grill, dimly registering how she recoiled from the booze fumes, he huffed in her face.

She took a step back, shaking her head furiously, her eyes darting from Abbott to Ibrahim and seeking help there, waving a hand at the same time. Abbott drew himself up, ready to insist that she told him what she knew, when he felt Ibrahim pull him away.

'Does this sort of approach get results in your normal line of work?' asked Ibrahim. He thrust his hands into the pockets of his suit. 'If you want it to appear less of a military matter, then perhaps you should have made an effort to look less like a military man. You wear a sidearm and there's no disguising that bulge at your side.' He pointed. 'These are people who are used to the itchy trigger fingers and the wild eyes of the Americans. The less they have to do with you, the less chance they have of getting shot. Look at the way you're talking to me now. Look at their eyes on us. *Look at how you just spoke to that woman.* Perhaps, if you want their help, you should make more of an effort to appear less of an oppressor.'

Abbott took deep breaths, knowing that Ibrahim spoke the truth, cursing himself for having lost his cool. He held up a hand. 'Translate for me,' he said, and tried again with the stallholder.

'I'm so sorry, ma'am,' he said. Ibrahim translated. 'Please accept my apologies. Do you have children yourself?'

He waited for Ibrahim to translate. The woman nodded yes. Abbott continued, 'Then you know how important they are. My boy is missing, and I know he was here. He may even have been taken from this very street. Please, I'm begging you, please help me to find him.'

After a moment, she seemed to decide but directed her reply at Ibrahim, who nodded, thanked her and then turned to Abbott. 'She saw Nathan,' he said. 'She saw him get into a car, a Mercedes, driven by a man.'

Abbott fiddled with his phone, finding a picture of Stone. 'Was this him?'

She looked at the picture, shaking her head uncertainly, speaking to Ibrahim.

'She's not sure,' relayed Ibrahim. 'This man had a thinner face. And a beard.'

Abbott brandished the photo of Stone, complete with stubble. 'The guy in the picture's got a beard.'

'Yes, but this man's beard was—' Ibrahim mimed on his own face.

'A goatee beard?'

'Yes, a goatee beard. And very neat. Very carefully trimmed.'

It didn't sound much like Stone, thought Abbott. But then a thought occurred to him: it couldn't be Stone. Because if Stone was taking some R & R in the Kurdish mountains, a trip apparently cut short by dying, he couldn't also have been in Baghdad meeting Nathan.

'A military man?' he asked. 'This man with the goatee beard. Was he a military man?'

Ibrahim asked the question, listened to the answer. 'She thinks so, yes. Dressed like you, she says.'

'Thank you,' said Abbott to the woman. 'Thank you so much,' but she was already waving him away, having reached the limit of her patience with his plight, and Abbott was left wondering about the importance of what he'd just learned. As in, did it mean anything? Or was it nothing? Gradually, as he stood there, a feeling crept over him. A feeling of being watched, and he felt a pair of eyes upon him. He looked around. The stall-holders had gone back to their business. To them he was invisible once more. And then he saw them. A pair of eyes, watching him.

CHAPTER 37

'Is everything all right, Abbott?' Ibrahim said. The pair of them had moved away from the stalls and to a line of parked cars, dusty and shabby.

'We're being watched,' said Abbott simply. He stopped, rested his hand on the butt of his Sig, gaze travelling across the front of the prison, and then turning to look around him. At the same time, he found himself acutely aware that he didn't want Ibrahim involved in any trouble. The translator was, after all, acting on a favour for Potter. 'You go, Ibrahim,' he said, clapping the other man on the shoulder. 'Go with my thanks for your help.' He pulled an apologetic face. 'And for your patience.'

Ibrahim nodded, sensing that trouble might be about to rear its ugly head. Sensing, also, that any trouble involving Abbott might well involve the gun at his hip or the one that hung at his side and was best avoided. He shook Abbott's hand, wished him well in his search for Nathan, and left.

And then Abbott saw it. Crouched by the wooden struts of a stall selling blankets, rugs and throws, was a kid. Was it the same kid who had visited him last night? Difficult to see. No doubt about it, though. This kid was watching Abbott like a hawk.

Moving casually, trying to give nothing away, Abbott came closer. He waited for a beaten-up old Peugeot to pass and then crossed, turning to his left and walking parallel to the wall, which brought him closer to the kid's hiding place.

He glanced to ensure the kid was still there. Their eyes met, and the kid got the message. He emerged from beneath the stall, threading his way between the legs of customers, and began moving quickly away, not quite running but faster than a walk.

'Hey, kid,' called Abbott. He felt last night's encounter wash over him like a physical event that was half bad memory and half his hangover reasserting its presence as he began walking in pursuit. 'Hey, kid.' Heads turned his way and he remembered what Ibrahim had told him. 'Hey, kid,' he repeated, putting so much lightness in his voice he sounded like a nursery-school teacher.

The kid glanced behind him, their eyes locked again.

Yes, definitely the same kid.

'You wanted to speak to me last night,' called Abbott, still in *hey, guys, it's play time* mode. 'Well, here I am now. Let's speak. Come on, kid. Look, I'm sorry, I know I was rude last night.'

Kid could speak English, right? He was speaking English before. But whether the kid understood him now or not, it was difficult to say. Either way, he knew he was being summoned and took off now at full pelt.

Behind, Abbott grimaced, steadied the rifle at his side and started off after him, not caring about the inevitable stares he attracted, or the excited chatter he left behind. A car honked its horn, but if it was for him or not he didn't know. Instead, he kept running.

Stupid to run in the centre of fucking Baghdad. Way to get shot. Still.

The kid took a sharp right, dashing down an alleyway strung with low-hanging washing lines.

Abbott followed, ducking the sheets, trying not to touch anything out of respect but needing to keep pace with the kid.

Ahead, the kid hung a left, dashing along an even narrower corridor that ran along the back of a row of houses. This one was strewn with bags of litter, even a discarded bed, and signs of bomb damage were everywhere, walls blackened and scorched.

At the end, the kid turned right, and Abbott felt last night's booze rise up his throat in bile form as he reached the exit, almost losing his footing as he, too, went right, scanning the street ahead. This one was wider, a busy thoroughfare, but he spotted the kid up ahead as he reached another junction and darted left.

By the time Abbott reached the junction he knew where they were. They had left the Kadhimiya district and were entering – or, in his case, re-entering – the Al Mansour district, once known as Baghdad's upmarket quarter.

There were more people here, including a pair of patrolling GIs who held their guns low, trying to provide a comforting, reassuring but absolutely non-aggressive presence. And if it was a trick that they failed to pull off, well, that was hardly surprising when the diplomats who gave them their orders were also failing at it.

They looked sharply at Abbott and he slowed to a fast walk, giving them a wave as though to say, 'Nothing to see here, folks,' and they nodded and moved on. He continued, mindful of the lined faces and watchful eyes of the locals upon him.

In front of him he saw a familiar sight and knew where he was at once. He caught sight of the kid turning a corner up ahead.

Sure enough, when he did the same, the walls of Mahlouthi's villa stood before him, instantly recognisable, thanks to the greenery that covered almost every inch, a sudden, verdant explosion of plant life in what was otherwise a world made entirely of stone and sand and dirt.

Hanging back now, Abbott watched as the kid entered the villa through a wicket door at the front. He considered simply marching up and banging on it himself – after all, the invite had already been extended – but decided against it. If this was the trap, he was in no mood to be the mouse.

So …

At the side of the villa, he knew, was a service hatch for access to the irrigation and heating systems below the complex. He went there now, dragging out his keys at the same time. There on the keyring was a special attachment, the kind of thing that back home he'd used to bleed the radiators, in a time when he carried out domestic, homely tasks such as bleeding radiators, except this one was slightly bigger.

It still fit the service hatch. He unlocked it, raised the metal cover and let himself down the ladder beneath, reaching up to close the hatch behind him.

Some steps later he was bent double as he made his way along a walkway to a door at the far end, his head brushing the piping above.

The same key worked again. He stepped through.

Now he was in the belly of the villa, in a small corridor behind the kitchen. As he knew, Mahlouthi had let most of his staff go during the war. For a while, the villa's only residents had been Mahlouthi and the four SF guys, and it was only a sense of order instilled in them by the army that had kept the place from falling to rack and ruin. Even then they'd grown sick of all the domestic chores, and after plenty of rumblings about being soldiers not cooks and cleaners, they'd insisted that Mahlouthi employ a guy to help run the household, which he did. A bloke called Tommy.

Standing at the kitchen door, Abbott tried to remember the location of the door compared to the layout of the room, weighing up his options: try sneaking in, or go in quick and take whoever was in there by surprise?

He went for option B, holding the Sig two-handed, sweeping the sight around the large room as he stepped smartly through.

Nothing.

The kitchen, as large as he remembered it, ordered and tidy, yawned emptily at him. At its centre was the table around which they'd sat during the evenings, sinking beers and taking the piss out of each other, sharing war stories and – in Stone's case, at least – making big plans for the future.

Was that where it had all gone wrong between them? he wondered. In the army, your main consideration was sticking together and following orders. The soil simply wasn't rich enough for individual personalities to flower. Afterwards, however, was when your horizons didn't so much broaden as alter, and all those different aspirations became apparent.

What had Abbott wanted? Enough money to finance his booze habit and pay maintenance. But beyond that? He wasn't sure then and even less sure now. Something different to Stone, that much was for certain.

Now, he thought. To business. If Nathan were in the villa – and Christ, yes, please let Nathan be in here somewhere – then where would he be? He knew the entrance to a wine cellar. He knew that very well, of course. Gently, he opened the kitchen door, seeing another but much more opulent corridor in front of him.

Quietly he moved forward – and then stopped. At his neck was the barrel of a gun.

CHAPTER 38

The voice was Cockney by way of Oz. 'Mockstralian', you might call it. And Abbott recognised it immediately. 'Well, how about that?' it said, 'It's the Monk.'

As a nickname, Monk had never really stuck with Abbott. Not like Badger for Mowles, Fingers for Stone, or the nickname they had given to Burton, the guy holding the gun on him now …

'Biscuits,' said Abbott, angling his neck away from the barrel of what he knew would be an AK-47. Burton had never met an AK he didn't love. 'Still working for Mahlouthi, eh?'

There was a chuckle. The gun came away. Relaxing now, Abbott holstered his sidearm, and turned to face Burton, who pulled the AK into the crook of his arm and saw Abbott's eyes on it. 'AK-forty-seven is the tool.' He grinned.

'Don't make me act the motherfucking fool,' finished Abbott.

Grinning, the two men embraced, Abbott pulling apart to appraise Burton more carefully. His old mate had 'gone native' with his long beard and flowing clothes. His hair had grown too, of course, and his sun-weathered skin crinkled as he smiled, only adding to the effect. 'Yeah, still working for Mahlouthi. Still providing personal security. It's a living, yeah?' He gestured.

'Keeps me off the streets. Personal security. Which includes dealing with intruders – like your good self, mate.'

Nevertheless, noted Abbott, Burton was not at all surprised to see him. Which figured. If Mahlouthi knew he was back in the city – and had even dispatched an envoy to speak to him – then Burton would, too.

'You were expecting me?'

Burton shrugged. 'Sooner or later.'

'Mahlouthi told you.'

'He tends to share little details like that with his chief security officer.' Burton smiled sardonically. 'What I don't know is what you're doing in Baghdad.'

'I'm looking for Nathan,' said Abbott.

'Nathan ...' Burton looked confused, trying to place the name.

'Nathan, my son. Nathan. Is he ...?' *No, of course he's not here.* 'Have you heard anything about him?'

One side of Burton's mouth pulled upward. 'Ah, no. Why would I have heard anything about Nathan, mate?'

Abbott told him, finishing by asking if the description of a security guy with a neat goatee meant anything to him. 'No, mate, can't say it does,' said Burton. He shrugged. 'I mean, a lot of guys have those kinds of beards, you know?'

'Do they? Most people can't be arsed with fussing around, can they?' Abbott ran a hand over his own beard. 'OK, what do you know of Stone or Mowles?'

'Well, Stone's—'

'Dead.'

'You heard.'

'I also heard that Mowles is the same way.'

'Really?' Burton was floored. 'Christ. How?'

Abbott explained, watching Burton carefully as he did so. Burton's mouth worked as he absorbed the news. 'That's not right, mate,' he said at last. 'Badger wasn't the type to jump out of a plane with dodgy equipment. No fucker would.'

Abbott was nodding. 'And Stone?'

'What about him?'

'Does that sound like an accident to you?'

Biscuits' face said that he didn't much care what had happened to Stone. 'Look, mate. Me and Fingers had what you might call a parting of the ways. A month or so after you—' He stopped, encountering a memory that curdled in his mind.

'I'm sorry about that,' interjected Abbott.

'All right, mate, sure you had your reasons.'

'Baghdad was the reason,' said Abbott, hoping the explanation, airy as it was, would suffice.

'Well, yeah, mate, I'm not saying you were the glue that held us together, but things got a bit fractious after you went, yeah? Me and Fingers, we kinda fell out and I haven't heard from him since.' Abbott's mouth opened to ask the obvious question, but Burton was ahead of him. 'Why did we fall out? Were you still around when he was going on about Executive fuckin' Alliance?'

'Yeah. I was and I've heard that he's since done very well with it.'

'You hear about Farlowe and Hercules?'

'Yeah, I heard.'

Biscuits made a money sign with his fingers. 'I fucking well wanted on board, didn't I?'

'Who wouldn't?'

Biscuits looked taken aback. 'Well, you, for one. You didn't.'

Abbott shrugged. 'Oh, come on, it was just a glint in his eye back then. How was I supposed to know the road was paved with gold? Plus, I had other shit going on.'

Like seeing a boy dying in a street. And then being chased away by the guilt.

'Yeah, well, it got real fucking serious. Stone used my name. He used Badger's name, and he used yours, for that matter. As far as Farlowe were concerned, they were getting four heads, not just one. Bit of smoke and mirrors there, mate. Fact is, I was as much the reason they wanted us lot as Stone was. Just that he was the figurehead, so of course he felt differently. He wanted it all for himself, which is why he fucked off to live it up in the Green Zone, and I was stuck babysitting Mahlouthi.'

'Sounds like you might have wanted him dead,' said Abbott and immediately regretted it, wishing he could put the words back into his mouth, and instantly he stitched on a smile to try and pass it off as a joke.

'Get you, Miss fucking Marple,' said Biscuits, but he grinned and, thankfully, the moment passed.

'What about Mowles?' said Abbott quickly.

'What about him?'

'Did he go onboard with Stone?'

Burton pulled a sour face. 'Far as I know, Badger stayed tight with Stone. He left about the same time, is all I can say.'

'The same, more or less.'

And now he's dead, thought Abbott. And so is Stone.

He found himself regretting having holstered his Sig and he brought his hands to his hips, feeling the little finger of his right hand brushing the butt of the gun. Burton noticed the movement, too, and perhaps it was Abbott's imagination, but he seemed to tense with the AK.

'Did you go to the funeral?' asked Abbott.

'Fingers? I wouldn't even know if there was one. Look, mate, there was no love lost. Fingers was never exactly the life and soul, was he? You know how just having him around put you on edge? Like he'd always see the bad side of everything? You'd be having a laugh and he'd bring you down by moaning about some shit. Anyway …' he gave a short shake of his head as if wanting to dismiss the thought of Stone. 'Does all this have anything to do with the reason for you sneaking around Mahlouthi's villa?'

'It's Nathan,' explained Abbott. 'That's all. I'm here looking for Nathan.'

'Didn't occur to you to knock on the door? Omar told me you followed him from the prison.'

'Omar. That's the little kid, is it?'

'Currently making his way home with a pocketful of money courtesy of Mahlouthi. And Omar tells me that you were a bit pissed last night. Didn't want to speak to him then. Next, you're chasing him through the city streets.'

'Sorry. What can I say? Indecisive.'

'And then I catch you creeping around when you've been practically invited to pay us a visit and you're behaving as though *we're* the ones acting suspiciously. If I wasn't so pleased to see you, I might get offended.'

'Well don't be. I was being careful, that's all. It's all about finding Nath, mate that's all I'm here for.'

'Well, I wish I could help you. But, like I say, I haven't heard anything.' He paused. 'I think we both know a man who would have done, though, eh?' he said, and used the barrel of the AK to point along the corridor and in the direction of Mahlouthi's quarters.

They had moved off and were nearly at the door when Abbott's phone rang and he took the call, holding up an apologetic finger to Burton and turning his back to raise the phone to his ear.

'Cuckoo?' he said.

'How are things?'

'Bit busy.' Abbott threw a look over at Burton who stood with his legs planted slightly apart, the AK in the crook of his elbow pointing skyward. 'Can you make this quick?'

'Sure. The quick version is that I found who partnered Mowles on the day of the jump.'

'Right,' Abbott eyes flicked once again to Burton, 'Go on.'

'He was questioned after the accident and allowed to go. Mexican authorities were probably glad he wasn't kicking up a fuss about it all, trying to sue their arse.'

'Name,' said Abbott simply.

'It was your mate Biscuits.'

CHAPTER 39

Abbott finished the call. His senses ratcheted up, approaching high alert as he joined Burton once more.

'Who was that, then?' asked Burton, with what Abbott thought was a note of forced lightness.

'Just a guy doing some digging for me.'

'Land ops, eh? Anything to report?'

'Not really.'

Burton flashed him a look that was just sour enough for Abbott to wonder if he'd seen a glimpse of Burton's real feelings, lurking beneath all that jollity. 'Still a closed book, aren't you, Abbott? Christ knows how I got landed with you and Stone. A right couple of shut-ins. If it hadn't been for Badger ...'

The two eyed each other. A new wariness had crept in between them. Abbott's mind was racing. Why would Burton affect not to know about Mowles when the lie was so easily exposed? One thing was for sure, nothing was certain right now. Something occurred to him. 'I haven't seen any staff yet,' he said. They had reached the pool area and he had a memory of seeing Mahlouthi's wives sunning themselves. 'None of the wives either.'

'The last of them left the other day,' said Burton.

'So that's it?' said Abbott.

'You remember Tommy?' said Burton. 'Did you and him overlap? I forget.'

'Yeah, I remember Tommy,' said Abbott. By now his suspicions were working overtime. Like how come Burton seemed to have so little memory of Abbott at the villa?

'So, yeah, Tommy's still here. But apart from me, Tommy and now you – oh, and occasionally Omar – that's it.'

'Why?' said Abbott. 'What happened?'

By now they'd climbed the steps into Mahlouthi's quarters, threaded their way through what looked like an ocean of ornate scatter cushions and crossed to the rear. Here was Mahlouthi's office. Burton knocked, calling, 'Moof, our guest is here. I'm sure you'd like a word.'

'Come,' replied Mahlouthi from inside.

'Let him tell you,' said Burton to Abbott, and in they went.

CHAPTER 40

Poor old Tommy must have been working like a dog, because Mahlouthi's suit remained pressed, his shirt was a crisp white, his spectacles still the height of fashion. In short, he was the same as Abbott remembered, as if untouched by the chaos of war and the equal chaos of peacetime. Perhaps his only concession to changing times was the fact that he did not wear his customary tie.

Between Abbott and Burton there had been wariness, caution, a sense of unfinished business and things beneath the surface. But that was nothing compared to the atmosphere between Mahlouthi and Abbott.

The big man tried to hide it, of course. He stood, came out from behind his desk in order to envelop Abbott in an all-too-familiar bear hug, but when he broke away, he immediately scuttled back. Mahlouthi's desk was big enough to make a pool table feel inadequate, but right now it acted as a handy barrier between him and Abbott, who had entered his office like a bad dream.

And as he stood there, Abbott realised that his first impression of Mahlouthi – that he hadn't changed – wasn't in fact accurate. He was nervy, ill at ease. In this light the absence of his usual tie assumed new meaning. Something was up. And it wasn't just Abbott being here. Something else.

'Have you told him?' Mahlouthi spoke to Burton but kept his eyes on Abbott.

Burton shook his head no.

'Did my boy tell you last night?' This question was directed at Abbott.

'Omar?'

Mahlouthi nodded.

'Whatever it was, no, he didn't tell me.'

'I wished you would have joined me last night.'

'I was indisposed. If it was important, then maybe a bit more meat on the bones would have helped.'

Mahlouthi rolled his eyes. Then, reaching for his phone, he jabbed at some buttons and slid it across the tabletop to Abbott.

Displayed was a text message. Just two words. *You're next.*

'You didn't tell me this,' Abbott said to Burton.

Burton shrugged, *no biggie*, and Abbott felt his suspicions flare a little more.

'I get this message and the same day discover that you are back in Baghdad,' said Mahlouthi.

'Abbott's boy is missing,' said Burton to Mahlouthi, who blanched at the news. At the same time, something passed between him and Abbott. Both were thinking the same thing. Both were seeing a motive.

'Your boy, he was called –' but Mahlouthi could not summon the name.

'He *is* Nathan,' replied Abbott and gave Mahlouthi a potted version of the story.

'I can help you find him,' said Mahlouthi, when he had finished.

'Can you?' said Abbott doubtfully. Only the greenery outside retained its former glory, and that was irrigated. Everything else about Mahlouthi spoke of a man who was – let's say *diminished*. Surely that had to extend to his famed network of 'contacts' as well?

'I still have influence,' said Mahlouthi, as though reading his mind. 'To the outside world,' he twirled his finger above his head to illustrate, 'everything about Mahlouthi is business as usual. And if Mahlouthi wants information he gets it.'

There. There it was. A little of the old fire.

'I have a request in return, though,' he added.

Of course he did.

'What is it?'

'You transfer your lodgings from the Al Mansour hotel to the Mahlouthi Villa.'

'No.' The word was out of his mouth before Abbott knew it. More of an instinct, a knee-jerk reflex, a gasp of pain at a prodded wound than a considered response. 'No, I'm not ...' *Coming back here.*

At the same time, Burton was letting out a sigh. 'Things are fine, Moof. I don't need an extra guy.'

Mahlouthi brandished the phone. 'You didn't, past tense. Things have changed.'

'Well, it's funny you should say that, actually,' said Burton. 'But there's something else you should know. Badger's dead.'

Again, Mahlouthi paled. 'Dead?'

'Yeah.'

'Dead?'

'Yeah, dead, Moof. It's the opposite of alive.'

Mahlouthi shot Burton a distracted look then returned his attention to Abbott. 'How?'

'Skydiving accident,' offered Abbott, giving Mahlouthi what details he knew.

All the details, that was, apart from one. And as he spoke, his eye went from Mahlouthi, whose mouth worked up and down, his bright white teeth looking faintly ridiculous when paired with his obvious shock, to Burton, and he saw nothing there to suggest his old comrade was hiding something. Was it possible that Cuckoo's information was false? Or perhaps – and this seemed more likely – that somebody had been impersonating Burton, using his name on the jump log? Still, he held back from confronting Burton with what he knew. It was like a piece of the puzzle lost in the living room. He just needed to find that one bit of the jigsaw …

And, yes, here was the best place to start looking for it.

'I'll do it,' he told Mahlouthi, who grinned in return.

'I'm not sharing the pay. Is that clear?' snapped Burton. 'I remain chief of security.'

'Your pay is safe,' said Mahlouthi. Abbott shrugged, not wanting to get roped into an argument. Not really having a dog in this fight, deciding to wait it out until the pair of them were finished. At last they had, and Mahlouthi, more relaxed now, said to Abbott, 'I gather you're still a fan of the hard stuff, Abbott.' He'd obviously heard about last night. Or perhaps it simply showed. Abbott wasn't complaining. The main thing was that Mahlouthi stood and walked to a sideboard, an escapee from the 1970s complete with coasters, soda siphon and a selection of cut-glass carafes, all of which, though eye-wateringly expensive, managed to look flea-market cheap, and began to dole out drinks.

It took him some time. Mahlouthi may have been many things but a drinks waiter was not one of them and if you didn't already know that he'd recently laid off most of his staff, then you did now. Abbott took his glass, having prompted Mahlouthi for ice, and the three of them sat drinking, not exactly friends, not even especially relaxed in each other's company. But together, reunited after almost a year apart.

Abbott had to reflect – and maybe this was just the booze talking, the whiskey reaching inside him with massaging fingers – that it wasn't too bad at all, really. He wondered if the other two thought the same as him: that once there had been five, now there were just three.

'Tommy will see to it that your belongings are transferred from the Al Mansour hotel to here,' explained Mahlouthi, and Abbott cringed inside. Only he knew the devastation he had left in his hotel room, the tell-tale empties, not to mention the mini-armoury hidden in the well of the room's wardrobe.

'Just my overnight bag and laptop,' he said. 'I'll be going back to my room in due course.'

* * *

Later, Tommy arrived, and he led Abbott out of the office and to his room. Abbott wondered about the topic of conversation between Mahlouthi and Burton when he left, reminding himself that although he was now a house guest, he was still very much the outsider in this dynamic. After all, he'd let them down by disappearing off to Singapore. They were bound to treat him with a level of distrust.

Following in Tommy's wake, he found they were taking a few twists and turns, but he knew where they were going. Sure enough, it was his old room, complete with his belongings which had been transferred from the hotel. As Tommy withdrew, he sat, wishing that he had been offered some of Mahlouthi's stash to take for his room.

Something occurred to him. The room had a fitted wardrobe, and in a cubbyhole inside was a half-bottle of vodka. He'd left it there when he was last a resident.

He recovered it, feeling ridiculously pleased with himself, almost like a prisoner having outwitted his captors, and he sat on the bed, sipping, letting the vodka keep the whiskey company.

Next, he reached for his laptop, placing it on the desk, opening it, checking his emails to find that Cuckoo had been in touch, a message titled 'Skydiving accident'.

There was no text in the body of the email, just a movie file that Abbott double-clicked on, expecting, no, hoping, that it was footage of the accident.

It was. This was footage from the body cam of Mowles's diving partner that day, and, right away, Abbott began to suspect that it had been doctored. For a start, in his experience, they tended to start the cam as they approached the drop zone. They'd include conversation, the skydivers hyping each other up.

On this one, however, that section of the trip had been chopped off, and the footage began mid-air. Was that because somebody didn't want those involved being identified?

He watched. The footage was from whoever was Mowles's partner. All that was visible of the cameraman was his arms, the fabric of his dive suit rippling. He saw Mowles a short distance away, lay flat in the air arms spread, falling but floating, and grinning – a grin that Abbott remembered well, that held no foresight of the horror that was just seconds away that suddenly faded as Mowles attempted to deploy his chute.

At the same time, the cameraman must have deployed his, and suddenly there was no sign of Mowles as his rate of dropping accelerated and the cameraman decelerated.

That was the last of Mowles: a grin that became a grimace, a last flash of terror-stricken eyes. Abbott watched it again and there was something about it, something that struck him, that he couldn't quite place until he watched it again and this time instead of keeping his attention focused on Mowles, he looked more carefully at what was visible of the cameraman.

Specifically, a finger. To be more precise, a missing finger.

So it wasn't Burton who was the second parachutist that day – it was Stone.

Stone had killed Mowles. And then ...

Then what?

CHAPTER 41

Abbott fired off an email to Cuckoo, then took his discovery to Burton, who was in his room. He knocked, then burst in with the question: 'Was there a body found?'

'You what?' Burton stood in the middle of the room in his pants, swaying slightly, looking like he wanted to be outraged that Abbott had burst in, but also intrigued.

'Stone and his "drowning accident",' explained Abbott. 'They ruled out murder, didn't they?'

Burton nodded.

'So they must have found a body?' pressed Abbott.

'Not as far as I know, mate, no.' Burton was still disorientated so Abbott filled him in, complete with the tale of how it had been Burton's name on the jump log, not Stone's.

'So all afternoon you thought that it was me who killed Badger?' said Burton. Still in his pants, he'd taken a seat on the edge of the bed, scratching his balls thoughtfully. 'And you didn't fucking say anything?' There was a look on his face that was somewhere between amused and genuinely upset and affronted.

'I didn't say anything because I couldn't believe it,' said Abbott.

Burton looked taken aback. Abbott could have sworn he saw his eyes swim. 'You mean that?' said Burton. 'You really couldn't believe it of me?'

'No,' said Abbott. In reality, he'd been keeping an open mind, but what the hell.

Burton looked sheepishly pleased. 'So what's your thinking, then?' He was drunk and slightly slurring his words. Abbott always found it vaguely surprising when other people were more drunk than he was. The evil drinking guy who lived inside took it as a challenge.

'I'm beginning to think that our mate Fingers faked his own death,' replied Abbott thoughtfully. His mind was going to Nathan, putting Nathan's disappearance together with the killing of Mowles, the maybe-staged-death of Stone, putting it with the address in the Kadhimiya district and a boy who lay dying in the dirt. Who said the final word, 'Dad.'

In the next instant he was tearing out of the room, his running footsteps echoing from the tiled walls and stone floors of the villa. He was drawing his gun.

* * *

Mahlouthi had retired to his bedroom and that's where Abbott found him. He knocked and announced himself calmly, but when Mahlouthi came to the door and answered, looking just as half-cut as Burton, Abbott barrelled in, pushing the bigger man back until he lost his footing and collapsed on the bed.

And then, with the soft, linen splendour of the businessman's bedroom billowing in the air-conditioning around him, Abbott put one hand to Mahlouthi's throat, and with his other brought the Sig to bear and pressed the barrel against his forehead.

Pressing down. Pressing hard. 'I need you to tell me something,' he growled.

Mahlouthi, normally so punctilious, so calm and self-assured, took several moments to find the words in reply, trying to focus without his glasses and stuttering, 'Tell you what?'

'Jeremy Robinson. Who was he?'

Abbott's finger tensed on the trigger. He knew that if he was right, then all of this was on Mahlouthi. It was Mahlouthi who had brought all this shit down on him. And for that he could put a bullet in the bastard here and now. He heard the grating sound of his own teeth. Felt his jaw clench. Knew he could walk away with Mahlouthi's blood splattered on his face and on his hands and not feel one iota of guilt.

But then something happened. Although Abbott had expected Mahlouthi to break down, cry and whimper, to his surprise, he went the other way. His eyes steadied, meeting Abbott's furious gaze, it was as though peace had come upon him, and for a moment Abbott wondered if Mahlouthi had wet himself with fear. That look was one he'd seen before on men whose bowels had spontaneously voided. They felt a brief moment of total peace and calm. A feeling of absolute relief. And that was how Mahlouthi looked now. 'I knew that you'd ask me this sooner or later,' he said. His voice was soft.

Abbott heard Burton burst in behind him and felt the barrel of a gun at the back of his head. His own resolve didn't waver. 'Whatever you're doing, don't do it, Monk,' said Burton, 'I'm half drunk, I'm only wearing my pants and you're a fucking good bloke who gave me the benefit of the doubt when you didn't have to. But I will blow your brains out.'

'I know,' said Abbott. The barrel of the gun still at Mahlouthi's forehead.

'I'll give you until the count of six until I pull the trigger,' said Burton.

The count of six. It was typical Burton. Had to be different. Even so.

'You pull the trigger, I'll pull the trigger,' said Abbott, without removing his pistol from Mahlouthi's forehead.

'You think, do you?' said Burton pleasantly. 'You think that a bullet bursting your head apart is going to make you pull the trigger?'

'Do you really want to take the chance?'

'This isn't the movies, Abbott. Muscles relax, even on instant death. Now just drop the gun before I tag you.'

Mahlouthi, pressed to the bed, looked straight up at Abbott, and his next words broke the deadlock. 'He was his son. Jeremy Robinson was Stone's son.'

'I knew it. I fucking knew it,' said Abbott. He let his arms drop, the barrel of his Sig leaving an indent in Mahlouthi's forehead.

His son. His son.

Of course, because Stone had been divorced and he had a son from that relationship. A son who would have been about the same age as Nathan. And that son was the boy that Abbott had watched die on the street.

The tension in the room seemed to dissipate. Behind him Burton sighed and relaxed his gun arm. 'Now,' he said, 'is one of you two fuckers going to tell me what the fuck is going on, or what?'

CHAPTER 42

Abbott awoke in the middle of the night.

He checked his Omega. 3.30 a.m.

But then, of course, he already knew that it would be 3.30 a.m. because that was the time they called Drinker's Dawn. The drink that pretended to be your friend by sending you off to the land of nod without the need for bedtime stories or nanny's cocoa turned out to be sleep's enemy. Your rest was disrupted and shot through with fragments of noxious dreams, and at 3.30 a.m. on the dot you came awake, and those shards and fragments of dream in your brain took greater shape, becoming the thoughts that plagued you.

He lay there, opening one eye blearily, just about focusing on the bottle of vodka that stood on his bedside table, almost empty now.

He'd told Burton everything, more or less.

'Stone's not dead,' Burton had said, incredulously. 'Why? I mean why the fuck go to the effort of staging your own death?'

'Two reasons, I reckon,' said Abbott. 'First, he'd somehow found out that he was under investigation. Second—'

'Yeah?'

'Second, because of all this. He needed to give himself time.'

'Yeah. And all of this being what?'

'Revenge, mate. An eye for an eye.'

How had Stone found out, though? How had he discovered that Mahlouthi was involved with Jeremy's death? More to the point, how had Stone found out that Abbott had anything to do with it?

He kept those questions to himself for the time being. Meanwhile, at last Burton had accepted that events were connected. What he'd had more trouble accepting was the fact that Abbott had accepted Mahlouthi's offer.

'We were the four fucking musketeers,' he said. 'One for all and all for one. You should have come to us. That was part of the deal. We didn't take side jobs – not without telling the others. Not in fucking secret so that we could keep all the money to ourselves.'

There had been nothing for it but to say sorry and to be grateful for Burton's grudging forgiveness.

'So, he's already killed Mowles, but you're next, eh?' Burton had said to Mahlouthi, moving on. 'And then who?' He pointed at Abbott. 'You think he's taken Nathan. A son for a son. What about after that? Is he coming for me?'

'If it is Stone, and he's on the warpath, does he have a reason to come after you?'

Burton looked affronted. 'No. Fuck that. It was him who left me high and fucking dry. I'm the injured party here. Stone can get to fuck if he thinks he's got a grievance.'

'Could be that he's not thinking logically.'

'Doesn't matter. There's what's right and there's what's right,' Burton had said.

If it *was* Stone. After all, there was always the risk that Abbott had been adding two and two together and making five. Either way, for now it was all he had to go on. The most likely explanation. And for now it was agreed that Mahlouthi would make his inquiries, while Abbott and Burton would stick around to – well, the official version? To provide security. The unofficial version? To wait.

Now, though, he found himself awake with the shit-thoughts battering at him like angry villagers attacking Frankenstein's castle. Until something else came to him. More of a sensation. A realisation that although there was nothing to hear, it was a pregnant sort of nothing. As though the corridors were slowly and silently filling with water.

He went to his door, put his ear to it and listened.

There. Was that it? A distant sound of movement that could be muffled feet on the marbled flooring. A sound like distant clicking.

Moving fast, he pulled on a sweatshirt and trousers, grabbed the Sig and looped the Kurz sling across his back and went to the door. Slowly, he inched it open to peer outside. He tensed, seeing a movement in the shadows, a figure. He raised the Kurz, feeling the tension on the bungee, ready to open up.

It was Burton. He was dressed, at least, and he held a finger to his lips, his AK-47 in the other hand, resting once more in the crook of his arm.

'Somebody's triggered an alarm,' he whispered.

'You've alarmed the place?'

Burton pulled a sardonic face, still whispering. 'We were short-staffed – and one of the places we alarmed was the service tunnel.'

'Which is how you knew about me.'

'Yes, mate, that's how I knew about you.'

It dawned on them both at the same time that whoever was coming knew about the service hatch and tunnel. They knew the layout of the villa but not about the development of the alarm installation.

Stone.

Suddenly Burton held up a hand for quiet, twitching to hear. Abbott heard it, too. A noise. Then around the corner of the corridor they saw the barrel of an AK. Half a second later, a figure wearing a black combat vest and balaclava appeared.

The guy saw Abbott and Burton. He gave a shout. He opened fire.

Contact.

The Kurz kicked as Abbott returned fire, a short burst that took plaster off the wall at the corner of the corridor.

In response, the guy in the balaclava pulled back sharply and then fired around the corner, blind, creating a deadly shooting gallery in the corridor. Abbott and Burton crouched, chunks of plaster raining down to the marble flooring around them. Using the wall for cover, with Burton on the left-hand side and Abbott on the right, the two SF men laid down intermittent covering fire, retreating in turn until they reached the end of the hall, and then, as Abbott fired off a final three rounds, Burton opened the door and they scurried through.

On the other side they took a breath, glancing at each other, both knowing that they had executed the move flawlessly, instinctively working as a team, that old psychic link coming back to them like a faithful black Labrador. There was no time for self-congratulation, though, and they were off once more, reloading on the run.

They knew without saying where they were going: to Mahlouthi.

'You never managed to persuade him to let you have a room nearer him, then?' asked Abbott as they dashed along the hallway towards Mahlouthi's quarters.

'He wanted the ones nearest for his women,' said Burton. He pulled up short. So did Abbott. At their feet was the body of Tommy, his throat cut, a huge puddle of dark blood spreading around him.

'He was a good bloke,' said Burton tightly as they moved on.

They reached the pool area. Here the pool lights beneath the water were the only illumination, and they gave the whole area a rippling effect.

As they arrived, they saw two intruders on the other side of the pool, also in balaclavas, also wielding AKs. For half a second the two sets of men were running parallel to one another, and then the balaclava crew opened fire on the run, spraying automatic fire randomly across the pool as Burton and Abbott scattered, both diving to the poolside. Glass smashed. Rounds ricocheted off ceramic tiles. A wooden towel-rail splintered and spun.

On the floor, Abbott steadied himself, Kurz extended on its sling, eye along the sight as he took aim at the guy on the right. To his left, he knew that Burton would be dealing with the guy on the left. Again, Abbott marvelled. Both were under fire but the human instinct to flee or return fire haphazardly was over-ridden by training and both men weren't just good at keeping a cool head while under attack; they thrived on it.

The two intruders fell at almost the same time, the one on the left spinning and falling backwards into the pool, blood erupting from his chest, the guy on the right smashing backwards in a welter of scarlet, landing half on and half off a sun lounger, army issue boots in the air.

Burton and Abbott shot each other a look – *top job* – both thinking how it never quite left you. How it always came back. Like learning to swim or riding a bike.

Then, just as the pool room seemed to have finished resounding to the short gun battle, the double doors to Mahlouthi's lodgings were thrown open, as though to make way for some grand procession. Only, instead of Mahlouthi in all his finery, flanked by minions, it was Mahlouthi in his pyjamas, used as a shield by two black-clad men bristling with AK-47s. Like their pals, they wore black combat vests and balaclavas.

Mahlouthi, red-faced, was shouting at Abbott and Burton, 'Do something. Do something.'

But neither Abbott nor Burton, crouched with their weapons trained on the group, were prepared to make the shot; there was too little of the target to make out in the dark; they had the wrong weapons for the job.

And now the intruders began edging Mahlouthi away from his quarters and to the far corner of the pool, where an exit door lay ajar. At the same time, Abbott saw Mahlouthi's eyes widen, as the realisation hit him. He was being taken. And in Baghdad, terrifying, horrifying things happened to people who were taken.

'Kill me,' said Mahlouthi, all of a sudden, changing his tune. 'Don't let them take me.'

Abbott shifted his aim. 'Your call,' he said to Burton. 'You know, what with you being chief of security and all.'

'Hold your fire,' said Burton in reply, a command that took Abbott by surprise. He had no love for Mahlouthi but to sentence him to God knew what fate seemed wrong.

One of the invaders had moved slightly, setting himself apart from Mahlouthi, putting a little distance between them. Abbott altered his aim a fraction, wondering if he could take the shot and bring the bloke down. From the corner of his eye he saw Biscuits waver, too, both wondering why the guy was making himself a target.

And then it became clear as the guy reached up and dragged off his balaclava, tossing it away. Of course. It was Stone. Older, more careworn. Weather-beaten. But still very much the man Abbott and Burton had once called a comrade.

For a moment, as Mahlouthi was dragged to the exit, Stone, Burton and Abbott faced each other across the pool, as though all were daring each other to open fire first. Abbott's eyes locked with Stone and what passed between them was a terrible knowing, a moment that removed all doubt from Abbott's mind. He knew it for sure now: for Stone this was all about the sins of the father.

'I've got him,' said Burton from the side of his mouth, 'I can take him.'

'No,' hissed Abbott. To find Nathan he needed Stone alive. 'Stone,' he shouted across the pool, 'give him back,' and of course he meant Nathan not Mahlouthi, and Stone knew that, too, because his burning, accusatory gaze was replaced by something altogether more terrifying. A smile that slowly spread across his face.

'All in good time,' he said.

And then he, too, was gone, and Abbott's shoulders sank, his Kurz dropping.

'Moof has a locator sewn into his pyjamas,' said Burton, already recovering. 'He needs to activate it. It's just a switch built into the unit. Fucking tiny thing. As soon as he can do that, we can find him.' They looked at one another, maybe thinking the same thing: find Mahlouthi, find Stone.

'He's probably forgotten he even has it,' said Abbott, pulling himself to his feet. 'You saw the state of him.'

Burton had reached the same conclusion. 'Yeah, maybe for the moment. But he'll remember. Have faith, mate. Come on, I don't think I've shown you our new ops room yet.'

The two bodies in the pool were left floating, blood spreading in the water around them as Abbott and Burton hurried away from the pool area. 'Ops room, eh?' said Abbott, as they ran.

'Too fucking right,' said Burton. 'An alarm in the maintenance tunnel isn't the only change we've made in your absence, you know.'

Next thing he was unlocking a white door. 'Welcome to the ops room,' he said grandly, flicking on light switches to reveal a small room containing two tatty office chairs, a *Loaded* calendar on the wall, and one side given over to a long desk on which sat a row of four monitors.

'This is the ops room?' said Abbott, who, despite everything, was unable to keep a note of amusement out of his voice.

'Get to fuck, will you, mate,' said Burton, reaching behind monitors and powering them up. 'It might not be the most technologically advanced ops room in the world, but it's ours, and we won't stand for outsiders taking the piss. Now this one—' he said, indicating the monitor on the far right, 'this is for the locator.'

The casing of the monitor was yellowing. 'Does it work?' asked Abbott.

Burton pulled a face. 'We'll soon see.'

The screen resolved to form a grid which Abbott took to be geographical. 'We're looking for a little blip,' said Burton, reaching to wipe dust off the screen.

'You ever have to do this before?' asked Abbott.

'First time for everything.' Burton peered hard at the screen. 'Come on. Come on, Moof,' he urged, 'remember the protocol.'

Mahlouthi would be terrified. He might simply forget to activate the locator in his terror. Or maybe his captors would search him and find it. Perhaps they'd cuff him in such a way that he couldn't even reach to switch it on.

All they could do now was wait.

CHAPTER 43

They found Mahlouthi's phone. It was Burton who turned it up. 'Why the great interest?' asked Abbott. He preferred to keep an eye on the tracker. Finding Mahlouthi brought them closer to Nathan; his main objective remained the same.

'You remember that message Mahlouthi showed you?' said Burton thoughtfully. He was scrolling through the contents of the phone. 'The one that said, "You're next"?'

'Yeah, I remember,' said Abbott.

'Well, it put the wind up him, for sure, but then something else happened that spooked him even more.'

'Finding out that I was in Baghdad, maybe?'

Burton made a noise like his mind had suddenly seized on something. 'That's right. He got the text message. Then he found out you were in Baghdad. But then something else happened and he started insisting on seeing you, and that's when Omar was despatched.'

'So what was the "something else," then?'

'Precisely, mate,' said Burton still flicking through the phone. 'Ah, bingo …'

It was a video file. Burton placed the phone to the desktop so that both he and Abbott could watch, and as it flicked into life it stirred memories of Abbott's first tour of Iraq – a kidnapping situation when they'd been sent footage of one of their own blokes being beheaded.

But this wasn't a beheading. In many ways, it was worse.

Worse because the torture being inflicted was clearly protracted. The prisoner, an Arab, wore just a pair of filthy shorts and was hanging in the bazoona position, suspended from an overhead beam with his hands tied behind his back. It looked like he'd been there a while. Probably his shoulder was already dislocated, but that wasn't stopping the man who was beating him, a man who was shirtless but nevertheless wore a balaclava. The length of metallic cable he held dripped with blood, and as they watched, he used it on the back of the hanging man, opening up a vicious strip of fresh, raw redness. Once, twice, a third time. The man's screams were given an unreal, tinny edge by the phone but still they went through Abbott. Still they made him flinch.

The guy with the metal cable took a breather. The victim's head slumped. Now the camera view shifted to reveal that nearby lay a body. Also shirtless, also badly messed up.

'Say the name,' came a shout on-screen.

'I have told you already,' pleaded the suspended man. His feet were tied. They hung just a few inches shy of the concrete floor of the room, and Abbott could see that the soles of his feet had been beaten. As they watched, he rotated, and for the first time, Abbott got a good look at his face. He couldn't be a hundred per cent certain, but it looked like one of the guys he'd seen attacking and killing Jeremy Robinson.

And then it was confirmed. 'Say the name anyway,' called the torturer. 'Who ordered Jeremy Robinson's death?'

'Mahlouthi,' screeched the victim. 'Mahomet Mahlouthi paid us to kill him.'

So that was it: Mahlouthi had been behind Jeremy Robinson's death the whole time. Why? Abbott didn't know.

From the side of the picture came another man, also wearing a balaclava. He raised a pistol, put it to the hanging man's head, and the hanging man said one word and that word was 'No,' before the killer put a round in his head.

The film ended.

Abbott thought. This was sent to terrify Mahlouthi. But it still didn't answer the question of how Stone knew that Mahlouthi had ordered the hit, nor how he knew that Abbott was in the mix. An inside man, perhaps?

One thing was for certain, Stone hadn't come to play. And wherever Mahlouthi was right now, he was in a world of pain.

* * *

Burton produced a handheld device that enabled them to keep tabs on the locator as they dealt with the bodies. The two men in the pool carried no form of identification, but they were both Westerners. What's more, they had the look of PSCs, which meant that they worked for Executive Alliance Group.

How many men did Stone have on the payroll? they wondered. How many did he trust? How many trusted him and how much was he paying them to help cover up his faked death and launch attacks on men they would once have fought alongside? Baghdad had a way of doing that to you. It warped your morals. It took you to dark places.

Abbott and Burton dumped their bodies, along with that of Tommy, in the bed of a Daihatsu pick-up in Mahlouthi's garage, covered them with a tarp secured with bungee cord, and returned once more to the ops room. And as morning turned to afternoon and Abbott and Burton sat anxiously, their hopes beginning to fade, Abbott felt the thirst creep upon him.

He yawned theatrically. 'How about we get a drink?' he proposed, trying to keep it casual. 'Something to take the edge off.'

Burton liked to drink, he remembered. They all did. Just that Abbott liked to drink more. Abbott didn't drink as a means of socialising, he socialised as a means of drinking. He liked to continue drinking when the party was over. He liked to drink alone because that way nobody got to see how much he drank. He could surrender himself to it without the anxiety of What Other People Thought.

'Nah, how about we don't,' said Burton, pretending he wasn't bothered. 'Might as well keep ourselves sharp, eh?'

Abbott knew Burton would love a drink. When he spoke, his voice was low. 'What's this all about, then, mate?'

'What do you mean?' said Burton.

'I mean, you want a drink as much as I do. You're not my sponsor all of a sudden, you know.' He couldn't help it. A surge of anger. Burton was right. In any sane universe, Abbott wouldn't touch a drop of drink, not when the life of his son hung in the balance.

So why did he feel so pissed off about it? Why did he feel like a kid being denied his favourite toys, like Burton was dishing out some kind of punishment? He wanted a drink, and it wasn't for Burton to tell him no.

'I know a problem when I see it, mate,' said Burton into the cloud of temper that had suddenly descended in the room. 'My dad was one, wasn't he? An alkie.'

'Hey,' started Abbott, 'who said anything about—'

'Oh, you're not, is that it? Because either you're lying, or you're in denial about it, and let me tell you, it had better be denial, because if you're lying to me when I'm hanging around here waiting to get tagged rather than doing what I should be doing, which is getting the hell out of Dodge, then you're fucked, mate, because I don't want any man at my back who tells me a barefaced lie.'

'All right, all right,' said Abbott. 'I've been putting it away lately. That's true. But I'm not a fucking alcoholic, all right? I'm not waking up desperate for a drink, trembling hands reaching for the whiskey.'

'No, mate, you ain't doing that, you're waking up at weird times of the morning hating yourself. You're spending each day telling yourself that today will be different, that you've got a handle on it, right?'

'Sometimes, maybe, yes. Sometimes. But that doesn't make me an alcoholic.'

'Because you care? Because you haven't given into it? Because you think rock bottom is a long way away just yet?'

'Exactly because of that.'

'Which?'

'All those reasons.'

'But you tell yourself you're going to change each day, don't you? Go on, admit it. You do. You tell yourself you're going to give the grog a miss today.'

'Maybe.'

'Except you never give it a miss that day, do you? You make that promise and you fail to keep it, every time, don't you, mate? Just like my old man. He was two people: catch him before eleven in the morning and he'd be grumpy – until he'd had his first drink. After that, good for a while, until he ran out of steam and sparked out on the sofa. He was quite a happy drunk, really. Generous with his money. Affectionate in a shaggy dog, drinky way. But he never wanted to do anything apart from sink the booze and sit on the sofa. Wouldn't remember half the stuff he'd said, even. Wouldn't know on those days that it got really bad and he started doing weird stuff that scared us kids. And he always, always put it first, you know? Whatever the day held in store. Necking booze was his first priority. Everything after that was just icing on the cake.

'And what really destroyed him wasn't the booze itself, it wasn't the way he used to behave. No, what really destroyed him was the fact that he couldn't stop. Or he knew that all our lives would be improved if he did, but he couldn't. That's what I think when I look at you, Abbott. I think of that bloke. And one thing I know about drinkers like my dad. They don't just stop at the one. They don't stop until the job is done. You think I want a drunken Monk fighting by my side? Or do I want the guy I knew from SF?'

Abbott had no answer.

'Am I right?'

Abbott shook his head.

'So no drink?'

'You fancy a drink?'

'Yeah, of course I fancy a drink. Difference is I like a drink. You *need* it.'

'You're wrong.'

'Prove it by staying dry for now, yeah?'

Abbott said nothing, indicating the monitor instead. 'No sign yet.'

'Nothing,' replied Burton. 'Mate, we're going to have to accept that it ain't gonna happen. It's been hours.'

'Either way we're going to hear something,' replied Abbott. 'Stone didn't take Mahlouthi just for the hell of it,' although as soon as the words were out of his mouth he thought of Nathan.

Half an hour later he excused himself. He made a call to Cuckoo, filling him in on all the recent developments.

'It might be time to call in the big guns,' said Cuckoo.

'No,' said Abbott. 'Nothing that endangers Nathan.'

Call over, he hurried along to Mahlouthi's office and downed several good gulps of whiskey straight from a carafe.

It wasn't just the booze, he told himself as his throat worked. It was a fuck-you to Burton. A little secretive way of saying, *No, mate, you're not the boss of me.*

He returned to the ops room, felt Burton's eyes on him. As he returned the other man's stare, Burton's eyes fell away, going to the monitor, more in disappointment than in embarrassment.

He knows, thought Abbott, taking his seat. He knows I'm weak. He found himself taking deep breaths, summoning an image of Nathan, putting his boy front and centre.

But isn't that the way it's always been, Abbott. You put the bottle before your family. You always have.

Like Burton's dad, he'd always put it first. He felt a sudden surge of warmth towards his old mate, knowing that Burton, for all his claims of self-preservation, was only looking out for him.

But he also knew that the sudden surge of warmth he felt was artificial – a product of the booze – and hated himself for it.

Either way, things were good in the room between them for a while, and Abbott found himself not quite dozing but closing his eyes, his thoughts going back to Tess.

CHAPTER 44

'So this is what it feels like to commit adultery in a cheap motel room,' she'd said.

It wasn't a motel, it was a hotel, and it wasn't cheap. The rest though? That was pretty accurate.

She was sitting up in bed, having pulled on her work shirt, the same one she'd been wearing the previous night in Kettner's, before they'd ended up back at his hotel, and the shirt had ended up on the floor. She'd buttoned it up over no bra, just a couple of buttons, not the whole set, enough to cover up. They were no longer living in a world of passion and nostalgia, catalyst: alcohol. They were back to reality.

The sex had been fun and fumbly and slightly drunken, as though they'd only just met in a club rather than being two people with so much emotional hinterland. Her body had felt unfamiliar to him. There were certain moves she had that were new. Of course. She had a whole life without him.

Afterwards, she had fallen asleep, halfway across the bed, as selfish with space as he remembered, and he had lain awake terrified of how she'd be by daybreak, when the morning forced them both to confront what they'd done. Would she open her eyes, hungover and full of remorse, and make her excuses in the name of a quick getaway? Would this be the beginning of something? Or the end?

As it was, she had surprised him. Her reaction was one of bemusement. Curiosity. She must have felt guilt – he knew her well enough to make that assumption – but for the time being at least she kept it hidden. 'Was that closure?' she asked, as if wanting to interrogate her own reasons as much as his.

He had no idea how to reply. Only that he didn't want it to be closure because that suggested something ending and he didn't want that. He needed more Tessa in his life, not less. He wanted her to save him. 'I only know that I think about you every day,' he told her, and even that was an understatement.

'I think about you all the time, too,' she said, but without too much conviction.

'So is this closure for you, then?'

She gave a short laugh. 'Not sure. Tell you what, though, I always thought we'd get back together that time.'

'Which time?'

'The time you went off with Fiona.'

'I didn't really "go off with" Fiona. You and I were on a break.'

'*We were on a break,*' she parroted Ross from *Friends*.

'Well, we were.'

'Yeah, and I got that. Which is how come I thought we'd get back together. I sort of assumed we would. And then we just didn't.'

The realisation hit him like a punch. The whole time he'd thought she'd been angry, wounded, betrayed, and absolutely resolute in her anger, whereas, in fact, she'd just assumed they would drift back together again. 'Because I suppose you went off to do the right thing, which was so noble of you, and absolutely the right thing to do, to try and give Nathan a proper start in life, and I went back to Cambridge and that was that.'

That was that.

She said it like it was nothing.

'And then I guess we just forged our own lives. You went off to war, I went off to law.' She laughed softly at her own joke.

I could have had you. But that was that.

'So maybe it was closure for me, yes. A last hurrah.' She cleared her throat. 'Because, um, I mean, I'm not being awful or anything, but that is, I mean that *was* the last time. You know, like although I came back here with you, and it's not like I put up much of a fight, and I might even have been the one who suggested it …'

'You were.'

'Well, there you go, and despite all that, and you being you, and everything we had before, I'm still a wife and a mum now, and I'm properly not in the habit of cheating on my husband and endangering everything we've built up, and if you still care for me as much as you say you do, then you'll respect that.'

A little fire in her eyes when she glanced his way.

'Of course,' he told her.

She nodded like a weight was off. 'And now, we need to think about breakfast. You'll excuse me if I don't join you in the restaurant. Perhaps you could order in?'

He did, and she dressed while they waited for room service to arrive, tied her hair back, applied some make-up – 'slap', as she still called it – and they ate, and he knew this was goodbye. Although he felt calmed in her presence, he knew it was just a temporary state of affairs, that he'd be cast adrift once again, when the morning was over.

'I guess if this is goodbye ...' He tried to ignore her look which said it was, and pressed on. 'I'm glad that you've at least got a better impression of me than the one I left you with before.'

She looked at him. A strand of hair had escaped from her ponytail and hung down her face. 'What do you mean?'

'You know, the whole angry young man thing. Always in trouble. Rebel without a clue and all that.'

'Well, you were a bit of a handful at times, that's true.' She chuckled. 'I'd tell other boyfriends about you and they'd be terrified of ever meeting you.'

'Well, there you go,' he said, trying not to think of her telling successive boyfriends about him, and how they were right to be worried because, yes, he probably would have lamped them. 'I mean, it's not a good look, is it? You know, I should have been pleased as punch to be going out with someone as cracking as you.'

'"Cracking"? What does cracking mean? It sounds a bit lad-mag for my liking.'

'It's not. It just means you were far too good for me and I should have seen it at the time; I should have cherished what I had, and maybe if I had, then I wouldn't have lost it.'

The silence that followed was uncomfortable, because they both knew that he had indeed lost it. That it was irretrievable now.

'There is something I've always wondered, though,' she said. 'Yes.'

'Well, I mean, talking to other guys. They weren't all as messed up as you. I always used to think it was – what? Hormones. Just growing up. Now I've sort of got to wondering if there was something – something that made you that way.'

The sound of cutlery was suddenly loud in the room. She was looking at him intently.

'Yes, there was,' he said at last.

'Something that happened before we met?'

'Before my family moved to Burton-on-Trent,' he said.

'OK,' she said, drawing out the word.

'It's painful,' he told her, looking away.

'You don't have to go there. Look, I'm sorry, I shouldn't be prying.'

'No. I want to. I owe it to you.'

'OK.' She used her napkin to dab her lips, took a sip of coffee.

'I had a brother,' he told her. 'Chris. His name was Chris. He was two years older than me. He was eleven when he died.'

Her shoulders rose and fell. Conflicting emotions played across her features. Shock. Pity. Maybe even a little anger that after all this time it was the first she knew that Abbott had ever had a brother.

'What happened to him?' she asked.

Again he looked away, knowing that he was going to tell her the story and summoning the courage to do it, taking a deep breath to start. 'We were playing by the river one day. Close to our house, like a bike ride away from our house. Our parents didn't like us playing by the river for obvious reasons, but we applied pretty intense pressure, and so they let us as long as we didn't go to the second bridge. There were two road bridges along the river, you see: the first one was the OK one. We hung out around there quite a bit. However hot it was outside, it would always be a bit cold and dank under that bridge. I remember it well.' He shivered in spite of the room's warmth. 'The second one, if you got as far as that one, then you'd gone too far, especially if you were just nine and eleven like we were, me and Chris. And it was fucking drummed into us. I mean *properly* drummed into us that we weren't allowed to go past that second bridge, not for any reason. The water was too deep and fast-running and the banks either side were too steep. It was pretty dangerous.'

She lowered her eyes, knowing there was only one place this story was going.

He continued. 'So anyway, there really was no place to play that was more fun than in that river, especially in the summer. You could kick off your shoes, go paddling and stuff. Fish for tiddlers. That kind of thing.' Tessa smiled along with the memory. 'But Chris, being older, he was like the one who was constantly pushing, testing the boundaries. You can imagine, yeah? Me, but to the power of five.

'So this one day we'd been running along the field playing some chase game.' He grinned ironically. 'Army soldiers, probably. That was always a favourite. And we pushed through the hedge that led to the riverbank, took off our shoes and were splashing through the river, until I kind of realised that we'd gone too far. Chris was just pissing about, though. He didn't seem to care, just taking it further and further, but sort of making me come along with him—' He paused, and maybe it was the whole situation, being back with Tessa, reliving that terrible moment, but he suddenly found himself having to choke back a tide of emotion, as though ice inside had suddenly cracked apart.

'Are you all right, Alex?' she asked. She reached for his hand and he took it gladly. 'Are you sure you want to go on?'

He nodded. Another deep breath. 'Chris had his plimsolls in his hands, and he kind of slipped. Just lost his footing, really. But it was enough for him to need to reach out and steady himself on the riverbed. The water was still only about knee height at this stage. I can see it now, the way he kind of wobbled, you know, and he put out his hand. Splash. Into the river. And the next thing I saw was one of his plimsolls, all white; we both had white plimsolls, like tennis-style plimsolls – "plimmys" we called them – and it was sailing down the river, bobbing along in the water like a paper hat.

'Now, the one thing that was drummed into us more than not going to the second bridge was don't come home without your shoes. Full-on like your life won't be worth living tackle. So I don't know about Chris, but, personally, when I saw that plimmy go sailing down the river, I pretty much shit myself. So of course he's going after it. He's racing down the river, and I can see that he's getting nearer and nearer to the second bridge. And I was shouting to him to stop. The water was like at the top of his thighs by now, but he went through the bridge. It was dark in there. I couldn't see him. And the water was almost up to my waist. I could feel it pushing-pulling me, you know, like it was a force stronger than I was, and I just couldn't go any further, I couldn't go under the bridge. I had to stop. I had to.

'I heard him shout my name. Just once. *Alex*. And I called for him. I must have shouted his name fifty times, but he was gone, and that was the last I ever saw or heard from him. They never found him.'

Tess gave a start. 'They never found him?'

'No. According to Mum and Dad they think he must have been carried off, maybe to the sea. And as a family we grieved for him, and I don't think we ever really stopped grieving for him, and I think there was a lot of blame that went unsaid.'

'Not directed at you.'

'I think, yes, in a way. All I can remember was so much bitterness. So much resentment. My dad started going out on night-time drives until he got done by the police for drink-driving. They were never the most loving, demonstrative parents in the world. A bit remote – but after that they got even worse. We moved house, of course, which is how we ended up in Burton-on-Trent. My mum and dad were keen that we should make a new start and so we never really mentioned Chris, didn't put up any photos of him, never really spoke about him. And by the time I met you, my life was pretty much the new normal; I'd developed ways to cope. But up until then …'

'Alex,' she said, 'I'm so, so sorry. For him, for them, but mostly – mostly for you.'

'Thank you,' he said. 'So am I. And I'm just sorry I never told you before.'

* * *

'Abbott.'

They had both been sitting, dozing, each lost in his own private thoughts, leaning back in the ops room chairs with their boots on the desks in front of them. Luckily, one of them – i.e. the one who hadn't been creeping off for surreptitious slugs of Mahlouthi's whiskey – was keeping his wits about him and had stayed half awake, and Abbott found himself roused by a Burton-sized nudge in the ribs.

He looked across, wondering if Burton knew that he'd been sneaking off for bumps of booze. If so, the other man had put it to the back of his mind. More important things were afoot. 'Look,' he said, leaning forward and Abbott did as he was told, focusing gradually on what was happening on the screen. A pulsing dot.

Mahlouthi's locator had been activated.

CHAPTER 45

It was early morning by the time they tracked the locator to a bombed-out area in the Al-Saydiya neighbourhood, part of the Al Rashid District.

Once upon a time Al-Saydiya had been a nice, middle-class area of Baghdad. But as with so much else in the city, the war had reassigned its status at the same time as it had destroyed the landscape. Bombed-out and burned-out, it was now a hotbed of insurgent activity and a favoured place for roadside bombs, while snipers were known to camp out in mosques and other buildings, picking off unsuspecting enemies at long range. It was the last place in the world – literally the world – that a couple of ex-SF soldiers would want to find themselves. And yet, here they were.

Christ. Abbott and Burton had cursed their luck. Here of all places.

Once in the area, they followed the locator, tracking the gently pulsing signal to a huge football-pitch-sized patch of waste ground. Across the other side was virtually the only building left standing. A bomb-damaged warehouse with a large ragged hole in the roof. Not far away from the warehouse was a rusting skip overflowing with trash of some sort, while in the middle of the open space was a burned-out van.

The warehouse door was inset with a smaller wicket door that hung open. Burton and Abbott looked at one another, neither wanting to literally walk in through the front door. Instead, they decided to walk around and, with the afternoon sun beating down hot upon them, they approached carefully, skirting the patch of waste ground, wary, scanning the rooftops of surrounding buildings at the same time, checking for anything unusual.

Around them, life carried on as normal. Men and women on the streets were going about their business as usual, cars passed, picking their way along pockmarked, battle-scarred roads, and far away, a helicopter clattered in the sky. In short, everything was as normal as it could be – Baghdad considering – and yet the locator that Burton held pulsed, and who knew what lay in store for them inside the warehouse. Maybe nothing. Maybe instant death.

'Could be that they've found the tracker and discarded it inside,' said Abbott.

Burton nodded. By now they were parallel with the far wall of the warehouse. Facing onto the waste ground was a single window high up. Looking at it, they were both acutely aware that anybody positioned inside could see them. And that whoever was in there might have a high-powered rifle. Even so, and despite that window, this was their best angle from which to approach the building.

'OK,' said Abbott, 'let's keep this casual.' It had not escaped his notice that two local women were gazing their way. 'Let's not attract attention to ourselves. We don't want to spook them. Last thing we need is them alerting the Iraqi guard or the cops.'

They made their way across the dirt, feeling as conspicuous as they looked, waiting until they were out of sight of the two busybodies across the other side before they drew their weapons, turned sideways on, and hurried up to the wall. Here there was a gash in the stone that offered access inside, just enough room for someone to squeeze through. They took up position either side. Abbott held his gun high by his shoulder, Burton the same.

Abbott had a thought. 'Did Stone know about the tracker?'

Burton shook his head. 'No. But even so. If he's found it, then we're walking into a trap.'

Abbott's smile was bitter. 'And that, mate, is the story of my trip to Baghdad.'

He listened, heard nothing then risked a glance inside. Nothing. Just darkness. The sunshine outside held at bay by the shadows within.

'Cover me,' he indicated to Burton and then, taking a deep breath and with his gun ready, he lifted a leg and climbed through.

On the other side he crouched, allowing his eyes to adjust to the immediate surroundings, checking for tripwires, ready for the ambush.

Which never came.

He straightened. Over his shoulder he called, 'Clear,' and Burton stepped into the warehouse beside him. For a moment they took stock, and then they heard a noise, a rasping human sound that made them crouch again, guns held ready. It came from the opposite side of the warehouse and as Abbott squinted in the half-light, what he saw was a dark shape, a seated figure with its arms pinned behind its back and its legs trussed, too. And although the figure wore a black hood – the kind of thing beloved of coalition troops – as well as what seemed to be a dark overcoat, Abbott knew it was Mahlouthi.

Abbott and Burton tensed, every nerve end shrieking and ready.

Silence.

'Moof,' called Abbott across the rubbish-strewn space. His voice was flat in the warehouse. A bird fluttered at the hole in the roof. Mahlouthi did not stir. 'Moof,' repeated Abbott, and there was still no reaction.

There was nothing for it but to step out into the open. Steeling themselves they scuttled across the floor, sweeping their weapons up into the rafters and to walkways overhead, knowing that no amount of pointing their guns was going to help if there was a sniper up there.

Closer to Mahlouthi now, and they could see that the Arab had been trussed with plastic ties, fastened tight to what looked like an old, tattered dining-room chair. His head lolled. Beneath the overcoat, an old macintosh, he still wore his pyjamas – heavily bloodstained, dirty, and tattered – on top of which was what looked like ...

A bomb vest.

Burton saw it too, eyes wide, he shared a terrified look with Abbott as both wondered what to do: try to save Mahlouthi or make a run for it.

Either way, this was it. Welcome to your trap.

'Abbott,' said Burton, a warning tone in his voice, 'we've got to get out of here.'

'But Mahlouthi.'

And Nathan.

'He's dead, Monk. Look at the fucking state of him.'

Abbott tore off the hood. Beneath it, Mahlouthi's face was an oozing mess of bloodied, bruised flesh, evidence of a terrible beating. Without lifting his chin from his chest, he stirred slightly, almost as though aware that he was the subject of conversation. Swollen eyes flickered. Prior to turning him into a human bomb, someone had done quite a number on him. Abbott thought of the guy suspended in the film. Fuckers had found the locator. Tortured Mahlouthi and then, when they'd found out what they wanted to know, switched on the locator and drawn Abbott and Burton to them.

'He's rigged to blow,' pressed Burton. 'Either way, he's dead. Let's go.'

'I can't leave him,' insisted Abbott. 'I can't leave him like this. Since when did we ever do that, Burton?'

'Oh yeah? Is this really about helping Mahlouthi, or about reaching Stone and finding Nathan?'

'Does it matter? I tell you what.' He jerked his chin. 'You go. Go on. Leave it to me.'

Burton curled a lip. 'Don't be daft. I'd leave him maybe. I'm not fucking leaving you.'

In front of them, Mahlouthi attempted to raise his head, his eyes opening fully at last as he tried to focus on Abbott and Burton. When he opened his mouth to speak, a bubble of blood formed at his lips. His nose was crusted with it.

And then, a phone rang. Abbott and Burton both froze and it was all Abbott could do not to screw up his eyes, knowing that he had rarely been so certain that death was but a breath away.

Nothing happened. Instead the phone kept on ringing. 'Is that your phone?' asked Burton through clenched teeth. 'Because I tell you this – it's not fucking mine.'

'Not mine either,' said Abbott.

'His?' asked Burton, looking at Mahlouthi.

The phone continued ringing, the jolly ringtone utterly incongruous in the dungeon-like surroundings. They looked down to where the noise was coming from. Abbott crouched, saw a phone beneath the chair. Steeling himself against the end, sure it would come at any second, he flipped it open and put the phone on speaker.

'Hello, Abbott,' said Stone.

CHAPTER 46

'I'm on speaker, am I?' said Stone. The old accent. Pure Cockney.

'Yeah, you are,' replied Abbott.

'Fucking-A. Hello, Monk. Hello, Biscuits. How are you both, then? Long time no speak.'

'Go fuck yourself backwards, mate,' said Burton. 'And hey, when you've finished doing that, how about we have a chat, man-to-man, just you and me, like. Maybe we could talk about how last night you tried to have us killed. And Tommy. Not forgetting poor old Tommy, eh? What'd he ever do to you?'

'Since when did anybody need to "do" something in our world? Being in the way of the main objective. That was enough. Yeah, sorry, Tommy. Blah blah. So long and thanks for all the tea. Maybe think twice about working for such a scumbag next time.'

'"Scumbag"? Pot. Kettle. Must have been gutting for you that Monk and I survived, eh, mate?'

'Don't be a dickhead, Biscuits. If I'd wanted you dead last night, you'd have your toes turned up now. You *and* Monk. Especially Monk.'

Yeah, thought Abbott. About that. Because if it was true, and frankly it probably was, then *why* leave us alive?

And the answer, of course, was for all of this. For this whole fucking sadistic circus, with Stone as the ringmaster and Abbott, Nathan, Burton and whoever else was unlucky enough to get in the way as the guys who tripped around the ring with custard dripping off their faces.

'Oh, I'm supposed to be grateful for that, am I?' Burton was saying.

'You?' came Stone's disembodied voice, metallic and faraway. 'I don't really give much of a mushy fart about you, to be honest. Sorry if that's a blow to your ego. You can leave now, if you want. Go on. Why not? You were never big mates with Abbott anyway. You don't owe him anything. Fuck off and take yourself out of the equation. It's him I've got business with. And believe you me, it gets nastier than this.'

Burton looked at Abbott, curled a lip and made a wanker sign. '"Leave?" You must be kidding. Mate, I'm sticking around to see you get what's coming to you for what you did to Badger. I reckon I owe him that, eh? Oh, and by the way, thanks for trying to pin all that on me. I won't be forgetting that in a hurry, mate, you can be fucking sure of that.'

'Fine, whatever, the day of reckoning approaches. I'll be sure to write it in my Filofax and I'll use my best pen. But before you get on your high horse, what happened to Badger was just business. Unlike you, Badger was getting greedy. If Badger had settled for the fucking large amount of money I was offering him, then Badger would be very much alive today, instead of decorating the desert in Mexico.'

Abbott spoke up. 'See, I don't quite believe that.'

'Really?' came Stone's reply.

'No,' he said. 'Badger wasn't like that. I think it's way more likely that he didn't like what you were planning for me and Nathan, and you decided to take him out of the picture. What did you do? Agree with him? Tell him to come for a skydive to celebrate him putting you back on the right path? Am I right? Did it go a bit like that?'

Stone went so quiet that Abbott was about to check the line when he spoke again.

'Badger didn't understand.'

'Didn't understand what?'

'How deep it fucking goes with you.'

And despite the heat, Abbott had to suppress a shudder.

'Look, Guy. Look, I'm sorry, mate. I couldn't say it enough, and I couldn't mean it more. I'm so fucking sorry for what happened to Jeremy.'

'Get his name out of your mouth.'

'Whatever it takes to make it up to you,' said Abbott.

'He was an innocent,' said Stone.

'I know. But – look, mate, he was playing with fire. You both were. He was spying for you, yeah?'

'He was helping, yes,' said Stone, although he said it with no relish, no pride.

Abbott checked around himself, wondering if they were being watched, at the same time, saying, 'And I guess you're going to tell me there were competing interests at work, yeah? That's how come Mahlouthi got involved?'

'Mahlouthi was in the pay of Hercules. Did you know that?'

Abbott looked down at Mahlouthi. *Of course – of course you were. How could I have not fucking seen it?* 'No, I didn't know that,' he said, and he could hear the note of resignation in his own voice.

'Oh yes, and Hercules suspected that I was being given the information needed to undercut them. They assumed it was a leak. They asked Mahlouthi to plug it for them.'

'Knowing that he employed you?'

'Uh-uh. Not at that time they didn't. All they knew was that someone – someone – was getting the drop on them, and they wanted to know who.'

Funny, thought Abbott. If it hadn't ended the way it had, then he would have made that discovery for himself, sooner or later. And if he had, then he could have had a word with Stone. Something like, 'Look, mate, they're onto you.' But of course he'd been trying to do Jeremy Robinson a favour, because he thought Jeremy Robinson seemed like a nice kid. What was the saying about the road to hell being paved with good intentions?

Abbott looked down at Mahlouthi, lashed to the chair. If the Arab knew what was going on, he showed no sign of it. Instead his head moved painfully, his eyes fluttered and his lips moved soundlessly, a thick rope of dark, viscous blood hanging from his mouth.

'Mahlouthi needed someone who could move more easily around the Green Zone to confirm what his spies were telling him – which is where you came in. It was you who took the money, ratting out your pals, eh? And when he found out that the man treading on his toes was living under his own roof, he wanted in on the deal. And he came to me.'

'Wait,' said Abbott. 'Mahlouthi didn't find out from me that Jeremy was your son. I had no idea myself.'

'Bullshit.'

'I fucking swear to you, Guy. I found out myself literally a matter of hours ago. As God is my witness. Biscuits. Tell him.'

'It's no fucking good, mate, he's lost it. Look at this shit.' He gestured at the broken, slit-open form of Mahlouthi in front of them. 'He's gone loco.'

No, thought Abbott. Stone hadn't gone suddenly nuts. These were plans that were long in the making. They had marinated in hatred, stewed in grief. But Burton was right about one thing. Stone wasn't listening to reason right now. He was beyond caring about the details of Abbott's involvement. All he knew was that Jeremy might have stayed out of danger if not for Abbott.

'So Mahlouthi came for his slice of the pie,' said Abbott. 'And you turned him down.'

'I denied all knowledge.'

Mahlouthi raised his head, the very effort of doing it causing him pain.

'But he wasn't convinced, of course,' continued Stone, 'and if he couldn't profit one way he decided to profit another way, by plugging the leak permanently on behalf of his paymasters. And my boy was left to die in the street.'

At least he didn't know that Abbott had been there. At least there was that.

'I couldn't even grieve, you know,' continued Stone. 'A quick trip home to bury my son, a few days off that I disguised as something else, and that was it.'

Burton's head had dropped. Perhaps remembering.

Feebly, Mahlouthi raised his head and spoke at last. 'Help me,' he rasped.

Abbott ignored him, feeling only contempt. 'What about Nathan?' he asked of Stone, but Stone made a disgusted sound and Abbott knew he shouldn't have brought up his own son so soon, cursing his lack of tact.

'You and Biscuits now have ten seconds,' said Stone. 'Think you can run fast enough?'

'Don't go,' pleaded Mahlouthi, the words vibrating on wet lips. 'Please don't go.' His eyes were fully open now, beseeching Abbott and Burton, and for all that he had done – practically the architect of the whole shit show – Abbott's feeling of disgust for him was gone and in its place he felt a rush of absolute pity.

And then, with no choice left, he grabbed Burton's sleeve to urge him on as the two of them turned and ran, not for the gash in the wall but to the closer front door.

Abbott was counting in his head: *one thousand, two thousand, three thousand* ... wondering how powerful the bomb would be as he and Burton hit the little wicket door. And as they dived through, he twisted, taking a last look at Mahlouthi and seeing the Arab bucking with fresh pain, his chest smoking, his face contorted as he screamed his final pleas. And then they were outside, blinded momentarily by the sun as they raced out onto the waste ground beyond, their boots pounding the dirt and the screams of Mahlouthi in their ears.

'The van,' shouted Burton. Ahead of them was the burned-out VW, the only cover for yards around. They made it, skidding around to the rear, curling up with their hands over their heads as behind them, the bomb blew.

Whump.

The air seemed to vibrate around them. A great heat pulsed across the waste ground, making the light shimmer. Debris rained down.

For a moment or so, that's how they stayed, knowing to wait in case of a secondary explosion. When none came, Abbott peeked around the side of the blackened van, seeing that while the warehouse still stood, a new hole had been punched into the front of it, a plume of black smoke issuing forth. Abbott still had the phone in his hand. From it came Stone's voice: 'Did you both make it, then?'

Abbott opened his mouth to reply but Burton had grabbed the phone from him, 'You're a fucking prick, Fingers,' he bawled.

'Prick, is it? Who's the prick really? The geezer who wants to see justice done? Or the geezer who gets in his way? There needn't be any danger to you, Biscuits, if you'd just stayed out of the fucking way like I said. Far as I'm concerned, if anything happens to you, it's your own fucking fault. You ride the roller-coaster at your own risk. I repeat, no harm need come to you as long as you stay out of my way.'

'Well, I wasn't out of your way, was I?' Flecks of spittle formed on Burton's beard. 'What am I? Just another Tommy. A poor bloke who's got in the way of your "main objective". We were part of the same team, Stone. Doesn't that fucking count for something?'

'It doesn't count for nothing when blood's involved. Anyway, fuck it, the team was history as soon as Mahlouthi and Abbott went after my son. Just you next, Monk. Just you and the boy.'

'Where is he?' demanded Abbott.

'Getting ready to keep Jeremy company.'

Abbott's jaw clenched. 'How do I know that you really have him. How do I know he's still alive?'

'You'll just have to fucking hope, won't you? But I'll be seeing you, Abbott, when you get your shit together. I'll be waiting.'

CHAPTER 47

Cuckoo was at Heathrow, having at last sorted out a temporary passport and having bid a not-at-all fond farewell to Singapore.

Dealing with the consulate in order to obtain his temporary passport, he'd been in constant terror of the cops wanting to talk to him. Surely they would have been able to ID him from outside the café? ID him, find him, interrogate him. Leaving the country then would have been out of the question. He'd stayed in that state of perpetual suspended terror the whole time he'd been waiting for his bit of cardboard. He'd been gripped by the same ass-cheek-clenching fear while waiting for his flight. During the flight itself? Ditto. Constantly asking himself, would they turn the plane around? No, of course not. But contact the authorities in the UK? Yes. Have somebody waiting for him at the other end? That was surely possible, too. Maybe even likely. After all, Abbott had certainly thought so. The pair of them had worked out a signal: Cuckoo was to clear his throat twice on the phone if he'd been picked up, in which case they were to assume that he was being monitored.

However, he'd made it this far. Back to Blighty, at least. After he'd disembarked, cleared passport control and sailed through customs unaccosted, he had allowed himself to relax a little.

Until, that was, he saw the two guys in plain clothes waiting on the other side of customs. How one guy nudged the other and pointed in his direction.

Cuckoo stopped. His little suitcase on wheels stopped, and for a crazy second he considered making a break for it. But that, he knew, was just his panic response kicking in. Instead, he stood still as the two men approached him.

'Alan Roberts?'

'Yes,' replied Cuckoo. 'That's me.' His heart was sinking. 'Who wants to know?'

His question was ignored. 'Just come with us, please,' they said. 'Let's keep it unobtrusive, shall we? There's nothing to be gained by making a fuss.'

They led Cuckoo away from the stream of travellers heading for arrivals, through a door marked for security personnel only, and into a side office where, seated behind a desk, was a guy in a scruffy suit with large Fred Basset bags under his eyes and a hangdog face to match.

'Mr Roberts,' he said, half standing and holding out his hand to shake. 'My name is Lansdale Thorpe from military intelligence.'

'Mr Thorpe.' Cuckoo shook his hand, parked his suitcase.

'I'd like a word, please.' Thorpe, indicated for Cuckoo to sit. It wasn't a question, but neither was it a threat, and as the two escorts disappeared and the door shut behind them, Cuckoo felt himself relax a little. Although he was in a little windowless room, he was pretty confident that nobody was going to try to kill him. Not here in Heathrow.

He settled into his chair, facing Thorpe, who shot him a tired smile and said, 'I'm sorry to grab you literally the second you step off the plane, but needs must, I'm afraid. What we have here is a very fluid, fast-moving situation.'

'And what situation is that?'

'Right. Well. We've been interested in a company based in Baghdad's Green Zone, a commercial security firm called Executive Alliance Group. Do you know it?'

Cuckoo tried not to let anything register on his face. 'Yes,' he said. 'Well, sort of.'

'"Sort of". Excellent. That'll do. What about EAG's CEO, an ex-SBS specialist by the name of Guy Stone?'

'I know of him.'

'OK, good. Well: EAG and its CEO Guy Stone have for some months now been the subject of a departmental corruption investigation. Not only that, but we're linking the murder of a Foreign Office worker, Jeremy Robinson, with them and their rivals Hercules. Do you know of Jeremy Robinson?' Cuckoo said nothing and Thorpe continued. 'At first we thought that Robinson was simply the luckless victim of a street robbery and nothing whatsoever to do with the investigation. It was a young whizzkid in our office who made the link.'

'Link being?' asked Cuckoo, who knew the link.

'He was Guy Stone's son.' Thorpe paused. 'Now. Park that for a second. And let's go to your wife, Fiona Roberts, who also happens to be the ex-wife of Alex Abbott. Mrs Roberts, your wife, has been making inquiries as to the whereabouts of her son with Abbott, Nathan, a serving soldier who is currently "whereabouts unknown", according to his base.

'Then there's you, hotfooting it to Singapore, which just so happens to be the current home of Alex Abbott. Abbott then entering Baghdad.' Thorpe nodded, acknowledging the look that flitted across Cuckoo's face. 'Yes, we know all about Abbott entering Baghdad. Added to that we know that two of Abbott's former team members, Mowles and Stone – the aforementioned Guy Stone – have both died recently, except we're not happy that Mowles's death was an accident, nor that he was actually jumping with his stated partner, a guy called Burton, on the day he died. Neither are we content with the explanation that Stone drowned. For us, what works is that Stone was behind Mowles's death. And then went on to fake his own. And now Abbott's in the mix, too ...' Thorpe sighed and threw up his hands theatrically. 'What's a man to think?'

Cuckoo cleared his throat, and shifted on his seat which suddenly felt a good deal less comfortable than it had before. 'Well, what *do* you think?' he asked.

'I don't. I let other people do that for me. But you're in this room, and I've got people on the ground in Baghdad who are desperate to lift Abbott. Literally pick him up in the street now ...'

'Don't do that,' said Cuckoo, quickly.

'Why?' said Thorpe quickly leaning forward. 'Why not?'

Cuckoo took a deep breath, feeling like he was on the hook and at the same time knowing that now was not the time to summon the big guns – it was time to spike them. *Forgive me, Abbott,* he thought. And began to tell Thorpe what he knew, which was what he'd been told by Abbott. How Executive Alliance Group was being supplied with the information they needed in order to supply the right people with the kickbacks, particularly the Farlowe contract. How Hercules weren't happy about that and no doubt had orchestrated the murder of Jeremy Robinson.'

As for Stone faking his own death?

'Because, as the head of Executive Alliance Group, Stone was under investigation by us,' said Thorpe, thoughtfully, the pieces of the jigsaw clearly forming a bigger picture for him now. 'By us, by the Americans, by just about anybody with an interest in the rebuilding of Iraq. You know I can have SF ready to move on Executive Alliance Group in an hour.'

'You have to let Abbott find his son first,' said Cuckoo quickly. 'Whatever you want with Stone. We just want Nathan back unharmed.'

'We'll come to that,' said Thorpe. 'According to his base, Nathan was taking time off for a bit of work on the side. Could be that the work is with Executive Alliance Group ...'

'It's not. Like I'm telling you, it's a kidnap situation.'

'Have you been in receipt of any demands?'

'Not as yet.'

'Do you know where he is?'

'No.'

'OK, well, we think we do know.'

Cuckoo gave a start. 'Really?'

'Yes. We think that he's in the EAG compound.'

'What makes you think that?'

'Good question. Let me show you.'

From beneath the desk, Thorpe produced a laptop. In moments he was showing Cuckoo drone and satellite footage. It was overhead, distant and far from distinct. 'Do you recognise this area?'

'No.'

'It's the Green Zone. What you're seeing there is the Executive Alliance Group compound and that *there* is a vehicle leaving the compound. Now—' he leaned forward and fast-forwarded the footage – 'different satellite. Different part of the city.'

They watched, and it was impossible for Cuckoo to make out what was happening but he was reliably informed by Lansdale Thorpe that he was seeing the kidnap of Nathan from outside the women's prison.

'He seemed to go peacefully,' said Thorpe. He reached to speed through the footage a little more. 'If Abbott is right, then what we're seeing here is his kidnap, although it's impossible to tell if he's going along willingly or not.'

Cuckoo looked at the date stamp. Made sense. He swallowed, hoping his face betrayed nothing. 'It's impossible to tell. Maybe.'

The footage showed the van moving off. The image switched to another source. 'Same SUV,' pointed out Thorpe, 'and if you watch, you'll see it's heading to the Green Zone.'

'And it ends up at EAG.'

'Exactly. You've got the picture.'

'Right. OK, so why would Stone be interested in kidnapping Nathan Abbott?'

'I don't know,' lied Cuckoo. 'I wish I did. Main thing is that we get Nathan out, though, yes?'

'Do you want the official answer?' replied Thorpe. 'OK, well, the official answer is that of course it's our number one priority to rescue one of our military personnel who's fallen foul of an outside agency. Or do you want the real answer? That he's low down the list. We need to take down Stone. We need to be seen to be acting on intelligence given to us by our American friends, and they very much want to see Executive Alliance Group out of the picture. That is our primary objective, and nothing must stand in the way, including Abbott.'

'All Abbott cares about is rescuing Nathan. He won't get in your way.'

'He'll be in the way. We need him out of the way.'

'You do know that I'm going to relate the particulars of this conversation to Abbott. You know he's going to want to go in.'

'You're to advise him not to,' said Thorpe pleasantly. 'That is your job, Mr Roberts. It's precisely why we're having this conversation. I'm prevailing on you as a member of the forces as well as a good upstanding, law-abiding citizen to work with us in ensuring that this operation goes ahead unhindered by Abbott. You are to tell him that we will be readying an SF team to go into the EAG compound in the next couple of days, and they will have instructions to ensure that Nathan is extracted alive. You tell Abbott that he doesn't mess this up for us, because if he does, then hell hath no fury. Do I make myself clear?'

'Abbott's not going to step away that easily. You'll have to give him something in return.'

Thorpe smiled. 'Then we'll give him something in return.'

CHAPTER 48

Breathe, recalibrate, deliver. That had been their mantra in the Special Forces. Abbott and Burton looked to it now. They made their way back to Mahlouthi's villa complex and had just dropped exhaustedly into the ops room chairs, taking a breather before they regrouped, when Abbott's phone rang.

It was Cuckoo. Beside Abbott, Burton's head dropped, maybe glad of the respite, able to catch a few moments' shut-eye before they formulated a next-step plan, and Abbott stood, taking the call in the hallway outside the room. 'Hello, Alan,' he said.

'All right, Abbott?' said Cuckoo. 'Dare I ask, how are things?'

'Well, I know now that Stone has got Nathan. He's behind all this,' said Abbott. He pincer-squeezed the bridge of his nose. 'You might say that he's been in touch.'

'With a ransom demand?'

'No. He doesn't want a ransom.'

'I see,' replied Cuckoo, and even through his fatigue Abbott couldn't help but notice a distinct lack of reaction from Cuckoo. 'Why? Why don't you think he wants a ransom?'

That was something that Abbott didn't particularly want to go into. 'That remains to be seen, mate. What about you? What have you got?'

'I'm back in the UK,' said Cuckoo with a touch of reproach in his voice that Abbott simply couldn't be bothered to respond to. 'And while I was half expecting them to be questioning me about Foxhole, what I got instead was a meeting with military intelligence.'

'Go on.'

'They're investigating Stone for financial irregularities,' Cuckoo was saying. 'Apparently, the Americans weren't happy with him. And they've managed to put you and Nathan together with all that. They think Nathan is at the Executive Alliance Group compound. They've got the place under satellite surveillance. They want you to stand down. Let them take it from here.'

'They know that Nathan's been kidnapped.'

'How the hell do they ...? Wait, you didn't tell them, did you?'

'I had to. They have a team preparing to go in,' interrupted Cuckoo. 'The team's due to be in place sometime tomorrow and will be moving in shortly after that. Look, Abbott, we've done our work. All we have to do is keep our heads down. SF will do the rest. You of all people know that they're the right people for this job.'

'Hostages die,' said Abbott. 'They especially die when a team goes in.'

'You're to stand down, Abbott.'

'You're not giving the orders here, Cuckoo. I'm not standing down. There's a guy who wants my balls on a platter. The same guy currently holding my son prisoner. And you think I'm going to stand down? Jesus Christ.'

'SF can handle this.'

'So can I.'

'OK, look, obviously I anticipated you might feel this way. So did they. So how about if you could closely monitor the situation?'

'And how would I do that?'

'Intelligence have agreed that if you give your word not to get involved, then you can come along as an observer on the SF incursion. That's all though, just as an observer. You can be there first-hand to see that Nathan's extraction is handled correctly. And in the meantime, you're to stay away from the Executive Alliance Group building – you're not even to enter the Green Zone. What do you think?'

'I have a condition,' said Abbott after a while.

'Look, mate, they're already ...'

'You pass it on. It has to be met or it's no deal.'

'Fire away.'

'Their SF incursion has to happen within the next forty-eight hours.'

'OK, I can ask. In the meantime, I have your word that you'll stand down?'

'Yes,' agreed Abbott. 'You have my word.'

Cuckoo paused. 'One thing: why would Stone want Nath? Is it some kind of reprisal for what happened to Jeremy Robinson?'

'I don't know, mate,' lied Abbott. 'I had nothing to do with any of that.'

He ended the call, knowing that nothing of what he'd just said mattered a damn.

It didn't matter because right at the start of the conversation Cuckoo had cleared his throat twice.

CHAPTER 49

'For the next forty-eight hours I need a constant watch on Executive Alliance Group. I need to know everything that goes on. Do you think you can do that?'

Abbott was sitting in the Country Club in the Green Zone, opposite Potter, who was looking at him carefully, almost as though checking him out. Unsurprising, really. On the drive over, Abbott had caught sight of himself in the rear-view and it wasn't a pretty sight. He'd flashed his pass at the coalition cop on entry and steeled himself for instant rejection but was waved through. Clearly Military Intelligence hadn't got their arse in gear to blacklist him yet.

Military Intelligence, he'd thought. No doubt they had Cuckoo by the balls. They'd be threatening him with the loss of his job, brandishing the Official Secrets Act at him. They probably had a picture of the Queen and Winston Churchill handy, so that Cuckoo could be in no doubt that he was expected to do his patriotic duty.

Even so, and despite whatever threats or inducements they tossed at him, there was a good chance that Cuckoo was fully on board with the idea that Abbott should wait and join the SF team. Trouble was, neither Whitehall nor Cuckoo knew what Abbott knew, which was that Stone was one step ahead and he wouldn't be hanging around in the Green Zone for long.

Just a question now of staying on top of the situation.

And still Potter looked at him, because, aside from Abbott looking a sight – bedraggled, tired and desperate – if the story of the mirror was to be believed, it was an extraordinary request. 'I'm sort of waiting to hear what's in it for me,' said Potter carefully. He sipped at his drink, perhaps doing so pointedly, since Abbott had drained his in one long draught.

'Is it still a going concern?' he'd asked.

'What? Since Stone bought the farm?' said Potter. 'Yeah, sure. CEO's dead but life goes on. He had a good number two, a guy by the name of Marsh. Tom Marsh. More than capable of running the show.'

Abbott held up a hand to stop him. 'What does he look like, this Tom Marsh? Goatee beard?'

Potter shook his head. 'Not that I've ever noticed. Probably not the droid you're looking for. But he is a good second-in-command and capable of running things. Look, there's way too much money swimming about for anything to stop the gravy train. You should have hung around. You'd be a very rich man right now.'

Yeah. Shouldawouldacoulda.

Potter took a belt of his drink. 'You didn't think Stone was dead, last time I spoke to you.'

'Still not entirely sure,' fibbed Abbott, 'which is why I'm hoping you could keep an eye on his hideout for me.'

'His hideout now, is it?'

'It's where I'd hide if I were him.'

'You think he's something to do with Nathan?'

'Point is, I'm asking for help, Potts,' said Abbott bluntly. 'Not the first time, and it may not be the last. Can't pay you, can't even promise to do anything for you right now, what with having a bunch of other stuff on my plate, but what I can say is that any time in the future you need me you only have to call. I'll be back in Baghdad faster than you can pick up a penguin.'

'I won't be in Baghdad,' said Potter. 'Plan is to move back to London. I've got the job. Even got a business card. Just arrived this morning, actually. Just packing things up here and I'll be moving back.'

'What's the job?'

Potter reached to a pocket of his shirt, withdrew a business card and tossed it across the table to Abbott. 'Hexagon,' said Abbott, thinking, *What are the chances?* and pushing the card into the back pocket of his cargo pants.

'You heard of them?'

'We've had dealings. Nothing direct.'

'Great. Well, maybe I could put a bit of business your way. Then again …' He tailed off, eye falling to Abbott's empty glass.

Abbott waved the moment away. 'Look, can you help me or not?'

Potter took a deep breath. 'You're a persuasive guy,' he said. Abbott said nothing. He kept his face neutral. 'I'll do it. I mean, look, it won't be me on duty; I'll have to use help, but I'll put somebody on it.'

'OK,' said Abbott. 'It's a deal.'

'I should fucking think it's a deal.'

'I need to know anything that happens. Any kind of activity.'

'What are we looking out for in particular?'

'Anything.'

'And do I need to watch out for any other parties?'

'Military Intelligence.'

Potter reared back. 'You're fucking joking.'

'It's all right, they won't have men on the ground, it's all eye-in-the-sky stuff.'

'Even so.'

'Mate, you'll be well clear.'

Potter raised his head. 'So Intelligence have taken an interest in you, then?'

'Could say that.'

'Well, don't look now – I said don't look now, but a couple of cops have just walked in.'

'Cheers, mate, that's my cue to leave quick-smart.' Abbott disguised it as a joke between mates, when he leaned forward, grabbed Potter's drink and drained it, but really he just wanted the drink.

He escaped the Green Zone and paid his hotel a visit, intending to collect his things. There he was waylaid by the receptionist, a guy he knew of old. 'Mr Abbott.'

'Hey, Ahmed.'

'Please,' said Ahmed, ushering him to the side of the desk, where he pretended to show him a dog-eared tourism leaflet. 'A man was in here looking for you,' said Ahmed.

'Did he by any chance have white hair?'

Ahmed's eyes widened. He nodded.

'Did he offer you money?'

'Yes,' said Ahmed.

'Did you take it?'

'I did.'

Abbott cleared his throat, not sure whether to be amused or outraged. 'OK, well, I guess that's fine. Um ... what did you tell him?'

'I told him that I didn't know where you were,' Ahmed lowered his voice, 'even though I saw Mr Mahlouthi's man, Tommy, who told me.'

'OK, well, thank you.' Abbott nodded. 'I appreciate that. 'But look, don't mess with this guy, OK? He means business. He comes back, you call me, OK?'

Outside his room, Abbott drew his sidearm and then let himself in quickly, sweeping the room by the numbers. Nothing. No sign of entry or of a search, but that didn't mean the guy hadn't been in. He knew what he was doing, this guy, and Abbott knew he should be more worried.

CHAPTER 50

He'd been putting it off, but things had gone too far. The situation could change at any second. He had to call her.

So on the journey back to Mahlouthi's villa, he parked near a rusting, bombed-out lorry that sat in a blackened hollow – a hollow that had long since moved from its original designation of 'bomb crater' to 'rubbish dump' – and he checked around himself, pulled out his phone, scrolled to her number and called.

'Alex,' she said, when she answered, a note of panic in her voice right from the offset. 'What is it? What's happened?'

'Nothing, Fi,' he said, 'no news just yet.'

'Oh.' She made a noise that was somewhere between relief and frustration. She probably wasn't sure herself, knowing only that all she wanted was for the phone to ring with news, and for that news to be good.

'Is Alan there?' he asked.

'He's in the other room, flaked out in front of the TV. I can wake him. Do you need to speak to him?'

He imagined Cuckoo back in his comfort zone, and for once he didn't think of him with scorn. Alan had handled himself well over the last week or so. 'Actually, it's you I need to speak to.'

'Me? Are you sure?'

'Yeah.'

'All right. Fire away.'

'How much has he told you?'

'Alan? He's told me that everything's in hand. That SF are getting ready to go in and rescue Nathan. That's right, isn't it? He's not trying to fucking soft soap me, is he?'

Despite everything, he found himself smiling. She still had the vocabulary of a particularly foul-mouthed navvy. 'No, that's about the size of it, but, look, there are a lot of ifs and buts involved. You know that we think Stone is behind all this, yes?'

'Yes, but we don't know why,' she said, with a half-question, half-warning in her voice. '*Why* would he be doing this to Nathan, Alex?'

'I don't know, but if you think it's personal, then I think you're probably right.'

'Christ's sake, have you brought this on us?' Her voice rose. 'Because if you fucking—'

'*No*.' His voice was sharp. He needed to nip this in the bud right now. Needed to get down to business. 'This is not on me, Fi.'

'Well it's on fucking somebody and I know it's not on me.'

'Let's not get into it. It's not why I'm calling anyway.'

She seemed to calm. 'Go on, then. Why are you calling?'

'It might go off before the SF team is in place. I need your blessing that if it does, I can move.'

'Well, you don't have it. I'm told that you've given your word you'll wait for them to move in. That they've even allowed you to come along as an observer as a matter of courtesy.'

'Yeah, yeah, but these people don't know Stone like I do; they're not as familiar with the situation as I am. It could be that I need to go in before they're ready.'

'It sounds to me like you're saying you think that's going to happen.'

'It's why I'm ringing, Fi. I'm not going to sit back and let shit go down that endangers Nathan.'

'And what "shit" might that be?'

'I don't know. But I'm not keen on letting Stone take his time to prepare for an attack. I'm not keen on giving him time to show a clean pair of heels. And I don't like the idea of a team going in because, SF or not, hostages die in situations like that.'

She caught her breath. He hadn't mean to be that blunt, but there you go.

'Are you still drinking?'

'What did Alan tell you?'

'He was vague.'

'This is Nathan we're talking about, Fi. He takes priority.'

'Look, no, I want you to wait for SF. Whatever happens, you wait. Because if anything – fucking anything – happens to Nathan because of some stupid shit you do, I swear to God—'

'All right,' he said. 'Point made. Look, I've got to go. I'll be seeing you, Fiona.'

Finishing the call, he sat for a moment in the baking-hot interior of the Merc. *Well, that didn't go well.* They'd fallen out over every other minor shit in their marriage. Of course they were going to disagree over how best to extract their son from a hostage situation.

But maybe it wouldn't come to that, he thought. Maybe he could wait for SF to make their move, and everything would go smoothly. He could only hope. For that, and to be reunited with Nathan. To have another chance at being a better father.

CHAPTER 51

Abbott had only been back at Mahlouthi's villa for a couple of hours when the phone rang. It was Potter. 'Something going on at Executive Alliance Group, according to my man on the ground,' he said.

'Like what?'

'Activity. Lots of tooled-up guys moving around. Trucks being manoeuvred into place. Hang fire. I'm going to take a drive around there myself.'

'We're on the move,' Abbott told Burton as he came off the phone, going on to slightly fillet what Potter had told him.

'It could be anything, mate,' said Burton. The pair of them were fully awake now, alert and looking to their weapons. 'I mean, fuck me, but our boy Stone has been building up quite the little empire, you know. Might just be an operation.'

'Sure,' replied Abbott. 'Could just be carrying out a job. Maybe they're making funeral arrangements for their dear, departed boss. Or maybe they just know the jig is up and they're on the move. And if that's the case, then they've caught Intelligence on the hop.'

Abbott was checking his weapons, readying himself for roll-out when the phone rang again. It was Potter. 'I'm outside now. No doubt in my mind, something's definitely going on, and it doesn't look like your average day at the office.'

'OK,' said Abbott, slinging his assault rifle over his shoulder. 'Describe what you see.'

'Well, a bit ago the big roller door opened and they rolled out an army lorry. Some old-looking World War II shizz. It's parked. And now we have EAG stooges loading it up. Boxes of God knows what, weapons and ammo, plus office stuff.'

'We're on our way,' replied Abbott. No doubt about it: Executive Alliance Group were on the move. They were shuttering the business. He waved at Burton and the pair of them began hurrying through the villa.

'The first lorry has moved off,' relayed Potter as they went.

'Do you see Stone?'

'Stone? What? I'm looking for zombies now?'

'Well, yeah, as I'm working on the assumption that he still walks among us.'

'OK, well, I don't see Stone,' replied Potter. 'Nobody I can put a name to so far. Looks like he's been busy hiring since I was an employee. Just regular security drones. Wait. You remember the number two I was telling you about? Marsh? He's there. And hey.'

'What?'

'Turns out he does have a goatee beard. Looks like he really is the droid you're looking for.'

Made sense, thought Abbott. Inside he felt a tight, coiling feeling, thinking. This was the guy who took Nathan. Then Potter was saying, 'Oh, crap.'

'What is it?'

'It's Nathan.'

Abbott had been about to enter the garage, Burton at his heel, but he stopped, the breath catching in his throat. Something struck him. Something other than the Nathan sighting. But he put it to one side for the time being. 'Tell me,' he said. 'Tell me what you see?'

'It was just a glimpse. He's in the back of the second truck. Heavily guarded. He seems all right, but ...'

'What?'

'Looks like he might have been drugged. He looks zonked out. Seems to need support.'

Haloperidol, thought Abbott. *Twenty milligrams. Knocks the patient into near-catatonia.* It's what he'd use to move a motivated prisoner like Nathan. It's what Stone would use.

But still. It struck Abbott that for the first time he knew beyond a doubt that Nathan was alive and well. How Nathan was so close now, almost within his grasp, and it was as though the wire coiled tight round his insides relaxed for an instant – and then tightened again.

'He's gone,' relayed Potter. 'Out of sight. And, my friend, the trucks are on the move.'

'We're on it,' confirmed Abbott. He and Burton were clambering into a Land Cruiser, and in moments were racing up the ramp of Mahlouthi's garage and into the street, Burton wrestling with the wheel.

'Can you follow them?' asked Abbott over the noise of the roaring Land Cruiser engine, Burton cursing and shouting at unwary pedestrians. 'Just until we're in place and have visual contact?'

'Roger that,' said Potter, 'I—' And then he stopped.

Abbott listened. Something was wrong, he could tell. 'Mate, what is it?'

At the other end of the line, Potter took a deep breath. 'Well, you know you asked me if I could see Stone?'

'Roger that.'

'Well he's in my rear-view mirror. And the reason he's in my rear-view mirror is because he's got in the back seat. Oh yeah, and he's holding a gun to my head.'

Abbott closed his eyes. In the driver's seat Burton looked quickly across at him, sensing something big was up.

'Let me speak to him,' said Abbott.

'He wants to speak to you,' said Potter.

'Who's that, then? Not my old mate, Monk. Here, give us the phone, let me have a word with him. Hello, Monk? Here, listen, I've got something to tell you. You know how we called you Monk? I bet you always thought it was because your name's Abbott, dintcha? It wasn't, you know. It was cos you was always drunk as a monk.'

Abbott's jaw clenched. He had one hand braced on the dash of the Cruiser as it clattered over the cratered streets. He held the phone to his shoulder, saying to Burton, 'Stone's got Potter.'

'So we head for the Green Zone and get him,' said Burton.

'No,' said Abbott. 'We head for the Green Zone, but to intercept the trucks. Potter can take care of himself.'

'Jesus, mate, that's cold,' said Burton, but Abbott said nothing. Instead he removed his thumb from the phone to talk to Stone once more. 'So you decided to close up the old place, eh?' he said.

'Yes, we have decided to temporarily move our operations.'

'Nathan not with you, by any chance, is he?'

'Wouldn't you like to know.'

'Don't you touch him, Stone,' he said. 'Don't you dare harm a hair on his head, or I swear to God I'll find you. I'll find you and kill you.'

'Find me? You're threatening to "find" me,' replied Stone. 'That's your big threat, is it? I'm *banking* on you finding me, you fucking moron. That's what this is all about. Right now, you're mine. You're doing exactly what I say. Here, why don't you say goodbye to your old mate Potter?'

Next came the gunshot.

CHAPTER 52

'What now?' Burton had pulled the Land Cruiser to the side of the road. Etched on his face was shock, the sense of a situation that was moving fast and getting out of control. 'What do we do?'

'Go there,' said Abbott in reply. His jaw was set. 'Just get to the Green Zone.'

'What the fuck is the matter with you, mate?' said Burton, his forehead creased. 'Don't you give a fuck about Potter? He's a mate.'

'He *was* a mate. He's gone now.'

'You cared more about Moof, as I remember.'

'Just get to the fucking Green Zone.'

Shaking his head in confusion and disgust, Burton pulled away once more. 'They'll stop us at the checkpoint,' he warned. 'What about your agreement with Military Intelligence?'

'We'll have to risk it.'

'Mate, you heard the shot. For crying out loud, I heard the shot, and I wasn't the one with the phone to my ear. You think Fingers will have left him alive, do you? No way, mate. The only prisoner he's interested in taking is Nathan, and ...'

You.

The word went unsaid.

Abbott's shoulders rose and fell as he thought, trying to make his decision. Wanting to make the right one. Burton was right. Chances were they wouldn't even make it past the checkpoint.

'OK,' he said. But still he clung to one last hope, and he lifted the phone. 'Potter,' he said. He heard the note of anguish and desperation and hopelessness in his own voice and hated it. 'Potter, are you there?'

Nothing came back. Nothing but the sound of dead air. A line that had been cut.

'Go,' he said at last.

Abbott and Burton stayed in the Land Cruiser. In his head, Abbott replayed the sound of the shot. Another one to add to the list, he thought. Another mark in the minus column.

You didn't do enough.

'Where to, then?' asked Burton.

'Kirkuk. Executive Alliance Group have an outpost there. That's where they'll be going. We'll catch them en route.'

Again Burton fought with the wheel and floored it. For some moments they rode in silence, Abbott bracing himself in the Toyota.

'It's on me,' he murmured as they drove, almost to himself, although Burton heard.

'No, mate, it's not on you. It's just shit happening, is what it is. It's just the way it works with fighting men, Monk. And you know what really gets me? You fucking know this. You know this now and you knew it then. Pouring booze down your throat in an attempt to block out something you should be dealing with. You don't drown your problems, mate, you confront them. What do you do with an enemy in the field? What are we doing now? You don't hide from your problems, you confront them. That's how you beat them.'

Shell-shocked as he was, Abbott knew Burton was making sense. Briefly, he wondered why he and Burton had never bonded before, but then remembered that he hadn't bonded with any of the crew. That was just him. The way he was. But although Abbott had always known that Burton was a good guy and a good man to have at your side, he was now beginning to wonder if he might also be a good mate.

'You know that Stone *wanted* us to chase after him, don't you?' said Burton as they drove, cutting a furrow into the road, kicking up sand and dust and dirt.

'Yeah, of course I know,' replied Abbott. 'And Stone knows I know. Everything that's happened since I came to Baghdad, maybe even before, all of it was set up. All of it staged to bring us to this moment.'

'And that fact doesn't bother you? That you're playing right into his hands, you're playing the enemy's game for him? And as for right now,' he pointed out, 'they're going to see us coming up on them, Abbott.'

'Yeah,' replied Abbott. He had been thinking the same thing. He grinned. 'Not exactly the kind of clandestine incursion we're used to, eh?'

'This isn't the way we like to do things, Abbott,' said Burton, 'not in SF.'

'It's my only option,' replied Abbott. 'It's the only thing I know how to do. The best time to recover Nathan is out in the open.'

'Well, you're in luck, because there they are,' said Burton. He pointed through the windscreen, which was covered in a layer of dirt, to where, in the distance, there were two pinpricks: the two Executive Alliance Group lorries, just as described by Potter: a pair of shonky old army trucks.

In one of those was Nathan.

The thought came to him. *I'm coming for you, son.*

It was followed by another one that he pushed away: *Maybe Guy Stone deserves his revenge.*

Ahead of them the old crocks were motoring, rocking on old springs across uneven ground but going fast, drivers pushing them to the limit.

Would they have spotted the Land Cruiser in their rear-view? Would they be concerned about it if they had? After all, they'd be armed to the teeth. Abbott didn't know any of the guys in either of those trucks, but he knew the type. He only had to look in the mirror for that. Give them a gun and an objective and there was nothing on earth that would stop them achieving it. They said that special forces don't scare easy, but that was false. They didn't scare at all.

* * *

'Hold it steady,' Abbott instructed Burton as they closed the gap. He reached for Burton's AK-47, meeting the other man's eyes and receiving a nod of consent in return. Now was the time. Now or never. Time for contact.

He thumbed the window down and leaned out. Grateful for the sunglasses protecting his eyes, he steadied himself on the sill of the door, getting his visuals sorted. As ever, he felt that familiar surge of adrenalin, a sense of stepping into his comfort zone. Peace at war.

He put his cheek to the stock, looked along the sites. Better to put a bullet in the engine block, but he was at the wrong end for that. It would have to be the tyres.

Steady now.

Steady.

The Land Cruiser rattled over the uneven road surface, ahead, the trucks were doing the same. Abbott was whipped by stones and dirt, his face being blasted by it. Trying to find his moment of calm within the maelstrom. Trying to go beyond it. He squeezed the trigger, firing a short burst just as the truck jinked. Rounds tore into the bodywork but none found their mark.

At the same time, Abbott saw barrels of AKs appear from within the tarp of the truck. Leaning out were Executive Alliance Group guys wearing combat vests familiar from the invasion at Mahlouthi's villa, their eyes protected by goggles.

'Contact,' said Abbott unnecessarily. 'Contact, contact, contact.'

'Roger that,' replied Burton, and he wrenched the wheel to the right, leaving Abbott's side clear for him to return fire. Conscious of Nathan but needing not to sustain hits, Abbott fired three short bursts along the skirt of the truck, hoping to send the shooters diving for cover. Instead, they returned fire.

'Christ,' spat Burton as rounds spanged into the Land Cruiser. Abbott steeled himself for a critical hit but, like him, they were finding the aim tricky. Still, Burton was in no mood to give them a second chance. He slammed on the brakes, yanked the wheel to the left and fell in beside the truck.

And now Abbott saw a face in the rear of the truck. Nathan. In almost the same instant he had disappeared from view once more, gone in a blur of hostile faces and tangled limbs. The whole moment had lasted just a fraction of a second but their eyes had met and Abbott prayed that Nathan had recognised him, that he knew salvation was close at hand.

I'm coming for you. Just hang on, Nathan.

Now Abbott saw another guy. This bloke didn't wear a combat vest, but he had a goatee beard, and at once Abbott knew that he was looking at Marsh, the famous second-in-command; the man who was probably responsible for meeting Nathan on the night of his disappearance. Marsh saw him, too. Their stares locked, but instead of defiance, Abbott saw something else. A shadow that crossed Marsh's face. His eyes dropped and he withdrew.

Once more, the combat vests opened fire. Abbott responded. At the same time, the driver swerved, as fully aware as Abbott that if they took a critical hit then they were stuffed. Mission over. Stranded in the desert.

'Bring it over to the other side,' Abbott called to Burton, let me get a clear shot.'

'And what the fuck are you expecting to shoot at?' shouted Burton, over the noise of the open window.

'Get up ahead. I'll take out the engine block.'

'Yeah, and that's if the blokes upfront don't take you out first.'

'What else do you suggest?' asked Abbott. The two men exchanged a look.

'All right, mate, it's your show,' said Burton. He dropped a gear, banged on the throttle, and the Land Cruiser shot forward. The guys in the truck opened fire. Burton held his nerve as Abbott returned fire. The butt of the AK thumped against his shoulder, a reassuringly familiar sensation as he pumped more rounds into the truck. Muzzles flashed in response, the truck swerving as the driver panicked.

And then they saw it. Up ahead, on the horizon at about ten o'clock, were three choppers: two Apaches and a Chinook.

'Jesus,' yelled Burton, grinning despite himself. 'Looks like Condoleezza Rice is arriving.'

CHAPTER 53

'Oh, that's bad,' said Abbott. He had pulled back into the cab, dipped his head to look beneath the glare of the sun. 'That's really bad.'

Neither of them needed to explain why. After all, they were two blokes in Mahlouthi's Land Cruiser. They'd just been exchanging fire with an army truck upfront. From a newcomer's point of view there could be little doubt who was the friendly and who was the hostile in this situation. What's more, they both knew that the security personnel upfront could make contact with the coalition forces in the choppers. *Great to see you guys. We're under attack. Any chance of an assist?*

And maybe that's exactly what they'd done. Or perhaps the airborne convoy had simply seen what looked like an attempted act of banditry in progress and decided to lend a hand anyway. As they watched, one of the Apaches tilted and peeled away from the others, adjusting its direction of travel. Heading for the road.

'Oh, fuck,' said Burton. 'Maybe I should pull up. Let them know we're not a threat.'

'No. Fuck that. We're already a threat. Keep us a moving target.' At the same time, he was reaching for the radio mic, but knowing the situation was hopeless. There was no time.

Suddenly, there was the Apache, its nose tilted. The guns started up, strafing the ground around the Land Cruiser.

Grunting, Burton fought with the wheel, both of them looking up and into the rear-view, squinting and trying to find the position of the Apache. There – there it was. Its tail swung round in a wide, lazy arc as the pilot lined them up once more.

Burton had realised that the better strategy was to stay near the trucks ahead but it was too late to rectify that. Now they were out in the open, sitting ducks, target practice. In a last-ditch attempt to try and prove that they weren't bandits, Abbott shoved himself through the passenger window, waving, trying to show the occupants of the Apache his Western face. But if they saw, then it was too late.

'Abort,' he was shrieking, waving his arms. 'Abort, abort.' He saw figures behind the cockpit shield. Anonymous outlines. Did they see him?

No.

The Apache pilot opened up again. The chopper's guns chattered, rounds churning up the ground in front of the speeding Toyota, kicking up giant divots like pillars of sand through which they had to pass. And Abbott watched, time coming to rest, as though played out in slow motion, as the twin lines of rounds burned a line in the sand, making their way towards them.

His mouth dropped open. He watched death approach. Beyond the chopper he saw the truck containing Nathan obscured by a cloud of dust.

And then it was as though they had been attacked by a giant can opener and their world tilted. The tyres blew, the front of the vehicle dipped, the bonnet was churned by firepower and the Land Cruiser flipped, rolling end over end.

The last thing that Abbott saw before blackness claimed him was Burton, his head whipping back and forth, smashing against the steering wheel at a terrible, unnatural angle.

* * *

The two lorries drew to a halt a couple of hundred yards away from the crumpled Land Cruiser. In the second lorry, Stone thanked the chopper team for helping them out. 'We thought we were dead meat there,' he told them.

'Happy to lend a hand,' replied the Apache pilot.

Stone looked over to where the Chinook was just passing by, bound for Baghdad. 'VIP visitor?' he asked.

'You might say that,' replied the Apache pilot evasively. 'You have a good day, sir.'

'You too, mate,' said Stone. 'You too.'

Next he looked around to check that Nathan was unharmed. Their truck was a bit torn up but otherwise OK. At the same time he nodded a thank you to the three EAG personnel guarding him for having acquitted themselves well in the firefight.

'Is everybody OK? Nobody hit? You did good,' he told them.

Two of them were new guys, and they both nodded back with smiles, pleased to have earned the boss's compliments. The third was an older hand who merely stared back, his eyes hidden by his sunglasses, his features betraying nothing and therefore everything.

'Not every hostile is a towel-head,' Stone reminded him.

The guy cleared his throat, spat out the back of the truck, shrugged. Stone awarded him a look that he held an extra beat or so. A muscle in his neck jumped. Then he turned back and thumbed the radio to speak to his second-in-command, Marsh, in the leading truck.

'Just hold fire until the coast is clear,' he said.

'Roger that,' came the reply.

They waited until the Apaches and the Chinook were out of sight. 'OK, go for it,' ordered Stone, and then both lorries turned, leaving plumes of dust in their wake as they returned to the site of the wrecked Land Cruiser.

It sat there, beached, a door hanging open and no sign of movement from within.

Stone jumped down from the truck. He drew his sidearm, held it aimed as he approached the Land Cruiser cautiously.

He stopped, glancing back at the trucks where Nathan had been allowed to come to the tailgate, to see flanked by two of his men, the two new guys.

Good. He wanted the kid to see this.

He ushered Marsh forward. As Stone provided cover, Marsh went to his knees and checked for signs of life. Stone turned his head to see Nathan watching from the rear of the truck, concern imprinted onto his features.

'This one's dead,' said Marsh, his voice carrying, made flat by the expanse of sand in which they stood.

Stone watched Nathan for a reaction. Saw the distress there and let it ferment. After all, wasn't this what had been done to him? To him and Jeremy? He let the moment hang before saying to Marsh, 'And Abbott?'

The second-in-command had straightened from having examined Burton, wiping blood on his field trousers as he moved around the Land Cruiser and bent to check through the passenger door.

Stone, with a smile on his face, his eyes hidden by the shades, watched Nathan, enjoying the moment.

'He's alive,' said Marsh.

'Good,' said Stone. 'Put him in the back of the truck. Not with his kid.' He looked at Nathan. Grinned. 'Put him in the other truck.'

CHAPTER 54

The Executive Alliance Group compound just outside Kirkuk was formed from the bones of an old, disused farmstead, complete with a low, flat-roofed main building and a series of other outbuildings and stable blocks. It commanded a large area to itself, and with acres of empty desert surrounding it on all sides it was nothing if not private, while, thanks to a sandstone wall that ran around the perimeter, typical of the area, it was secure. The site had not been part of the old Hercules set-up when Stone had performed his takeover; instead he had overseen the acquisition himself, thinking of it as a new addition to what he liked to refer to as 'the group' and sometimes as 'the brand', depending on how fancy he was feeling. He considered the Kirkuk compound something of a bolthole, an outer outpost, and although when he had first arranged for its purchase the plan to take his revenge on Abbott and Mahlouthi had been but a glint in his eye, he had always assumed that it would one day come in handy.

Today was that day.

As the two trucks approached, Marsh and another man jumped from the leading lorry to unlock the compound gates. The trucks drew up inside, men spilled out of the rear and the air was filled with a sense of industry as they set about establishing their base.

There was another feeling among them. Something more difficult to pinpoint. An uncertainty – a feeling that this train was only just on the track. Sure enough, the men were looking to Marsh. He was the only one among them who could be said to have Stone's ear, and they needed him to guide them, to put their minds at rest and reassure them that their leader was still firing on all cylinders, because on that score, they had their doubts: this, after all, was a guy who had faked his own death for reasons that had not been adequately explained.

Marsh did right by his men, and as they were engaged in establishing their new base, he requested an audience with the boss. The two men moved away from the group, Marsh waiting until they were out of earshot before he spoke. 'Boss?'

Stone turned, sensing something amiss, resisting the urge to let out a huge sigh, knowing what was coming. He lifted his sunglasses up to perch them on his head, squinting in the sun to give Marsh his full attention. 'Yes?'

'It's the lads,' started Marsh, and Stone, not for the first time, rued the fact that he wasn't able to carry out his plans unaided. He had only the very best men from the old Executive Alliance Group operation, as well as recruiting a few key personnel. But the trouble with good men was that while they may have been excellent warriors, they had the annoying habit of thinking for themselves.

'Yes.' Stone smiled. 'What about them? Correct me if I'm wrong, didn't I just give the green light for a pay rise? What is it now? Television and a record player in the common room?'

'Yeah, you did, mate, but even so ...'

Stone didn't especially like his second-in-command referring to him as 'mate'. But it was his bed and he'd made it. None of these guys would be following him if they thought they were back in the army, no matter how much he paid them. For the time being, at least until this phase of his operation was complete, until his honour was satisfied, he was going to have to put up with it, and since he was also self-aware enough to realise that he was not a leader who had what you might call the common touch, he knew that he needed his consigliere, in this case Marsh, to act as a go-between.

Marsh looked uncomfortable. His dust-streaked face was mainly hidden by shades, and he fiddled with the toggle of the boonie hat he wore. 'The thing is, things are getting a bit irregular. Like, a couple of the lads were saying that it was obvious Mahlouthi wasn't a high-value target. And these new guys you've brought in. How come they have the run of the place? Seem to enjoy special privileges, like. Are you sure you did all the checks for that lot?' Marsh asked. 'Because they seem a bit dodgy to me.'

Stone had, of course, done the checks. And those checks had told him exactly what he wanted, no needed to know: which was that all three men – five to begin with, two of them had been killed during the attack on Mahlouthi's villa – were of what you might call low character. Drummed out of the army for a variety of reasons, mostly involving the gratuitous use of force. Men who could be easily paid to not ask questions. As a result, they did indeed form an unofficial inner circle.

'Things are getting a bit irregular,' repeated Marsh. He lowered his voice. 'We go after Mahlouthi. Next thing you know, we're having to up sticks and leave the Green Zone, just like that. Then we're being fired upon by two guys who look like friendlies.'

The whole time, Stone worked to keep his face neutral. He held up a hand. 'OK, listen, Marsh, mate, you've got to ask the guys to trust me, OK? I needed to bring in some muscle. The new blokes,' he pointed, 'you're right, they're not quite up to our standard and that's why it's fine with me if they keep themselves to themselves and don't mingle; who gives a fuck about that? Do you? Do I? No. I just needed some extra muscle.'

Marsh lent even closer. 'But, mate, if they're not quite up to snuff, why did you ask them to do the Mahlouthi job? Our lads would have loved that job.'

'Come again? Because a moment ago you said they were getting a bit antsy about being fired upon in the desert. And that Mahlouthi wasn't a high-value target. Make up your mind, eh?' He heard the irritation come through in his voice and tried to damp down on it.

'I didn't mean—' returned Marsh, awkwardly. 'This is not about the contact. We absolutely love a bit of that, every man here. It's about who we're fighting and why.'

'Well, on that score, you'll just have to trust that there are certain cards I have to keep close to my chest. All will be revealed, you have my word, but for the time being, all that trust that I have built up with you and with the guys, some of whom I kept on, some of whom I employed – and all of whom I pay very fucking well indeed – I need that trust now. I think I've done enough to earn it. OK?'

He tilted his chin, challenging his number two, and when Marsh nodded, saying, 'Yes, mate', he reached to clap him on the shoulders. 'OK?' He said, needing that extra confirmation.

'OK,' agreed Marsh.

Stone turned and walked away, and Marsh watched him go, unconvinced. Something about the boss's expansive gestures didn't sit right by him. And yes, even though they had just come out the other side of a firefight, there was also the fact that Stone's hands had been trembling.

Something wasn't right, Marsh knew. Not right at all.

CHAPTER 55

Abbott had briefly recovered consciousness on the drive. He remembered seeing a burned-out coalition troop carrier with the words 'Dave Angel Eco Warrior' spray-painted on the front and having no idea what the words meant. And then he drifted off again, the mists reclaiming him, taking him back into their world.

And then he was released once again. More time had passed. He was no longer in transit, for one thing. Slowly, events returned to him. The chase across the desert. An Apache and its mounted guns. Burton's face making terrible, crunching contact with the steering wheel. The burned-out troop carrier. After that, nothing.

Where was he now? The answer was in some kind of ... Well, it appeared to be a small wooden cell. He pulled himself into a seated position, boots scraping on the stone floor, noting the straw underfoot.

He was in a stable block, locked in one of the stables. A small enclosed space with wooden partitions either side. As his eyes continued upwards, what he saw was the fact that the door to the bay had been secured with cable ties, while metal container sides had been slung over the top of the bay, again secured with cable ties in order to stop whoever was inside from climbing over the top.

'Whoever was inside' being him.

It was a pretty makeshift-looking prison, but effective – at least in the short term. He wasn't handcuffed or secured, nor had he been injured. He felt bruising at his ribs but otherwise seemed OK. Gingerly, he touched fingertips to his face, feeling grazes there. Another one on his forehead. His eye, too, was tender when he touched it. Still, nothing permanent.

Using the partition wall for support, he pulled himself to his feet in order to get an idea if he had sustained any other injuries, testing his weight first on one leg and then the other, ensuring he had feeling in his fingertips and arms, moving his head gently at first and then a little more vigorously left, right, up, down.

Looking through the secure door of the bay, he could see the rest of the stables. At the far end was a door, ajar, that seemed to lead out into a courtyard, and from there he could hear voices and movement.

Now he moved to the other side of the cell, two paces away. There on tiptoes, he was able to look through a barred section and into what turned out to be the bay next door.

Nathan.

The boy was sitting against the far wall of his own stable, which had been secured similarly to Abbott's. He sat with his legs pulled up, his arms over his knees and his head hanging low. Nathan was in his mid-twenties and yet Abbott had never seen him looking more like a frightened child.

'Nathan,' Abbott called, keeping his voice low. He looked to his left from where he could see out into the stable, but there was no sign of anyone. Could it be that Stone and co. had underestimated how quickly Abbott might regain consciousness? Maybe he had won himself some precious minutes. His hand went to one of the cable ties. Given time, he could probably gnaw through that. Maybe. Those things were tough.

'Nathan,' he repeated. 'Nathan, can you hear me? It's ...' He found himself struggling over the word as though just by saying it he was claiming to be something he wasn't but he said it anyway. 'Dad.'

Again, a glance out into the stable. Still no sign of anyone.

Very slowly, Nathan raised his head. His eyes took a while to focus on Abbott although Abbott was not sure if they did indeed focus at all. It was a look he'd seen before on squaddies in Iraq and Northern Ireland. Nothing behind the eyes. PTSD they called it nowadays. Back in the old days they called it the thousand-yard stare. Or shell shock.

Abbott's heart sunk to see that same look in his son's eyes now: just vacant space where once there had been humour and love and defiance and every other semblance of humanity awarded to a boy with spirit.

There was, however, just a tiny flick of recognition. That alone was enough to give Abbott hope.

'Nathan,' he repeated, pressing his face to the bars of the opening and wincing, 'can you hear me?'

'Dad,' Nathan said distantly, talking to his knees, as though talking about Abbott rather than addressing him. 'He told me you were in trouble. I came for you.'

The words seared Abbott's heart. Of course he had always known that Stone had used false pretences in order to trap Nathan. And, of course, it was likely they would have involved him. To hear it spoken, though – to know for sure – was different still. And he thought of Nathan, swallowing all of Stone's lies, believing that Stone and his father had been great comrades, when, in fact, nothing could have been further from the truth. 'I came for you,' he repeated, and again his voice had a spaced-out dreamy tone.

Still on tiptoe, Abbott reached his arms through the bars. 'Nathan,' he said, 'come here, son.' Trying to be a dad now. Tragically too late, but still. 'Let me hold you.'

Nathan stood and though he moved on autopilot, he did at least go to Abbott, allowing himself to be held in his arms, Abbott knowing that this was the first time since Nathan was little that he had held him. And all those years in between had been the booze and his demons and death, his fights with Fi – all of which had come together to stop him being the father that he found in himself now.

'I'm sorry, son,' he said, tasting the wetness in his mouth. 'I'm so, so, sorry. Things will change. I've changed. I promise you that things will be different from now on.'

On the other side of the partition, Nathan began to sag but Abbott held him upright, the muscles in his arms bulging. Now that he had hold of his boy, he didn't want to let him go.

'They told me you were in trouble,' repeated Nathan, the wooziness still in his voice.

Again, Nathan's body seemed to relax and for a moment Abbott thought he was about to fall away, and it occurred to Abbott that Nathan might go into shock. 'OK, OK, Nathan,' he said gently, 'I want you to listen very carefully. I need you to sit down, OK? Just sit down, take deep breaths, listen to my voice and do what I say. Is that clear?'

As he spoke, Abbott's eyes went again to the stable outside. Something caught his eye. Something he hadn't seen before, that made the words of comfort die in his throat and instead his fingers went to the tightly wound cable ties holding the doors in place.

What he'd seen was a petrol canister.

CHAPTER 56

'Hello again, mate. How are you doing?'

Stone had entered the stable block and now stood before Abbott's stable. He wore a faded black polo shirt open at the neck, his circular dog tags visible. Funny. He'd always worn them. Abbott had torn his off the day he left the army.

The two men regarded one another in silence. They had trained together. They had served and fought together. And now one was a prisoner, the other his captor, and yet there was no triumph or vindication present, and as Stone stood looking impassively through the bars of the makeshift cell at Abbott, his eyes betrayed nothing. There was no sense of a man who felt his plan had finally come together. He looked tired but beyond that was almost as vacant as Nathan.

What was the expression? Before you set out for revenge, first dig two graves.

'They'll be coming for you,' said Abbott. 'It's over. The whole jig is up. They're bringing in an SF team for you.'

'Yeah,' Stone said, 'but it ain't in place yet, is it? I've got time.'

'You're wanted for murder.'

Stone shrugged, almost sadly. 'Yeah, among other things.'

'Well, in that case, you don't have time for games. You need to put as much distance between them and you as possible. I mean, what were you hoping for after this? You'd just kill me and then go back to normal? You won't. You might have me here, but the plan hasn't worked. You've been exposed. You can't just move three hours down the road and expect it all to go away.'

'All I need is the time it takes for you to watch your son die. That's all I want. Beyond that—' he shrugged again. 'I don't care. This is about doing to you what you did to me. An eye for an eye.'

Abbott nodded. Perhaps he would have been the same himself. Perhaps. 'You know, what you've done, it's – I admire it. You thought like a soldier, a military man. You've done way more than I ever could have done and that's because you're a better soldier than me.'

'A better father, too, I guess,' said Stone, and for the first time he showed emotion. A smile that crept slowly across him. And it was as though he was looking deep into Abbott's soul, somehow able to study the shit-thoughts inside.

'Yeah, a better father.' Stone turned suddenly, walking slowly off to the side, at the same time saying over his shoulder, 'I needed you here, Abbott. I needed you and Mahlouthi both to know what you'd done. I wanted both of you to die with regret and pain and sorrow in your hearts. Because you're right, ain't you, Monk. You couldn't have done what I done. Like how would you have reacted, Abbott, if I'd killed Nathan on Mahlouthi's orders? We both know, don't we? You'd have disappeared into a bottle. And in your cups you'd have dreamed of doing what I done, but you wouldn't have done it, would you? You wouldn't have done it because you wouldn't have been able to find your way out of the bottle. Makes me fucking laugh, this does. The icing on the cake, you might say. You're standing there hating me, but really deep down you admire me, you fucking envy me, because you know that my way is the military way. And you know that makes me a better soldier than you.' He paused. 'And yeah – a better father.'

Abbott looked at him, wondering whether to say what was on the tip of his tongue but deciding against. 'OK, fair enough, maybe I am a little bit in awe. I mean, fair play, mate, you got me where you wanted me: behind bars. Mahlouthi's insides all over Baghdad. But at what cost? You're finished.'

'Yeah, finished here in Baghdad. That's right. Looks like I'll just have to go home, dry my tears on all my money. You may not have heard, but I've been bought out, mate.'

'Oh yeah? Who?'

'You'll know the firm. Hexagon Security.'

Abbott felt his jaw tighten. His shoulders rose and fell.

'Yeah, I've heard of them,' he said, the irony not lost on him. 'OK, so you've got a bit of money in the bank. They'll get you. They'll catch up with you.'

'For what?'

'If not the murder of Mowles, then corruption charges.'

'Badger? Good luck with proving I was even in Mexico at the time. As for the corruption? When SF stage their raid on Executive Alliance Group, they'll find all the paperwork burned, I'm afraid. And good luck making anything stick without a paper trail. Oh, and their star witness for the prosecution – well, there are two problems there: first, he was my son. Second, you killed him.'

There's also the body-cam footage, thought Abbott.

But now wasn't the time to say, because Stone had returned holding something that he set down.

It was the petrol can.

Abbott swallowed. He glanced through the bars at Nathan, who sat motionless. 'OK, fair enough. I can get with all of that. I understand. But why kill Badger?'

'Badger didn't like the idea of taking Nathan. He was fine with the idea of killing Mahlouthi, of course, not so keen on involving you. Even when I told him the reason why. So he had to go, made to look like an accident. After that, why not kill myself off – put myself out of the frame before the intelligence agencies got to me, so I could deal with you and Mahlouthi? The thought of you running around like Nancy Drew was just the icing on the cake, really.' He paused. His eyes were on the petrol can. His hands were in his pockets and he was fiddling with something. 'And now it's over. Or soon it will be. And I'm going to get out of this fucking country for good. I'm going to go back home. Settle down, crack open a beer and lie back knowing that I did my bit for my country, I satisfied personal honour, and I made a packet into the bargain.'

'All the while being dead?'

'Nah, I'm going to reappear, aren't I, after taking time out to find myself on a solo hiking tour. What? You all thought I was dead? God, I'm so sorry for all the trouble I've caused.'

Abbott was trying to control his breathing, trying not to think about that petrol can. 'So how come you're not happy, then?' he asked Stone.

All of a sudden, Abbott regretted the question, knew that he should have been cleverer than to push Stone's buttons this way because when Stone looked up, his eyes glistened and his next words were growled.

'Because the only thing wrong with that picture is that Jeremy isn't here to share it with me. He can't share in the fortune that he helped create.'

From his pocket he pulled a Zippo. In the next instant he had torn the cap off the petrol can, advanced on Nathan's stable and had begun spraying the fuel inside.

CHAPTER 57

'No,' cried Abbott and he thought he remembered from some-where that simply saying the word 'no' was supposed to have a profound effect on a human, any human, so conditioned are we to it. But that was clearly bullshit because Stone kept on slinging the petrol can back and forth, liquid death spraying inside Nathan's stable, splattering to the floor. 'Stone, no,' repeated Abbott, 'This isn't you. This isn't the way we do things.'

Stone ignored him. Kept slinging. He had taken out his phone, as though wanting to film what was about to happen. Abbott changed tack. 'Come on,' he said, hearing the desperation in his own voice, 'be a man about it. Come on. You're not going to burn a kid to death, are you? Put a bullet in me.'

Stone had finished. He slung the petrol can which landed a few feet away skidding along the stones behind him. 'And leave him alive so that he can come after me?'

'Then put a bullet in us both.' Abbott's voice was rising. 'Just not this way, Stone. Not like this. You're not a monster.' But at the same time he wondered, because maybe their way of life made monsters of them all, just in different ways. Could he have found it in himself to act in a way that was utterly inhumane, repugnant to the man in the street? Answer: yes – yes he could. 'I can help you,' he tried instead. 'Let me help you.'

'Help me by shutting up,' said Stone. He raised the bronze Zippo lighter.

No, no.

Abbott glanced to his left, through the bar of the partition to Nathan. His reaction to the fuel had been to shrink into one corner, but when Abbott found his gaze there was no fear or alarm in his eyes.

'Nathan,' said Abbott uselessly. Then something occurred to him. His guys, the other Executive Alliance Group personnel. They couldn't be down with this. No way. Stone had to be a lone actor on this one.

He thought fast. 'Are you sure this is about revenge?' he said quickly, needing to keep Stone talking. 'Are you sure this is about revenge for Jeremy?'

And it was as though Stone knew where Abbott was headed. 'Get his name out of your mouth.'

'Because he was doing your dirty work for you, wasn't he? That's why he was there. Maybe even why he was in Baghdad.'

'We were working together.'

'Oh yeah? And whose idea was that, then? His? No, I don't think so somehow. You blame me, don't you, for bringing him out of the Green Zone that night. But what about yourself? What about the reason he was in Baghdad in the first place? Are you sure all of this is really revenge for Jeremy, or is it for you – to help you with your guilt? You let him down, didn't you?'

'Well, you should know all about that.'

The Zippo was aloft. Stone's eyes burned. There was no way back.

'Help!' called Abbott at the top of his voice, raising his chin as if to shout it through the stable ceiling. 'For Christ's sake, *help*!'

At the same time he saw a crack of light at the door, and saw a figure move through. A figure with a knife that came up behind Stone quickly. Was it the second-in-command? Marsh? Abbott couldn't tell, and anyway, Stone had raised his Zippo, flicked it so that the flame flared, and his eyes were on Abbott as he pulled back his arm. Suddenly he sensed movement, realised that somebody was behind him. He turned to see the man who was about to attack him. And, for the first time, so did Abbott.

It was Burton. He was covered in blood. His beard was matted with it, his teeth streaked with it. His eyes were wild, and his knife was held high in no regulation attack formation that Abbott knew of.

'*You fucked me*,' he screamed at Stone.

Stone dropped his phone at the same time as his arm slapped to his side, reaching for his sidearm. But he was too late and it was all he could do to block the downward slice of Burton's combat knife. He caught Burton's arm, the two stood for a moment, grappling, and at the same time the lit Zippo dropped. Stone saw it on the ground and kicked it towards the bay.

Whump.

The bay went up.

'*Nathan*,' screamed Abbott, pushing himself to the partition wall. Through the flames he saw Nathan gaze almost quizzically at the fire that somehow seemed to have appeared in the cell, that now gathered itself around him.

'Burton,' Abbott was screaming, 'Burton, it's Nathan, he needs help.'

But Burton was otherwise engaged. He and Stone were locked in battle, the pair of them had wrestled each other to the floor and were rolling, each trying to get the upper hand like kids fighting on the school field at lunch break – only with death on their minds.

In desperation, Abbott began yanking at the cage door. The cable ties held fast. He leaped, fingers going through the metal of the cage side overhead, trying to use his weight to shift it, and when that didn't work, shoving at it. As he dropped back to the ground, flames licked through the partition bars. At the same time, Nathan next door began screaming, the agony of the fire finally dragging him from his trance-like state.

And then Abbott saw it – the cable ties were melting in the heat. With an extra burst of strength, he began yanking at the door, again and again, feeling flames singe first his arms and then hair, but still yanking, back and forth, back and forth, trying to work at the cable ties, trying to help them on their way as the heat gave them elasticity, the gap between the door and its frame growing slightly wider, slightly wider, feeling hairs at his eyelids and eyebrows burn, feeling the flames lick his hair until, finally, the cables gave, his door opened and he was rushing out, wrenching on Nathan's door again and again, back and forth, back and forth, until those cables snapped too, and he was yanking open the door, ignoring the fire that leaped to embrace him like an old friend and reaching out to Nathan, grabbing him, pulling him from the bay to safety.

He used his own body to smother the flames that lay in patches on Nathan's clothes, saying, 'Nathan? Nathan, can you hear me? Can you hear me?'

Nathan's skin was blackened. In places it was as though it had been flayed away, revealing striations of red flesh beneath.

Abbott went to put his hands to his face then stopped himself, seeing Nathan's face properly for the first time. His eyebrows and eyelids had been burned away. His lips were black, as though they had shrunk over his teeth. There were blisters and bubbles on his eyelids and small plumes of smoke came off them, as though they were still burning inside. He put his cheek to the boy's mouth, trying to feel for breath, checked for a pulse. Nathan was alive. Just. Alive but unconscious, barely hanging on.

And now Abbott looked over, seeing an epic struggle between Burton and Stone – Stone had the advantage. There was a sound like tools being dropped and the combat knife slid across the flags. Burton saw it, knowing it was his only chance, but Stone pressed home the advantage, bucking his hips and grasping Burton in a scissor hold with his legs.

Most likely, Burton had sustained internal injuries during the crash, for he was instantly in agony, his shoulders went back and his arms were suddenly useless to him amid an onslaught of pain. Stone squeezed his thighs together and wrenched to the side, bringing Burton to the ground and twisting so that he came out on top.

He managed to free his sidearm from its holster. But Abbott had seen, had launched himself from where he knelt with Nathan. As he dived over, he grabbed the petrol can, swinging it at Stone and catching him on the head with a sound that was almost comical, like a cartoon, spraying Stone with fuel at the same time. Stone, rising, was unsteady for a moment, blood already coursing down his temple as Abbott crashed to the floor on the other side of him. Abbott twisted in time to see Stone aim blindly, Abbott bringing the fuel tank to bear just as Stone's finger whitened on the trigger.

The round spanged off, ricocheting somewhere in the stable block. Abbott gave him no chance to fire twice, throwing the petrol canister, following it up by barrelling into Stone, who pinwheeled backwards.

And was suddenly on fire.

He'd been too close to the blazing bays; the greedy flames reached out and took him. But even now his gun arm was coming up, his mouth open, tendrils of smoke escaping, and still his last final urge was to kill Abbott. The gun came up, and Abbott thought of Nathan.

Abbott barrelled forward. He caught Stone in the midriff, propelling him backwards so that Stone's feet came out from under him and the two of them fell, Abbott landing on top of Stone in the stable. Around them the fire raged, and Stone writhed, trying to keep his head out of the flames, but Abbott's hands were around his throat, Abbott screaming with the effort, shrieking with the agony of the fire on his hands as he held Stone's head in the fire listening to his agonised shrieking.

Stone was still screaming, his mouth open, revealing a black hollow void beneath as though the fire was eating him from the inside out. Still Abbott's hands constricted around his throat until, suddenly, he felt a hand at his back and then was pulled backwards and clear of the flaming stable bay by a panting, blood-covered Burton.

'I think he's dead, mate,' said Burton.

CHAPTER 58

In the next instant, Abbott skidded over to where Nathan lay. Burton, moving painfully, was at his heel.

'We need to get him to hospital,' said Abbott. 'Come on.' He looked at Burton. 'How the fuck did you get here?'

'In the Toyota at thirty miles an hour the whole way,' winced Burton. 'That is one very fucked vehicle, mate.'

In moments, Burton and Abbott were hobbling out of the stables. Abbott burned, Burton injured, but both of them in better shape than Nathan. Supported in between them, he was still out cold, head lolling on his chest, his clothes like smoking beggars' rags, charred and burned from the fire that behind them began to consume the entire stable building.

In the compound they stopped for a second blinking in bright sunlight. 'There,' called Burton, and he began to make his way over to the truck. At the same time, the door to the main building burst open and two men came running out, both with assault rifles plugged into their shoulders. '*Don't fucking move.*'

Behind them hurried a third man. 'No,' he called. 'Let them go.'

'What do you mean, Marsh?' said one of the men over his shoulder, putting his cheek back to the stock of the AR.

Standing in the door of the main house, Marsh was looking carefully at Abbott, Burton and Nathan. His eyes travelled to the stable block, ablaze, and then back again, as though divining what had happened. That Stone was no longer part of the equation. Behind him, three more men poured out into the courtyard, 'Where's Stone?' one of the men was saying.

'He's not here, and if you think I'm giving the order to open fire on friendlies without him, you can think again,' replied Marsh. He hoisted his AR, finger coming close to the trigger guard.

'This is the security we went up against at Mahlouthi's villa,' said one of the gun-toting trio. Like his two pals, he wore a black combat vest.

'Where is he?' asked Marsh, ignoring the guy. 'Where's Stone?' Behind him appeared more Executive Alliance Group men, fanning out behind them. These guys had stripped down to T-shirts or were bare-chested, but they were all armed. Abbott couldn't help but notice how they kept themselves apart from the three combat-vest guys.

'Your boss is dead,' Burton called across. All eyes went to him, seeing the state of him. Marsh in particular.

'I thought you were dead,' he said across the courtyard. 'I'm sorry. I would never have left you there if I'd known. I genuinely didn't feel a pulse, mate.'

Abbott wondered how Burton was going to take it, but the big man cracked a grin. 'I'm as tough as that Land Cruiser out there.' He gesticulated beyond the gates. 'Both presumed dead but still very much alive.'

Meanwhile, the combat-vest crew were getting antsy, making eyes at one another as they crouched, as though each was daring the others to make the first move. Abbott felt the barrels of the rifles upon them, knowing they were more than willing to open fire – gagging for it, in fact.

'This one killed Blakey,' said one of them, gesturing at Abbott.

'It was combat,' said Marsh. 'Blakey would have taken him out, if he could have done.'

'Fact is, they were security for Mahlouthi,' said another.

'So they were just doing their job,' said Marsh. 'Was your mission to kill them?'

'No.'

'There you go. Just doing their job.'

'Well, I'm just doing mine. And we brought them in here as prisoners, we're not letting them go until I get the go-ahead from the boss.'

'Didn't you hear, you idiot? Boss is dead,' said Marsh, and as though to explain his own lack of sadness, added, 'he wasn't playing with a full deck.'

'He'd lost it,' confirmed Abbott. He felt the attention of the men go to him. 'I'm telling you. Completely lost the plot. He tried to burn us alive. All we did was save ourselves.'

Marsh seemed to be considering.

'OK, then, you can go. Take a truck.'

They began to make their way towards one of the trucks but a voice from one of the three combat vests stopped them. 'No way. No way are they going anywhere.'

'Stand down, soldier,' said Marsh. 'And that's an order.'

'You don't give me orders.'

Marsh turned to one of the men behind him. 'Go check in the stables. If you can, see if he's telling the truth.'

'I can't stay here for much longer,' Abbott said to him. He shot Marsh imploring eyes, trying to appeal to his better nature. Hoping there was one. 'I need to get my son to hospital.'

'Just a moment.'

Seconds later the man reappeared. 'Fire needs putting out,' he said.

'We'll get to that,' replied Marsh testily. 'Let's start with whether there is a body in there, shall we?'

'Oh yeah, there's a body in there, all right.'

'And is the body him? Is it the boss?'

'Gotta say, I think it is. Either way, I didn't see him inside, did you?'

'And that's the way it goes, is it?' snapped combat vest. 'The guys who killed our boss – we let them go. Case closed.'

'They need to get the boy to the hospital.'

'And fast,' pressed Abbott.

'Nah, man, I'm not having this.'

'I said stand down,' repeated Marsh.

'No.'

Marsh took a deep breath. 'Lads,' was all he said, and the guns of the men behind him swung to cover the three men in combat vests. 'Drop your weapons.'

'You fucking pussy,' said one.

'Say that again, and I'll put a round in you just for the hell of it,' said Marsh. 'We're taking one to the hospital, might as well take two.' He returned his attention to Abbott and Burton, who were already taking advantage of the changed dynamic and had begun limping towards one of the trucks, carrying Nathan. Of the two, it was the one that had led the convoy, and escaped the battle unharmed.

'Is there a medic here?' called Abbott across to the men.

But Marsh had already moved after them, and was now bending down to Nathan. 'Closest you'll get is me.'

Abbott looked at him sharply. 'You're a paramedic?' he said. 'You know what you're doing?'

'No. But I've had some training,' said Marsh. He called across to his men for a first-aid kit, saying to Abbott, 'I can do my best for him until we get him to hospital,' he pulled a face, shook his head gravely, 'but I can tell you now that he needs expert medical attention fast, or he's going to die.'

Watched by the Executive Alliance Group crew, Abbott, Burton and Marsh loaded Nathan gently into the back of the lorry. Abbott clambered in beside him. Marsh, too. 'You OK to drive?' said Abbott to Burton.

'No,' shot back Burton, 'I am not fucking OK to drive. But if I can drive that fucked-up Land Cruiser, I can drive this.'

CHAPTER 59

Moments later, the truck was roaring into life and they were on their way. Abbott sat with his back against the side of the truck, with Nathan's head in his lap, taking some comfort from the fact that his son's chest rose and fell, and his eyelids would occasionally flicker.

'Mate, you're hurt,' said Marsh, 'you need to get these wounds dressed.'

Abbott shook him away when he tried to inspect the burns on the back of his hand, saying nothing but wanting the medic to concentrate on Nathan. 'All right,' said Marsh, 'but at least try to get some sleep.'

Abbott told himself that wasn't going to happen, but as he lay there, he began to feel himself phasing out. His head lolled. Into his mind came visions of Jeremy Robinson vainly hanging onto life as he died. A little boy on a riverbank. Tessa …

The bodies …

Suddenly, he jerked awake, realising that he hadn't checked on Nathan.

'He's hanging in there,' said Marsh gently. He removed a pair of scissors from his mouth to speak, carefully unrolling a bandage at the same time. He looked like you'd expect a medic to look. As for Nathan, Abbott moved to check for himself. The boy was still alive. Just. His heartbeat was faint, hardly even apparent under Abbott's fingertips. His pulse fluttered like the wings of a dying butterfly.

But he didn't have long. That much Abbott knew.

He sat back, lost in thought. He remembered something and reached into his pocket, pulled out a phone that he flipped open.

'Who are you calling?' asked Marsh.

'Nobody,' replied Abbott. 'This is Stone's phone. I grabbed it before we left the stables.'

'Stone's phone?' Something in Marsh's voice made Abbott look up. 'Hey, maybe you should give it here? Perhaps I'll know the pass code.' He made as if to reach over and take it.

'Or maybe I'll just hang onto it,' said Abbott, holding the phone away. His eyes were on Marsh, wondering about the change that seemed to have come over him.

'Of course,' covered Marsh. 'Yeah, of course, buddy. Whatever.'

Something occurred to Abbott. How long had he'd been dozing? 'Shouldn't we be in Kirkuk by now?' he said, and before Marsh could answer, he had scrabbled to the side of the truck and yanked up the tarpaulin in order to look outside.

No sign of Kirkuk. No sign of anything. He looked up to locate the sun, confirming his suspicion: they were not travelling towards Kirkuk. They were going in the wrong direction. They passed a burned-out coalition troop carrier. It had the words 'Dave Angel Eco Warrior' spray-painted on the front.

They were going back to Baghdad.

Now he pushed Stone's phone back into his pocket and leaped to the separator between the truck's cab and the back of the lorry, looking through the dirty glass to see that Burton was on the phone. He rapped on the window. 'Kirkuk,' he screamed. 'We need to get into Kirkuk. What are you doing?'

In the front, Burton threw a furtive look over his shoulder.

'Negative, mate,' he said, laying down his phone quickly. 'Baghdad. It's the only place they have the facilities. He needs a life support.'

'He's right,' confirmed Marsh from behind him. 'Sorry, mate, I should have said. We talked about it while you were out.' He placed the bandage down and shifted position, as if wanting to get the blood back into his legs. At his thigh, a Glock.

'Baghdad is a three-hour drive,' said Abbott. 'He hasn't got that long. We get into the nearest hospital. They can fly the gear to us.'

'Baghdad, mate, trust me,' insisted Marsh. 'Sit back. See to your boy. Come on, we know what we're doing.'

Abbott rounded on him. 'Oh yeah? Like you knew what you were doing when you pronounced Burton dead, mister para-medic.' At the same time something occurred to him and he went back to the separator. 'Who were you talking to just now?' he bellowed through it.

'What are you talking about?' said Burton. The retainer of his sidearm holster was loose. Had it been like that before?

'I mean that you were on the phone just now. Who were you talking to?'

'The hospital. I was hoping they could meet us halfway.'

Abbott dropped back, unconvinced. His mind raced and his eyes went to Marsh, who was watching him. Marsh's forehead shone. There was something in his eyes. A wariness.

Abbott thought back to the fact that Stone had always seemed one step ahead of him, and yet the path to him had seemed smooth somehow. How did Stone know that SF were planning to come for Executive Alliance Group? Because he had been tipped off, right? And who might it have been that had tipped him off? Abbott started to wonder about Burton's words when he burst into the burning stable block.

He'd screamed, '*You fucked me.*'

Which, at the time, Abbott had taken to mean one thing and now thought meant another. Neither of those things being that they'd actually fucked.

But if Stone and Burton had been in league and then had fallen out, what the fuck was Burton doing now?

'The blond guy,' said Abbott. 'You know him, don't you? You know who I'm talking about?'

'I'm telling you, mate, just settle down,' Burton called back over his shoulder. 'My priority now is saving your son, and if you've chosen this moment to go completely loco, well, I'm sorry, but I have to do something about it.' He reached down to his sidearm, calling at the same time, 'Marsh!'

Abbott looked back to see that Marsh was holding a gun on him, his other arm braced on the side of the truck for support.

CHAPTER 60

For a moment or so they looked at one another in silence. The truck groaned and creaked, bumping over uneven road. 'You and him, then?' said Abbott at last, indicating forward to the lorry cab with his chin.

'Yeah,' said Marsh. 'I'm not quite the number two, despite what you've seen. I'm more what you might call your replacement. Mowles, Burton and Stone were the ones who formed the Executive Alliance Group. They wanted you, of course, but you were too busy getting pissed even to notice they were doing it, let alone get involved, so I got to step in, like Ringo.

'The thing is that as soon as Jeremy was killed, they knew that military intelligence would be onto them. But they'd already built in an insurance policy. Stone was the figurehead. Me, I was on board, too, keeping shop. Burton and Mowles were the invisible backroom boys. The idea was that if military intelligence ever got to sniffing too hard, then Burton would duck out of sight. He would be the disgraced and corrupt former chairman, and we would step into the breach in order to keep the business going but at the same time ensure that Stone was getting paid, and everything could go ahead as planned.'

Abbott found his eyes going to Nathan, who lay still on the truck bed. His eyelids fluttered. One finger moved, and although these were feeble movements, almost those of an animal, trapped and dying, Abbott was grateful for them, for the signs of life still there.

'What "everything"?' he asked Marsh. 'What was planned?'

'The Hexagon takeover. That was the whole idea. Big business is moving into Baghdad and they've got big money to spend. It was no good just turfing out Hercules and setting up shop ourselves, we wanted somebody even bigger to come in and take over so we could retire to Monaco. But of course they weren't going to shower us with money if we had a crook at the helm, even if that crook was the guy who built the business up in the first place. Hey, listen, none of us made the rules. You play the hand you're dealt, all that kind of stuff. But yeah. That was the game plan. The idea was that we swept in, built it up, gave the business a lick of glossy paint, waited for the sharks to start nosing around and then,' he made a whooshing sound, 'get the hell out.'

'And Mowles?'

'A combination of greed – just wanted too fucking much – and you. He wasn't happy about Stone and his plans.' Marsh shrugged. 'He was just in the way, basically. Just needed booting off the project.'

'And me? Where did I fit in?'

'You didn't "fit in".' Marsh rolled his eyes as though the whole issue had been the bane of his life. 'I mean, yeah, you – you and him,' he inclined his chin to gesture at Nathan. 'You two were Stone's pet project, and given that he was somewhat essential to the programme, we had no choice but to go along with it. And so here we are.'

'Except that's not it,' said Abbott. 'Not "here we are", because there's something else, isn't there? Stone's dead now …'

'Burton and I would have killed Stone at some point. Once the deal went through he was another inessential part of the programme. The thing is, we saw a way to maximise the profits.'

'The white-haired geezer,' said Abbott. 'Mr fucking clean jeans.'

'"Clean jeans"? What are you on about? I don't know what the fuck you're talking about.'

'Yes, you do. You're dying to tell me. It's the blond guy, isn't it? Tell me, how much?'

'Now you've lost me.'

'I'm talking about the bounty on my head. How much is it for? And when did you find out about it?'

Marsh seemed to consider, maybe knowing he'd already gone further than he'd intended. 'OK, yes, there is a bounty on your head.'

'And that's where we're going, isn't it? You're taking me to him.'

Every muscle in Abbott's body was taught. In his mind, total focus. And then he made his move. He launched himself forward at Marsh, catching the other man's gun arm and rolling around it, the two of them both falling backwards simultaneously so that for one strange moment it was like they were sitting together at the back of the truck, like a couple of old pals in the aftermath of a drunken fall. Until Abbott snatched up Marsh's arm and, exerting as much pressure as he was able, snapped it.

Marsh had not been expecting Abbott to be so fast, so decisive – so ruthless. The gun dropped and skidded, his sleeve was suddenly soaked with blood, and Abbott knew from experience that the bone beneath would be showing.

Up ahead, Burton had heard the commotion and the truck swerved. He was shouting something, but his words were drowned out by Marsh's agonised screaming as he slithered away clutching at his arm, only just attached. When he looked at Abbott it was with sheer disbelief as he was unsure whether to fight back or simply tend to himself and scream like a wounded animal. His mind was made up when he saw Abbott make a dive for the gun. Burton chose that moment to swerve the truck, perhaps seeing what Abbott was up to, and the sidearm slid away. Now Marsh went for it, too. Diving over Nathan's prone body in a bid to reach it first.

Abbott got there ahead of him, scooped up the gun and put a round in Marsh's face.

Marsh's chin disintegrated in a cloud of blood, bone and teeth – the kind of damage only a hollowpoint can do. But it was his gun. Served him right. Still not quite dead, he emitted an even higher-pitched screech, so Abbott shot him again then kicked him over the tailgate of the lorry, feeling nothing as Marsh's body tumbled in a cloud of sand to the desert below. Nothing but the need to get the truck turned around and to the hospital in Kirkuk. He pulled himself up, shouting out in pain but ignoring it as he pulled the tarpaulin to one side and swung out of the lorry, around to the cab.

'Fuck,' yelled Burton, caught by surprise. He tried to reach for his pistol, but Abbott put a boot in his face. The truck swerved once more, lurched and hit a pothole, the poor under-stress suspension unable to cope with the sudden demands on it. Abbott tried to grab the wheel but Burton hung on, yelling obscenities, seemingly fixated on something outside. Abbott glanced out of the windscreen and saw what they were heading for – a car wreck by the side of the road. The whole route was lined with them and maybe Burton was hoping that if they hit one, then he could throw Abbott off.

With a shout, Abbott tried to pull the wheel over. Shouting back, Burton hung on. Both men were badly wounded, covered in blood and stripped of everything except need and instinct and bloodlust now.

Abbott's effort wasn't quite enough. The truck clipped the car wreck. It seemed to hop. The rear stepped out. For a second Abbott thought it might maintain traction, ride out the storm, but something had to give and give it did, and the whole thing tilted, throwing Abbott forward onto Burton and smothering the other man's attempt to reach his weapon. The truck fell to its side in a confusion of twisted metal and shattered windscreen glass.

CHAPTER 61

Abbott and Burton pulled themselves out of the cab and faced each other across the sand. Burton's face was speckled with broken glass, blood running freely from the cuts, his long beard glittering with it. Abbott put a hand to his own face and felt chunks of glass fall away. Every muscle, every atom of him seemed to hurt but Nathan was in the back of the lorry and right now the only thing standing in the way of saving Nathan was Burton, which meant that Burton had to die.

No doubt about it. The feeling was mutual. 'You're a fucking cunt, Monk,' said Burton. He spat blood and glass. 'You know you were a good bloke once, but you sold out your mates, first to the grog and then to Mahlouthi. I bet you think it was you who was betrayed, don't you? Wrong. You were the one. You were the bloke who did all the betraying.'

'Oh, come off it, we were never mates.'

'Not in your mind, maybe. But we should have been. We fucking could have been.'

Abbott shook his head. 'And you're mad at *me*? What about Fingers, eh? Fucking tried to kill you. Left you for dead in the desert. Why'd he do that, do you think? Out of the kindness of his heart?'

'Yeah, it's like a rot that spread, though, isn't it? And where do you think it fucking started?'

'And that's why you took part in this, is it? Why you let Stone kidnap and burn my son?'

Burton made a scoffing sound. 'It's why I let him, yes. It's why I didn't give a shit.'

Abbott saw the hurt inside Burton and maybe for a second he understood it, but there was too much at stake now, too much shit had gone down to worry about it. He saw Burton's pistol lying in the sand. At the same time, Burton saw Abbott look, and in the next instant Burton saw it and they both dived for it at once.

Burton was closer but Abbott reached him before he could get to it and the two of them fell as Abbott grappled Burton to the ground. They were close to the wreck now. Burton put one hand to the hot metal to steady himself, kicking out and making painful contact with Abbott's cheek. He did it again. Abbott hung on grimly to his other leg, knowing he couldn't take much more punishment. Sure enough, the boot hammered down again and this time Abbott was forced to relinquish his grip as with a shout of triumph Burton pulled free and made a dive for the gun.

Abbott scuttled back at the same time as Burton reached the gun. He'd already seen what Burton had failed to see. Snug against the sand piled up against the side of the wreck: a flash of metal and a single protruding red wire.

It was an IED.

And Burton, if he continued his current trajectory, was going to blunder right into it.

'Right, you fucker!' screamed Burton.

Which were his parting words. In the next instant Abbott was cowering as with a flash followed by a hollow-sounding bang the IED detonated, sending a shower of dirt and blood and flesh raining down around him.

It was over in an instant. As the fury of the explosion receded, Abbott picked himself up, coughing, shaking debris off himself and thanking God that the wreckage had absorbed most of the blast and Burton had absorbed the rest. All that was visible of him through a cloud of debris was a leg – just the calf portion. The rest of him was drying scattered on the sand.

But Abbott wasn't sticking around to enjoy the sight. He limped to the truck, bits of Burton dropping off his tattered clothing as he hurried, coming to the back of the truck. 'Nathan,' he called, his voice hoarse. 'Nathan.'

His son lay in the back of the truck, tangled in the wreckage. Abbott dragged him clear, bringing him out into the sun. He rolled him over, checking for a pulse. Was there one? He couldn't be sure. His hands shook.

'Nath,' he said, his voice hoarse. He could hear himself on the verge of panic, forcing it back, bringing his SF training to the fore.

Starting CPR. Chest compressions. Rescue breaths.

Droplets of something fell to Nathan's unmoving body. Tears or sweat, Abbott didn't know. 'Come on, mate,' he was saying. 'Stay with me. Stay. With. Me.'

Dark blood oozed from Nathan's mouth. His head lolled. And Abbott continued with CPR. He continued until he was too exhausted to do any more.

A vehicle approached where Abbott knelt beside Nathan. It drew to a halt, the driver's door opened, and the sole occupant of the vehicle stepped out, with his gun drawn and pointed at Abbott. Slowly, carefully, he approached, until he stood behind

Abbott, who even though he must have been aware of the vehicle had neither moved nor said anything.

The new arrival had a shock of blond hair and wore a pristine pair of jeans. He waited a moment or so, and when there was still no response from Abbott, coughed politely.

'He's dead,' said Abbott. In his voice was only emptiness.

'I see,' said Kind.

'I never got to—' started Abbott. He stopped. Below him, Nathan was burned almost black. Grotesque bubbles of traumatised and charred flesh had formed on his face, but to Abbott he looked almost beautiful. And his hair. His hair had grown a little so that despite his burns he looked more like the old Nathan than he had before. In death he reclaimed his true self.

'I never got to be a better father. I never got to be the father he deserved,' said Abbott.

But Kind wasn't listening. Still with his gun held on Abbott, he had pulled out his phone. Pressed to dial.

After some moments he spoke.

'Contact,' he said.

CHAPTER 62

Two months later

Abbott held a bunch of party balloons as he made his way along a corridor of the Swallow Hotel in Shoreditch. Ahead of him went a member of the cleaning staff.

The balloons he held were the foil, helium-filled type. They had the words '40 today' printed on them. In his other hand was a bottle of champagne. Completing the picture, he was smartly dressed, but that was also because he had a dinner date at Kettner's in Soho later on.

The cleaner stopped at a door and, with a look left and right, her forehead creased with worry, used her pass card to open it. She poked her head in the door. 'Housekeeping,' she said. 'There was no reply from inside. She looked at Abbott and nodded.

'Brilliant,' he said. He gave her a sloppy grin and a wink. 'You're an absolute star. I'll take it from here.' He passed her a wad of money which she pushed into the hip pocket of her uniform and then moved off.

Abbott watched her go and then stepped into the room, careful not to touch anything until he had pulled on a pair of surgical gloves. Without the key card there was no electricity in the room, and it was beginning to get dark, so he moved quickly. Early evening Friday and there was a party atmosphere in the air, both in the streets outside and in the hotel itself. Muffled music came from the room next door.

He secured the balloons by the side of the bed. Next he searched the drawers and then the wardrobe, finding a suitcase which he rifled through. From the suitcase he removed a pistol. He put it to one side, relieved to see that it was the Glock nine he had expected. Then he placed a chair facing into the room so that anybody entering would not immediately see him and manoeuvred a side table into position beside it. He found the minibar, raided it, safe in the knowledge that he wouldn't be paying, and laid out various miniatures and mixers on the table, helping himself to a glass and starting on the first of his evening's drinks. From his pocket he took a suppressor and fitted it to the Glock, which he kept within reach. He placed a phone on the table. Beside it he placed another phone, this one with a particular number on speed dial.

And then, in the dark room, he waited.

After about an hour Abbott heard movement at the door as the key card was presented. He reached for the gun and held it steady as a man passed through the door and into the vestibule, activating the electricity with the key card.

The lights came on. The door swung shut. The man walked into the room, preoccupied with the phone that he held. And then the balloons shifted with a rubberised tin-foil squeak and he became aware that he was not alone.

He looked up sharply. Saw Abbott. Saw the gun.

'Hello, mate,' said Abbott.

Potter blinked. 'Hello, Abbott,' he said. He looked at the balloons, arched an eyebrow. 'Forty? I'm not quite there yet.'

'Not quite,' said Abbott, and although Potter looked the same as always, cool and unruffled, he knew that his death was surely just moments away.

'You're not dead, then?' he said to Abbott.

'You assumed I would be?'

'They brought back Nathan and another body.'

'Bits of one. It was Burton.'

'Ah. So you got out of the desert alive. How did you manage that?'

'Yeah, funny thing, actually. Sit down.' Abbott indicated with the barrel, pausing while Potter took a seat. It occurred to him that if this were a film, he'd be the baddie. 'Hands where I can see them. So, yeah, there I was in the desert, Nathan just dead. Still warm in my arms.' He held the moment a beat or so, composing himself, taking a deep breath through his nose. 'And who should appear but my assassin, a guy called Mr Kind, would you believe. Mr too fucking Kind. Now this Mr Kind had been employed by a very rich bloke called Travis Bryars. You heard of Travis Bryars, Potts?'

Potter shook his head slowly. His eyes flicked to his wardrobe, perhaps thinking of the gun that had been there.

'No, well, Travis Bryars is a bonds trader who was the target of a surveillance operation for which Hexagon were hired. A surveillance operation that was to begin in Singapore. Hexagon used a local team who used me, which is how I know about it. Were you aware of that, the whole Singapore operation?'

Again Potter shook his head.

'Only I thought you might, being a Hexagon employee. Except, of course, you're quite new there, aren't you? Plus, you have overall control of the Middle East operation so maybe that's outside your remit.'

Potter said nothing but Abbott knew his words were landing.

'So anyway. I dropped a bollock on the Singapore job.' He picked up his glass and shook it. 'Not only did I balls it up, but I made a right Charlie out of Travis Bryars, who went fucking ape. He employed this Mr Kind to wipe me out. Old Mr Kind did a lot of killing to get to me. A lot of killing and a lot of asking questions. He found his way to Baghdad and put a little bounty out on me, which is how come Burton and Marsh got involved. According to Marsh – right before I shot him in the face – they wanted to "maximise their profits", which they planned to do by arranging to deliver me to Kind. Did you know anything about that?'

Another 'no' from Potter. Abbott stared at him for a moment, wondering whether to believe him or not, but then let it drop.

'Those "profits" they wanted to maximise, by the way, were from the sale of Executive Alliance Group to Hexagon. And you certainly knew all about that, didn't you? In fact, let's talk about that, because Stone didn't turf you out of Executive Alliance Group like you told me, did he? No, the truth is that you'd already left and joined Hexagon. That night in the Country Club you told me that you were due to start there. But you already had a business card. Who has a business card for a job they haven't even started yet?' He slapped his own forehead. 'How could I be so fucking dumb as to let that one go?

'But you know what? I had other things on my mind back then and no reason to suspect you at the time. So I didn't. Not until later.'

Potter blinked.

'It was you, wasn't it? You were Stone's man on the inside. You were the one who told him that Mahlouthi and I were responsible for Jeremy's death. At what point did you get involved, Potts?'

Potter took a deep breath. His eyes were level. 'He threatened me,' he said. 'It was just after Jeremy's death. I was still at Hercules. Stone got to me and told me that if I didn't give up the kid's killers, then I was a dead man.'

Abbott made a scoffing sound. 'Is that the best you can do? Fucksake. OK, look, I'm seeing an old friend for dinner so I need to hurry this up. You knew that Mahlouthi was in bed with Hercules, right?'

Potter shook his head.

Abbott's mouth tightened. 'Next time you tell me a lie I'll put a bullet in your leg. Swear to God. Start again. You *knew* that Mahlouthi was in bed with Hercules, didn't you?'

Reluctantly, Potter nodded.

'And you were the one who asked Mahlouthi to plug the leak, weren't you? Yes or no.'

'Why do you think that?'

Abbott gave a lopsided smile. 'Good question. I'd ask it myself if I were in your position right now. After all, why go incriminating yourself if I don't have proof. Here—' He picked up one of the two phones from the side table and tossed it onto the bed beside Potter. 'That's Stone's phone. Good to see the two of you corresponded by text, and it's all on there: you ratting out Mahlouthi. Ratting me out. You giving up the two guys who killed Jeremy. Details of my arrival in Baghdad. Lots of little helpful nuggets. It's all there, mate. Jesus Christ, I hope he made it worth your while.'

'And that's how you found it, was it? Looking on the phone?'

'That's when I knew for sure. But do you know when the penny dropped? I mean, I guess I'd started to have my suspicions early doors, but it was when you were suddenly so familiar with the comings and goings at Executive Alliance Group. And then what *finally* did it was when you knew what Nathan looked like. I never showed you a picture of him, but you knew what he looked like all right. You knew how to press my buttons. Matter of fact, you were being told what to say to me, weren't you? Stone was using you to puppet me. So, yeah, by the time that Stone pretended to put a bullet in you, I'd pretty much already worked it all out. But there's still one thing I'm not sure about. You knew that Mahlouthi was in it, but how did you know to tell Stone that I was involved? Only Mahlouthi knew that.'

'We went through his room afterwards. There was a note from you in there. Your number, your handwriting. You were unlucky. Most other guys wouldn't have known your number, but I did. It was in my phone.'

'Of course,' said Abbott.

Potter was dead-eyed, knowing there was nothing he could say now. There was a fatalistic look about him.

'Presumably you told him that you had nothing to do with the stabbing?' said Abbott.

Potter nodded.

'But of course he wouldn't have believed you.' Abbott gestured at the phone. 'You told him that you'd managed to "discover" the details of the hit, but my guess is you were involved right from the start. That you were in it up to your armpits, and if I came to that conclusion, then Stone would have done, too. You were living on borrowed time, mate. Except he still needed you, didn't he? Because once you joined Hexagon you were his man on the inside, plus you were still feeding him intel about me. Proper busy bee, weren't you?' He paused. 'I'd ask why, but I think I know the answer.'

'You already got there,' said Potter. He made the money fingers. 'Farlowe, Hexagon, EAG. The whole shit is worth tens of millions, mate.'

'Yeah, sure,' said Abbott. He picked up the second phone. His phone. He pressed the speed dial button, and to the person who answered he said, 'Contact.' Opposite him, sitting on the bed, Potter swallowed.

'All of which brings me back to Mr Kind, who was about to put a bullet in me. Before he did, though, the one thing he wanted to know was the identity of the New York party who had hired Hexagon for the surveillance job on Bryars. Now, of course, I didn't know that. But I did remember my treacherous mate, and not the one whose bits were all over the sand around me. The other one. The one whose Hexagon business card I had in my pocket.'

'I can't tell him that. I don't know who hired Hexagon,' said Potter. He shrugged.

'Yeah, I know, but that won't stop him torturing you.'

'He's on his way over here now, is he?'

'"Over"? No, mate, he's on his way *up* now. Did you pass the bar? You'd have recognised him from his jeans.'

Potter nodded. 'And you're going to let that happen? You're going to let him torture me?'

Abbott smiled a wintry smile. 'I don't even feel like I've started mourning Nathan yet, Potter, but I do know that I'll be doing it for the rest of my life. I'll be spending the rest of my life trying to make it up to myself and to his mother and to everyone else who loved him. Of all the blood on my hands, his will never wash off. Never.'

He raised the Glock.

'I've got to tag one more bloke tonight, Potts. But it isn't you.'

There was a knock at the door. Abbott stood, collected the balloons and went to answer it. At the door stood Kind who was ready to step through, one hand already inside his jacket, suddenly taken aback as the balloons bloomed at him from the door. Abbott glanced quickly up and down the corridor, raised the gun and plugged Kind, a swift double-tap in the chest. *Thk thk*.

He stepped forward and in a bustle of balloons stopped Kind from falling, sweeping an arm around him and bringing him into the room, letting the door slam shut.

The body of Kind lay on the floor, one leg twisted up under him, a look of vague confusion and surprise frozen on his face, the look of a man whose TV remote control wasn't where he thought he'd left it. Abbott trained the Glock on the corpse for a minute or so. The air-conditioning kicked in. And then, satisfied, he relaxed.

He looked down at himself. Plenty of blood on his hands. Luckily, none on his clobber. Directing his attention to Potter, he raised the gun. Potter quivered, knowing the end was close, but Abbott stayed his hand. The killing had to stop. And instead he said, 'I guess this'll have your fingerprints on it. I'm taking it with me for insurance purposes, just in case I need it in the future. In the meantime, you'll have to explain this little lot to the cops. I trust you'll keep my name out of it. And nor do I want to be getting a visit from you or any other Hexagon employee in the near future, you get me? Because next time I won't be so merciful.'

Abbott left.

CHAPTER 63

Abbott arrived at Kettner's early, took a seat and waited for Tessa to appear. He wasn't quite sure how he felt. Numb. Drunk. In shock and yet somehow alive. It was as if he wore a mask, an Alex Abbott face mask, and the mask remained composed and blank, while beneath it the nerves and muscles of his real face twitched and writhed.

He sank one drink quickly, called for another and made a significant dent in that, knowing he could pretend that it was his first, and all the time he tried to work out how he felt about this meeting.

For a start, it had been called by Tess, who had said nothing about it other than that she needed to see him. It wasn't a romantic 'needed to see him', he knew. Something else. She'd heard about Nathan, so he'd need to bear her sympathy, watch it bounce off his own emotional paralysis, but other than that, he didn't know. All he knew, in fact, was that he was desperate to see her. More than ever, he needed to be saved by her. Before the void could claim him.

And he got that, for a while, when he inhaled her scent as she enveloped him with her pity. The force of her caring awoke something within him. Her eyes, which glittered with compassion, terrified him, for what he lived most in fear of was the moment that his own grief took him. But they also reminded him that there was good in the world. Just that you had to look for it.

They talked as they ate, skirting the subject of last time, only briefly touching on Nathan's death. He didn't go into details on it, and as for the future he told her he was going freelance, thinking about returning to Singapore, collecting his poor Accord from whatever pound it had been taken to.

The thought of returning to Singapore made him close his eyes momentarily. He had first gone there with nothing, to escape his misdeeds in Baghdad. He would be returning for the same reason, only with even less. He wondered if all the old gang would still be meeting at AA. Rodney from *Only Fools and Horses*. The misery tourist.

And then Tessa got to the reason why she wanted to see him. As before she'd come straight from work, only this time she reached down to a briefcase and extracted some papers, laying them face down on the table with her hand upon them, before she spoke.

'You remember last time we met?' she said, colouring a little, just a little.

'Yes,' he said.

'What you told me? About your older brother.'

'Yes, of course.' He heard a rushing sound in his ears, not sure he wanted to hear what might come next.

'Well, something you said, about how your parents told you that he must have been swept out to sea. It didn't ring true somehow. Either way, I looked into it.' She was awkward, uncomfortable. She glanced down at the papers under her hand. 'I found something.'

'What is it?' he asked, and it was as though somebody else were saying the words.

'I think ...'

'Yes.'

'Alex, I think that your parents lied to you.'

ALEX ABBOTT WILL RETURN.

AUTUMN 2021

ACKNOWLEDGEMENTS

Writing *Scar Tissue* (in lockdown, no less!) has been a journey of discovery in more ways than one. I'd like to thank my fellow travellers, without whom none of this would be possible: the wonderful Laura, Matthew Phillips and Madiya Altaf at Blink, Andrew Holmes, David Riding and Sam Graham at MBA, and, of course, my amazing family. Thank you one and all.

Where is your break point?

Is it here? Facing the gruelling SAS selection process on one leg, with a busted ankle and the finish line nowhere in sight?

Or here? Under heavy fire from armed kidnappers while protecting journalists en route to Baghdad.

Or is it here? At the bottom of a bottle, with a family in pieces, unable to adapt to a civilian lifestyle, yearning for a warzone?

Ex-Special Forces soldier, Ollie Ollerton has faced many break points in his life and now he tells us the vital lessons he has learnt. His incredible story features hardened criminals, high-speed car chases, counter-terrorism and humanitarian heroics.

How do you make a commitment and achieve your goals?

How do you end procrastination and hesitation that feeds self-doubt?

How do you learn to be courageous in all aspects of your life?

Ollie Ollerton knows more than his fair share about keeping going. As a recruit he survived the infamously tough SAS selection process on a busted ankle with the Directing Staff pleading with him to give up. But it's in Ollie's personal life that he really had to dig deep. At his lowest he was battling a failed relationship, substance abuse, depression and a reckless disregard for his own life.

In *Battle Ready*, Ollie tells the story of how he turned his life around and passes on the lessons he has learned. He shares the step-by-step plan that changed his life. From finding purpose and visualising an outcome, to breaking bad habits and establishing positive new routines, his advice will help readers to overcome their own obstacles; to become ready for any battle.